BOOK THREE

GUARD *me*

USA TODAY BESTSELLING AUTHORS

J.L. BECK & C. HALLMAN

Copyright © 2019 by J.L. Beck C. Hallman

All rights reserved.

No part of this book may be reproduced in any form or by any electronic or mechanical means, including information storage and retrieval systems, without written permission from the author, except for the use of brief quotations in a book review.

Editing by: Word Nerd Editing

Cover Design by: C. Hallman

PROLOGUE

Violet

THE MUSIC POUNDS LOUDLY in my ears. It's so loud I can't hear myself think, let alone hear whatever it is my best friend is trying to say to me. I don't know why I was so excited about coming here for my birthday. It seemed like such a good idea when my friends suggested it.

However, now that I'm here, everything seems so much less appealing. My ears hurt from the loud music, and my throat is scratchy from the smoke that clings to the air. The skin-tight dress and black high heels I'm wearing are getting more uncomfortable with each passing minute. All in all, coming here was a shit idea.

Sweat beads against my forehead as I survey the crowd. Everyone here seems to be way older than me. I'm only eighteen, but this club allows people under twenty-one to come in as long as you let them stamp both of your hands.

Some older guy offered to buy me a drink a couple minutes ago, and I'm starting to wonder if maybe I should have let him. I really don't want to get drunk in here and lose my wits, but it's so hot, and I can't help but wonder if I'd loosen up with a little alcohol in my system.

I grip my cell phone tightly, deciding there won't be any drinking for me tonight. I'll just call my sister Ella and have her pick me up. She's going to be pissed at me for not telling her what I was doing, but she'll get over it; she always does. I unlock my phone and start scrolling through my messages when a man appears at my side.

"Here." He shoves a glass at me. It has some red liquid in it, and I know better than to take some drink from a random stranger. I shake my head and hold up my hand to motion to him that I am not interested but he just shoves the glass closer to my face.

Annoyance boils deep inside me. I take the glass, hoping it will make the asshole leave. I don't take a sip, nor do I plan to.

"Want to dance?" The guy leans into me and slurs right next to my ear. He smells of smoke and sweat. I almost gag at the mixture of scents.

"No, thank you," I decline politely.

"But I just bought you a drink, the least you can do is dance with me." He gives me a creepy smile, and I shudder, attempting to take a step backward. The entire place is packed, bodies rubbing against each other, making it hard to escape this asshole.

I need to find another way to get away from him. My eyes glance over a neon restroom sign off in the distance.

"You're right. I'm just going to the bathroom really quick and then I'll dance with you." I give him a wide smile and set the drink on the table a few feet away from us.

"All right, I'll be waiting right here for you, baby," he slurs, as I start to walk away.

Walking in the direction of the bathroom, I weave between people, pushing and shoving just to get a step ahead. Once I reach the restrooms, I turn and start walking back toward the entrance of the club. Music vibrates through me, and I find it harder and harder to breathe with all the bodies around me. I'll just go outside and call Ella; that way, maybe I can tell her I wanted to go to the club but changed my mind. Her shift at the diner will be over in a few minutes, so she'll be able to swing by here on her way back to the apartment.

Then we can forget tonight never happened.

I make it through the crowd and walk into the hallway leading outside. There are only a few people lingering near the exit. Nobody seems to be paying me an ounce of attention, except one man. He is leaning against the far wall, his entire body encased in the shadows, but I can see his eyes scanning me up and down. He's staring at my body in a way that makes me feel exposed and I don't like it, not one bit. I make my feet walk faster as I hurry past him, his gaze remaining on me the whole time. The hair on the back of my neck stands up, and a bad feeling fills my gut. This guy is pure evil... it oozes out of him, like a bad smell. I can feel it, see it.

The moment I step outside, and fresh air fills my lungs, I feel a little better. I peer up into the night sky, pressing against the brick exterior wall of the club. I flip my phone around in my sweaty hand to call my sister, but when I scroll down to her name, I realize that I have no signal.

Shit.

I start walking down the sidewalk, holding the phone up in front of me, hoping to find a spot where I get at least one bar. I take little steps, watching the phone screen more than my surroundings.

"Shit," I mumble to myself, knowing I'm going to get my ass chewed whenever I do get ahold of Ella.

"Need a lift?" an unfamiliar voice calls out, making me jump. I quickly turn around, dropping my phone in the process. It's the creepy guy from the hallway, and now he is standing a few inches away from me.

My voice is stuck in my throat, and all I can do is shake my head. The man gives me a sinister smile that has my stomach coiling with nervous knots. Looking past his shoulders, I realize that I've wandered away a good bit from the front of the club, and I'm completely alone with this unknown man. My heart rate spikes as fear surges through my veins. I don't know how, or why, but I just know something bad is about to happen.

I take a step back, desperately trying to get some distance. I feel paranoid, like I'm losing my mind. I think he is going to grab me, but he makes no move to do so. I take another step back, and he smiles at me, his eyes darken as if he is enjoying this little cat and mouse game.

I take another small step backward, realizing then why he didn't try and grab me. A set of strong arms wrap around me from behind. Fear and panic creeps in when a large hand covers my mouth, stopping the scream burning to escape from my lips. I start kicking and flailing my arms, attempting to hit any appendage I can.

Time seems to stand still when I feel a prick in the side of my neck.

I fight for another five seconds before my limbs get heavy and my eyes close. I'm vaguely aware of a car pulling up next to us and my body being thrown into it like a rag doll. I want to fight, scream, and cry, but my body is completely useless and not following any of my commands. I feel my mind drifting away as panic settles deep inside of me. My last thought before the darkness completely claims me is to wonder if I will ever wake up again.

1

Violet

I GROAN, my eyelids feeling as if they have been replaced with sandpaper. My head is pounding, making it hard for me to think...I shiver as a coldness sweeps over my exposed skin. Exhaling, I pry my eyes open and find that I'm lying in a bed, looking up at a white ceiling.

For a moment, I think I'm in the hospital.

Was I in an accident?

I turn my head, expecting to find an IV sticking out of my arm, or some type of medical equipment. What I see instead makes my heart stop mid-beat. A deep panic settles into my bones, sinking deep into my core. I'm in a concrete box. There are no windows. In fact, all four walls are white, with no paintings or decor.

It is a completely empty room minus the mattress beneath me. I scurry into a sitting position, pressing my back against the wall. It's cold, and I stifle a whimper by biting my lip. My eyes move over the room once more.

The mattress beneath me is stained and doesn't even have a sheet on it. There is no blanket or pillow. Nothing about this room says I'll be staying for a while, and that terrifies me. If whoever has me doesn't plan on keeping me for a while then that means... I can't even finish the thought without feeling like I might pass out.

I look down at myself. I'm wearing nothing but a damn skin-tight dress, and my shoes are long gone. Looking at my attire jogs a memory from my mind. I remember... *my birthday... the club... that creepy, scary guy.* Everything comes rushing back to me all at once.

Oh, god, no, where am I? What happened to me?

My gaze swings around the room again. I have to find a way out. There seems to be only one exit and entrance out of the room, and it's through the large metal door on the far side of the room. I eye the thing, knowing there is no way I'll be able to break it down or get it open. There is a small door in the center of it that reminds me of a food slot of a prison cell door.

Next to the door is a large mirror set inside the wall. I eye it with apprehension. I can't help but wonder if it's just a mirror or a one-way mirror, where people can watch you from the other side. There is another room off to the right that leads into a small bathroom. I slowly stand on wobbly legs to take a closer look inside of it.

"Shit," I grumble when my bare feet touch the cold cement floor. It's impossibly cold in this room, and I've never craved a blanket more in my life then I do right now.

Inside the tiny bathroom are a toilet and a sink. There is no toilet paper, soap, or any of the things that a normal person would have in their own bathroom at home. I back out of the tiny room, feeling more unsure then I did before I stepped foot inside of it. I scurry over to the mattress, crawling across it, before sitting down in the farthest corner, pulling my legs up to my chest. I'm cold, so cold.

Times seems to blend together. I don't know how long I sit like this, could be minutes, hours, maybe even days. There is no real way of telling time here. My eyes start to droop closed again when I hear something happening in front of my door.

I jump up and run to it. I hear the rattling of keys followed by a lock opening. I want to scream, beg, plead... but a part of me is terrified to find out what is on the other side of that door.

Disappointment fills my veins when instead of the large metal door opening, the small flap opens and a plate is shoved inside the room.

"Hello?" I call out, my voice coming out scratchy and raw. "Please, you don't have to help me, but please tell me why am I here? Tell me who took me," I beg and get down on my knees, hoping to catch a glimpse of the outside world through the tiny opening.

My pleas go unanswered and the door quickly slams shut, nearly knocking the paper plate onto the floor. I eye the sandwich and the bottle of water that's now on the floor in front of the door. Tears build up in my eyes and threaten to spill over as I make my way back to the mattress, leaving the plate of food. My stomach tightens nervously. There is no way I could keep anything down right now.

∼

I DON'T KNOW how many days pass. All I know is that I'm on the verge of insanity. If I'm not sleeping, I'm crying. When I'm not doing either of those things, I'm driving myself crazy while trying to figure out why I am here.

Every time a meal is brought, I try and talk to the person on the other side of the door, but as always, they don't respond. I've stopped eating the food they bring in hopes that someone will be forced to come in and talk to me. My eyes often go to the mirror that overlooks the room. Sometimes I get the feeling that I'm being watched, and I most likely am, since I'm almost certain the damn thing is not just a mirror. I remain on the mattress, just as I always do, attempting to get warm. I'm so cold; I'm not sure I remember what it feels like to be warm anymore. The little thin dress I'm wearing gives me little protection or warmth, and I shiver uncontrollably.

Between being cold and always afraid of the unknown, I get no sleep. I'm in a constant state of panic, my body so stiff and exhausted that even tiny movements cause my muscles to ache. I wonder if my sister is looking for me, searching for me? I wonder where I am? Who took me? There are a million questions running through my mind, and no answers. I shiver against the mattress, but my head perks up at a noise outside my door.

My last meal of the day was brought a few hours ago... and this has never happened before. I hear the jingling of keys and deep husky laughter... laughter that belongs to men.

God, no. My entire body clams up when the door opens, a loud creak vibrating through the room. I look up, paralyzed with fear, as two dark-haired men enter.

"My, oh, my, look what we have here, Luca." The two men walk unsteadily toward me. I can smell the alcohol on their breath and they're still a few feet away from me.

I've wished for the door to open for so long, hating that it kept me trapped in this room, but what I didn't know was that it protected me, shielded me, because now that it's open, I want it to close, taking the two men before me with it.

"Look at those full lips. I bet they will look great around my cock," the other man snickers.

"How angry do you think Ivan will be if we pop her cherry?" the first man asks.

Fear like I've never felt before spirals out of control inside of me. They edge closer toward me, and I wish the wall would swallow me whole, making me disappear from this room and out of reach from these assholes.

"We're gonna have some fun with you, baby. You want that, don't you?"

I shake my head, looking up into a pair of dark eyes. There is no emotion, no caring nature in those eyes, just pure lust, and I know then that the two men before me are monsters.

I look past the two figures in front of me and realize that they've left the door open behind them. Hope blooms inside me. They take another step forward. They're much too close now, and I know if I want to survive this I need to do something. Fighting the ache in my muscles, my body starts to move on its own. I jump up from the mattress, trying to run past them, but even drunk, the men are faster than I am. I barely make it a couple of feet before one of them grabs me by the arm, yanking me backward.

Luca pushes me into the second guy's arms. Panic swarms me, my chest heaves, and still, through it all, I know that I need to fight them even if my chances of escaping are slim. I'm not going to go out without fighting.

I might not have the strength I need to overpower them, but I have long nails. I use them to my advantage, lashing out with my hand and sinking them into his ugly face, while slashing downward. He hisses out in pain, and I relish in that sound.

Of course, he rewards me by backhanding me across the face. Pain radiates across my jaw, the impact making my head snap back. Tears fill my eyes, and before I can recover, my arms are roughly twisted behind my back, making me cry out in pain. I can barely see through the treacherous tears spilling from my eyes, but I know I got the bastard good. Five bloody scratches line his face, and I almost smile. Almost.

"You're going to fucking regret doing that, you whore." Another slap lands on my face, the pain intensifies, and before I can even get my bearings, my dress is being ripped down my body in one furious pull, leaving me in nothing but my underwear.

"Fuck, look at that little body. I bet she's tight." Luca grips me by the chin, his fat fingers digging into my skin. I snarl my lip and spit right in his face. He looks at me with murderous rage, and I wonder if this is where I'm going to die.

He wipes a hand down his face and with that same hand, he punches me. Literally punches me. My jaw aches at the impact, and the copper taste of blood fills my mouth.

"Please... please, stop..." I cry, trying to wiggle out of their hold, but my futile attempts just seem to egg them on. The one behind me is grinding his erection into my backside and the one in front of me starts smiling while he squeezes my boobs painfully. When one of his hands travels down between my legs, roughly grabbing me there, another rush of anger floods my system, giving me just a little bit more strength.

I grit my teeth and push through the pain. In my final attempt to fight them, I throw my head back as hard as I can, hitting the guy behind me somewhere in the face. He releases me with a grunt, and I use that moment to bring my knee up and kick the guy in front of me between the legs. He falls to the floor, swear words filling the air. Without looking back, I bolt toward the door and out into a well-lit hall. I'm out... I'm outside of the cell. I glance back at the man over my shoulder and see out of the corner of my eyes that I can see through the mirror into my cell like it's a window.

They've been watching me this whole time... watching me, seeing me struggle and cry. Adrenaline floods my body, forcing me forward. I start running, without thought to where I'm going, only that I need to get away from those men. I hear someone following behind me, heavy footsteps, and words in a language I don't understand.

Once I reach the end of the hallway, I take a sharp turn around the corner, ready to pick up speed. Instead, I slam into a wall... or what I think is a wall. When I lift my eyes, I discover that it isn't really a wall, but a wall of muscled chest.

All the air leaves my lungs at the impact, and my knees buckle. Strong arms grip onto me, engulfing me in warmth...in safety. My hands land flatly on his huge chest, and I curl my fingers into his shirt when I hear the two men trying to hurt me approach behind us.

I look up at the face of the man holding me. His eyes are gunmetal gray, reminding me of the sky before a storm, but as he looks into my eyes, his gaze softens.

"Help me, please help me," I whisper, my voice trembling. I grip onto his shirt tighter, willing him to help me, to save me from these horrible men. He doesn't say a word, he just stares at me, no emotion whatsoever in his eyes. When the heavy footfalls of the two guys chasing me stop behind us, I see his eyes move past me to where the two guys are standing.

I feel their presence without looking, and it terrifies me. I pray he isn't going to give me back to them, I don't know what will happen if he does, but I won't just let them have me. No way. I bury my face into the unknown man's chest. His scent washes over me, like expensive whiskey and cinnamon. Feeling his muscles move underneath my touch, I know he is so much bigger and stronger than those two. He could protect me from them.

An eerie moment of silence falls over us, and my body starts to shake uncontrollably.

"That bitch tried to run, boss. We were just going to put her back in the cell," Luca says into the silence.

"And who opened the cell door for her?" the man holding me asks. His voice is deep and dark, and dread fills my veins at his words. He is not going to help me. Maybe he is the one who put me in that room. The one who kidnapped me. Sobs rack my body at the disappointment. I'm never going to get out of here. I'm never going to be safe again.

"Ivan... boss, we were just going to have a little fun... we weren't going to hurt her..."

"You don't touch the merchandise and by the looks of her fucking face, it seems like you did a whole lot of hurting her," Ivan growls.

One single word stands out from his sentence: Merchandise? I know what the word means but I can't comprehend what it means for *me*. They can't possibly be selling me... or anyone for that matter, right? It's illegal to sell humans... men, women, it doesn't matter.

As I listen in shock to their conversation, I realize that I'm still holding on to the man who obviously has something to do with me being here. Why do I feel safe in his arms? I should push him away, fight him like I did the other two men. I should try and escape, but instead, I lean into him for comfort. I feel safe in his arms, even though the rational part of my brain tells me I shouldn't.

I enjoy his big hands sprawled out over my back, and the warmth his body gives me. For a moment, I can forget the throbbing in my face and the split in my lip. I can forget that I've been kidnapped and held prisoner.

"She tried escaping, boss. We had to stop her. Maybe if she didn't try and claw our fucking eyes out, she wouldn't look like she does," the other man starts, but Luca cuts him off by clearing his throat, as if he knows better than to disobey.

"It won't happen again, boss. We just wanted to have a little fun. Clearly, we made a mistake. We'll put her back in her cell and lock it up."

My body stiffens at his words, and my fingers clutch Ivan's shirt. *Please say no.* I beg in my head like a prayer. If he gives me to them, I'm going to run. I'm going to run as fast and hard as I can.

"I'll take her back myself and if I see you two around her cell again... I'll kill you both. We don't touch the merchandise. If you want to fuck something, go to the whorehouse," he warns them.

"Of course, boss," they both mumble and when I hear their feet pounding against the floor, going in the opposite direction of where we're standing, I sigh. I cling to the man before me, my fingers refusing to let go of him.

A whimper escapes my lips when he pries my fingers from his shirt and lifts me into the air, holding me like a groom holds his bride... like I weigh nothing at all. I probably don't, considering his size. I briefly catch a glimpse of a large tattoo on the side of his neck before I lower my face so he can't look at it.

He cradles me to his chest like I'm a small child. His skin feels so warm against mine, and I want to sink deep inside him and stay there forever. I twist and burrow my face into his chest. I remember then that I'm completely naked, other than my panties. I've never been naked in front of a man before, and now I've been naked in front of three all in one night.

"Please, don't put me back in that room," I murmur into his shirt. He doesn't respond or stop walking in the direction I just came from. He just continues walking as if he didn't hear me at all. With every step he takes, I lose a little more hope that I'm ever going to get out of here.

2

Ivan

HER BLUE EYES pierced through my heart like a dull butter knife. I'm so fucking angry right now. More than angry, actually, and I don't understand the emotions I'm feeling.

I carry her small body back into the cell. With her fingers curled into the fabric of my shirt, she is holding on to me as if her life depends upon it. I glance down at her, but her face is buried into my chest. She is crying, sobbing, her whole body shaking with the force of her tears, and I can't get her stupid pleas out of my head. She's stupid, so stupid. Without knowing who I am, she begs me to help her, like I'm some kind of fucking hero. She has no fucking idea how wrong she is. I'm just as bad as those assholes who bruised up her face and tried to have their way with her.

Still, hearing the desperation in her voice, seeing how scared she, feeling her cling to me like I'm the only one who can save her gives me an ounce of hope that maybe there is some good left inside of me, when I thought all of it had been snuffed out a long time ago. I saved her, protected her, and that does something to me, even I don't want to acknowledge it.

Typically, I don't deal with this part of the business. Mainly because I don't like how they treat the women. It doesn't get me off to see women sexually abused or beaten, so I try to ignore this part of the job and leave my men to deal with this shit. Which makes me no better than them. Yeah, I might not hurt the women, but I don't do anything to stop it either. I knew she was here, of course, I'd gotten her file thrown on my desk the second she was brought in to be processed, but I'd never seen her, besides the small picture of her driver's license, not until now. Most of the women here never saw me, the man who made sure the entire operation went as smoothly as possible.

I carry her to the bed, my molars grinding together when I see the ripped dress discarded on the floor. I quickly scan the room, getting even angrier when I see there isn't even a blanket or sheet on the dirty mattress. I don't want to put her back on it, but what else am I going to fucking do with her? I didn't realize the women lived in such shitty conditions, but I suppose offering them anything gives them false hope. Most of these women will end up dead or worse after they're sold. So, something as superficial as a blanket or pillow won't matter anyway.

I kneel down next to the mattress, ready to lay her down on it, when her shaking intensifies.

"Please, don't leave me here, please." Her words cut through me.

"I can't help you," I tell her with a stern voice, but I can't bring myself to peel her from my body or put her down on the mattress. Something about her makes me want to break every rule.

"Can you stay with me... just for a little while?"

I don't dare look at her. I should put her down and walk out that door without ever looking back, but the way she clings to me has awakened a protective instinct inside me.

An instinct I thought I'd lost long ago, one I shoved down so deep inside me that it would never see the light of day again. I guess I was wrong. I hadn't lost the ability to care, I just hadn't had a reason to.

I sit down on the mattress, resting my back against the cold wall, while continuing to hold her in my arms. She cuddles into me as if she can't get close enough.

"I'm so cold," she whimpers.

I tighten my arms around her and rub my hands up and down her cold skin, trying to get her warmed up. I need to find her something to wear and get her a blanket. There's no way I can leave her in here naked like this.

I sit there for a long time, just holding her, attempting to warm her fragile body while she sobs into my chest. I don't say anything to her. Mostly because there is nothing to say. There is nothing I can offer her that will change the outcome of her future. Selling women is part of my job, and she was brought here, plucked off the street. She might not have asked to be brought here, but she's here now, and I can't just let her go.

After a while, her sobs quiet down and eventually, her crying ceases altogether, but her grip on my shirt never eases up. Her breathing evens out and when her head rolls from my chest onto my arm and I see her eyes closed, I know for sure she is out.

I look down at her face, studying her features, taking in her natural beauty. It's no wonder the men selected her. With her long blond hair framing her heart-shaped face, she looks like a sleeping angel in my arms. My eyes drift down to her split lip. There's smeared blood across it, a small cut in the corner, and her swollen jaw is turning black and blue with bruising. Looking at her, at how fragile she is, pulls a memory from deep inside my head.

Mira. I try to shake it away, but this situation is all too similar to hers. I'm holding a small broken body in my arms, her eyes are closed, and blood covers her face just like it did Mira's. And just like back then, I can't help her. I can't save her. I can't save anybody.

"Stop, Mira," I yell. I hate having to play with my baby sister.

She's so annoying, all she ever does is follow me and Tyler around.

"Ivan," she whines, looking up at me with big blue eyes.

"No, Mira, go play by yourself." I turn back to Tyler. We start walking down the sidewalk in the direction of the playground.

"I want to come with you," she demands, her tiny feet sounding behind me. I whirl around, and she stops dead in her tracks.

"No. You're too little," I boom over her, watching tears glisten in her eyes. I clench my fists at my sides. I feel bad for hurting her feelings, but I don't always want to play with her. Sometimes, I just want to play with my friends.

"You're so mean, Ivan. The worst," she pouts, turning around, bouncing the giant purple ball in her hands. It bounces away from her and toward the street.

My heart pounds inside my chest...

I squeeze my lids shut for a short time, trying to catch my breath as the memory washes through me. Once I've calmed myself a bit, I get up, still holding her in my arms, and very gently lay her down onto the mattress so she won't wake up. She immediately curls up into a tight ball, her tiny hands tucked under her angelic face. I look down at her naked form, knowing that I can't leave her here like this. It's an irrational thought, knowing that she will be sold, but while she is here, the least I can do is give her some type of modesty and make sure she doesn't freeze to death. So, I pull off my black long-sleeved thermal shirt and cover her small body with it like a blanket.

When I straighten, I take another look around the empty room. How long has she been here? I can't fucking remember but I know the auction is not for another three weeks.

I exhale a ragged breath, scrubbing a frustrated hand down my face. I shake my head in anger. I can't worry about this shit. There is nothing I can do to change the outcome of this for her. I just need to go have a drink and forget this whole shit show ever happened.

I take a few steps toward the door and glance into the tiny bathroom. It's fucking filthy, and there is no soap or a towel... not even fucking toilet paper? How the fuck can she be expected to remain sanitary when they don't even give her the necessities needed to do so?

Fuck, what am I thinking? She isn't being treated like a human because she isn't going to be seen as one here. I've never thought about the women brought here because I never saw them. I never paid an ounce of attention to them because I didn't want to.

But now that I have, I'm appalled. My blood boils, and I have to stop myself from slamming the door shut behind me when I leave the cell. I want to find someone to punch and yell at, but I really have no one to blame other than myself, and that makes this ten times worse. Guilt is a bitch, and it's hitting as hard as it never has before.

The men working for me just follow my orders; they don't come up with this shit on their own. If I don't order them to do something, then they aren't going to fucking do it. This is on me.

I walk from the first floor up the stairs to the second floor, my feet pounding across concrete. When I reach the door to my room, I unlock it, and twist the knob, walking inside. I slam the door closed behind me and walk into the bathroom connected off the bedroom. I shouldn't be feeling shit for this woman... and still, I can't get the image of her without a single fucking thing to give her comfort out of my head. There are other women here, all on that same floor, experiencing the same things she is, so why the fuck don't I care about them, too?

Because they aren't her.

Holding her in my arms, feeling her cling to me, reminded me of the one person in my life that I failed to save, failed to protect. I grit my teeth, grabbing onto the sink that's barely fastened to the wall. Things were easier before she escaped and ran right into my arms like I was the hero in this twisted fucking story.

But I'm not the hero. I can't save her. I can't even save myself. I force air into my lungs and swallow down all the emotions swirling out of control inside of me. This is my job. The only life I've ever known, and some tiny, fragile fucking woman isn't going to ruin it for me.

I lift my eyes to the mirror, and I see the man I'm meant to be. The hardened criminal, the killer, the fucked-up asshole.

I was born to do this. It's in my blood.

3

*V*iolet

I BLINK MY EYES OPEN, feeling a little warmer than I have in a long time. My jaw throbs, and I fight back tears at the pain. When I shift against the mattress, I feel an unknown fabric rubbing against my naked skin. I gaze down at my body, which is now covered with a large black shirt. I look around the room expecting... *hoping* the owner of that shirt would still be here, but I'm met with nothing more than disappointment when I realize the room is completely empty, as always.

I suck in a ragged breath, and the faint scent of cinnamon and whiskey tickles my nostrils, which I quickly realize comes from the shirt covering me. I get up and shimmy the shirt off of me while trying to keep my boobs covered.

Now that I know for a fact this mirror isn't really a mirror and that someone might be watching me right now, I am not going to give anyone a show. I turn my back to the door and slip the oversized shirt over my head. The soft fabric falls over my body, swallowing me whole. The shirt is so long on me it fits me more like a dress than a t-shirt, coming to rest just below my knees.

I sit there for a long time, wrapped in Ivan's shirt. It still smells like him, and I can't help but revel in his unique scent. It calms me, makes me feel safe, and reminds me of how he made me feel when he was holding me in his huge arms. He said that he couldn't help me, but he doesn't realize how much he already has.

Not only did he save me from being raped by those two men, but he also held me for I don't even know how long. After being without any human contact for so many days, his gentle touch meant everything to me... not to mention the warmth he provided me with. Because of him, I felt a little more human again. For the first time since I got here, I smile. He even left me his shirt; he cared enough to leave his shirt, knowing how cold I was. If that's not kindness, then I don't know what is.

I pull my legs up to my chest and rest my head on my knees, trying to relax, when I hear someone unlocking the door. I'm instantly on high alert, staring at the door, waiting to see who is going to come walking through it. Ivan told those guys not to come back. Surely, they would listen to him? They called him boss, so I'm assuming he's the one in control of this entire thing.

When I see the food door flap open and a tray being shoved through it, I'm equally relieved and disappointed. It's not Ivan, but it's no one coming in here to try and hurt me either.

I almost don't get up, leaving the food sitting there, when I take another look at the contents on the tray. It holds the normal paper plate and water bottle, but there is something else on it.

I jump up and run to the door, my bare feet slapping against the cold concrete.

Toilet paper. Fucking toilet paper. I never thought I could be so happy about such a ridiculous little thing as toilet paper... but I am. I'm so happy about it that I decide to actually eat a few bites of the sandwich. The inside of my mouth hurts like hell and my jaw is swollen, but I manage to chew anyway. I twist the cap off the clear bottle of water and wash down the dry PB&J pieces in my mouth. They land in my belly with a heavy thud.

I eye the door, knowing there is no way one of the men put that toilet paper on the tray. They wouldn't care enough about such a small thing. After all, I'm nothing but a piece of meat to be sold. I know for certain Ivan had to have done it. He was kind enough to leave his shirt for me, so there is no way it was anyone but him. Which leaves me wondering how he became the boss of this godforsaken place? He seems different than the other men here... or at least the ones I've met. He's kinder, gentler, and that gives me hope where I've had none.

~

DAYS BLEED TOGETHER, and I completely lose track of time. I don't know how many days I have been here; all I know is that with each passing day, I hope for Ivan to return. He is the only person who has treated me like a human being since I arrived here, and I crave human interaction.

I'm so fucking lonely. I just want to see another person... they don't even have to talk to me. I just don't want to be alone anymore. My stomach is so empty it aches, throbs, but I can't bring myself to eat anything.

What's the point anyway? It's not going to change the outcome of what happens to me. Maybe if I don't eat anything, I'll lose some weight... and maybe then I won't be appealing to anyone?

Dinner or lunch, whatever it is, was served a few hours ago, telling me it's either late afternoon or night time. My face still hurts, but not as badly as it did a few days ago. I look at my reflection in the mirror. An ugly array of purple and green bruises mar my chin, jaw, and right cheek. The swelling has gone down immensely, but I still don't look like myself. My hair is a greasy mess on my head, and my body has become sickly thin.

With nothing else but my own mind, I spend every day asking

myself the same questions over and over again. Why did I go to that stupid club? Is Ella looking for me? When am I going to get out of here and what's going to happen to me when I do?

I have no answers to my questions, and that terrifies me. I don't know why any of this happened to me and, most of all, I don't know what my future holds. Parts of me wonder if I'm better off dying?

I crawl into a tiny ball and let the tears stinging my eyes fall. I cry for the unknown, for my future, and for the past I'm certain I'll never get to go back to.

4

Ivan

I'M JUST LOOKING over the weapons export reports on my desk when someone knocks on the door of my office.

"What?" I growl.

Gabe opens the door, popping his head in as if he's making sure I don't shoot him on sight. I have been in an extra foul mood for the last week, and my men have all noticed and most likely felt it, since I've been handing out ass kickings more often.

"What do you want?" I don't even look up at him. I just keep sifting through the papers, wishing he would just turn around and leave already.

"Sorry to interrupt, boss, but I thought I should tell you that one of the girls hasn't been eating."

My head snaps up at his words and suddenly, he has my full attention. "Which girl?" I ask, irritated. I really hope it's not the same one as before. I've been trying to get her out of my fucking head all week, but the image of her beautiful face, her big blue eyes looking up at me and how she felt cradled in my arms, is permanently embedded into my brain. Everytime I close my eyes, I see her in that damn room, cold and alone.

"Number five."

I sigh at his words. Of course, it's her. Out of the ten women on that floor, it's got to be her.

"For how long?" I ask, trying to sound uninterested

"Almost a week." *A week?* A whole fucking week? I remember her face and how swollen it was when I left her. Maybe she can't eat. Fuck, I should have let the doc check her out. No one is going to buy her if she is dead.

"I'll take care of it."

Gabe stares at me for a second longer than I'd like, looking at me like he is waiting for an explanation or something. I don't owe this guy anything.

"Get the fuck out of my office," I snarl at him and watch him scurry away, shutting the door behind him. I shove the papers on my desk away from me and open the drawer underneath. I rummage through it until I find the pill bottle I'm looking for.

Demerol is going to numb her up and help her sleep. I wrack my brain on what I'm going to say to her. I'm not sure what I'm going to tell her, but I can't let her starve herself.

I get up and walk out of my office, making my way down to the cells. When I get to her cell, I stop in front of the one-way mirror and watch her for a few minutes. She is curled up on the mattress in the fetal position.

Most of her body is covered by my shirt, and even though her eyes are closed, she doesn't look like she is sleeping. Her features are too tense. Her cheek and jaw are still bruised, but her lip has mostly healed. Her face looks skinnier, and I'll bet anything she's lost weight. *What the fuck am I supposed to do with her?*

I shake my head and unlock the cell door. Immediately, she sits up, looking at me with wide eyes, When I step closer, she scoots back on her mattress until her back hits the wall.

"You need to eat," I tell her, walking until I'm standing right in front of the mattress.

"Why?" Her voice is quiet and raspy, as if she hasn't been drinking enough water either.

"If you don't eat, you are going to die."

"Aren't I going to die soon anyway?" She looks up at me with those big blue eyes of hers and even with the dark circles underneath, the beauty of them still pours out of her.

"Not necessarily." I know the chances that she is going to end up dead are high, but I don't want to think about that, not right now.

"I doubt men buy women like they're at a meat market just so they can take them out on nice dates. I'd rather starve to death then die at the hands of some sicko."

I know she is right, and it would probably be a kindness to let her die this way instead of selling her to the highest bidder. Yet, the thought of her dying has my chest aching.

I pull the pill bottle from my pocket and hand it to her. She looks down at it but makes no move to take it. Jesus, this woman is infuriating. Instead of forcing it into her hand like I want to, I throw it onto the mattress beside her and turn around, heading for the door.

"Don't leave... please," she begs.

I almost lose it right then. Balling my hands into fists, I grab the tray of food from the door. When I turn back around to look at her, her eyes are watery like she is about to start crying. *Fuck me.* She looks like a mess, but a beautiful mess, like the sky after a horrible thunderstorm. I close the distance between us and hold the tray in front of her face.

"Take a pill and eat," I order.

She looks down at the tray, examining the food. "Will you stay if I eat?"

Bargaining. She's bargaining with me. I consider her offer for a moment, even though I already know what the answer should be. I sit down next to her on the mattress, holding the tray of food on my lap. As soon as I settle, she scoots over to me, so her body is pushed up against mine.

I should push her away... I should get up and walk out of here, but I know I can't. I feel compelled to see this through to the end, to at least make sure she's safe for the rest of her stay here. I break off a piece of the sandwich and hand it to her.

Her small hand reaches out to grab it, and her thin fingers brush against mine as she does. Her skin is still cold, and suddenly, I have to fight the urge to pull her onto my lap and throw my arms around her. I want to hold her close, protect her, make certain she's taken care of. Everything I shouldn't do for her, I want to.

She starts taking small bites of the already bite-sized piece I've handed to her. I watch her chew, and it seems as if even this simple task takes an enormous effort for her. After a few bites, she leans her head against my shoulder and closes her eyes while she eats.

"You need to take one of these. It's just some pain medicine." I don't tell her that this is more like morphine and less like Tylenol.

"I don't want to take any drugs," she tells me sleepily.

"It'll help you feel better."

"Yeah and make me weaker... easier to be taken advantage of." Her words spark a fear deep in my belly. She's right. If she's sleepy, knocked out on pain meds, then any of the fucking bastards in this place can come in and take advantage of her.

"No one will touch you." The words vibrate out of me.

"Don't lie to me, Ivan."

I straighten up a bit at her use of my name. I didn't think about it when the guys called me by my name in her presence the other night. And now, I suddenly wish I knew her name.

"I know that far worse is to come for me. The least you can do is be honest with me, if you aren't going to let me go."

"No one will touch you or hurt you again. I won't let them." I don't realize how much I mean those words until I say them, and I know deep down that I won't let anyone hurt her or touch her again. I can't let her go, no matter how compelled I feel to, but I can protect her at least while she is here.

"What's going to happen to me?" she asks, and I hand her another small piece of the sandwich. She eats it slowly. I'm not sure I want to tell her what's going to happen, not when I shouldn't even be in here to begin with. If any of the men saw me in here, I'd have to come up with some kind of excuse, I have no real reason to be in here. It's unlike me, and I think the men are already starting to notice a change in my behavior.

"Just eat." I hand her another small piece, but she doesn't reach for it. I want to offer her more than this dry piece of shit sandwich, but I can't. Yet another item on the long list of fucking things that I can't bring myself to do for her.

"I'm done." She shakes her head slightly.

"You need to eat more than a quarter of a sandwich. You haven't eaten for nearly a week."

She sighs while continuing to shake her head. "I can't... I'm not hungry." Her body sinks more into mine, like she is too weak to keep holding herself up. She stretches out her legs in front of her and the shirt rides up to above her knees, revealing a little more of her skin. I almost throw the tray across the room when I see some dried blood on the inside of her thighs.

I twist to look at her, and she slides down the wall. I catch her before her head hits the mattress. My hands are on her thin upper arms, pulling her up straight before I can stop myself from doing so. Her eyes fly open, and she looks up at me, shock reflecting in her eyes.

"Who hurt you? Did someone come in here again?" My voice comes out much harsher than I intend it to, but I'm fucking furious.

I ordered them not to touch her, told them I'd kill them myself if they did, and yet here she fucking is, clearly hurt. I grit my teeth, wanting to leave the room right this second and find the fuckers who did this to her. All I feel is burning rage. Her eyes go impossibly wide, her body stiff with fear underneath my touch. Fuck, and now I'm hurting her, too. I loosen my grip, and she shakes her head slowly.

"No one came in here again, no one but you."

"Then why is there blood between your legs?"

She looks down at her thighs and squeezes them together as if out of reflex, as if she's trying to hide the evidence of whatever the hell happened.

"It's... It's nothing." She tries to pull away from me, but I don't let her. I watch her face closely, but she won't meet my eyes. She tries to pull the shirt down to cover her legs more, and her cheeks turn a faint pink. Is she blushing? Now that I've taken another look at her, I realize she looks more embarrassed than scared.

"I'm... well, I'm on my period," she says without looking at me.

I release her at once, feeling like an even bigger asshole than before. I squeeze my eyes shut, trying to make all of this go away. When I open my eyes again, I find her staring back at me with tears in her eyes. I look up and down her body. Her hair is matted in spots and greasy. Her legs are filthy, and she has been wearing the shirt I gave her for over a week now.

Christ. I pry my eyes away from her and look around the empty room that holds nothing but a dirty mattress. I can't take it anymore. Something inside me snaps. It cracks, and the contents seep right out of me. I have to get her out of here and cleaned up, even if it's just for a few hours.

I stand up, and she immediately starts pleading with me. "Please don't go, I can get cleaned up in the sink. I'll try to eat some more. Just please don't leave me alone. Please, Ivan. Please." Her words just add to the growing pain in my chest. The way my name falls from her lips makes it a million times worse. She reminds me of all the good I could do for her, that beneath everything, I am human, and I am capable of caring. That scares the fuck out of me, because caring for her will only mean one thing... and that would get us both killed. In my line of work there is no room for others. If my boss were to discover I cared for anyone...well let's just say it wouldn't end well.

Already having made my choice, I look down at her. "Get up."

She looks up at me, confusion marring her delicate features, and she gets up anyway. Her small arms push her up to stand on shaky legs.

"You're going to come with me to take a shower and then I'm going to bring you back down here... You will not run. You will not scream. Do you understand?"

She nods her head furiously, and her eyes light up just a little. I grab her by the arm and start guiding her outside the cell. Her steps are small and hesitant. At first, I think she is afraid, but after watching her for a few moments, I see her face contort in pain, and I quickly realize that she is far too weak to be walking.

"I'm going to carry you." I slide my arms underneath her. She lets out as small gasp as I pick her up but doesn't complain. I walk out into the hallway, and she leans her head against my shoulder.

"Close your eyes," I whisper as we walk. I don't need her to be looking around here. I'm already taking a huge fucking risk letting her out of her cell. She doesn't need to see anybody or anything around here. Looking down at her, I see she has followed my command and turned her face into my chest just like the last time I carried her.

I carry her all the way up to the third floor, where some of us have small apartments. I briefly set her down on her feet so I can grab my keys from my pocket and unlock the door. I twist the knob, opening the door. I gesture for her to walk in and she does, her eyes wide, her legs shaking as if she is unsure of what will happen next.

"You live here?" she asks, her eyes moving over the contents of the apartment. The place isn't much, just a one bedroom with a small kitchen and living room. It's only me living here, and I don't need all that much. She takes a few more steps, her fingers gliding over the back of my leather couch. I wonder what she's thinking?

Will she try and run away from me? Will she take my kindness for weakness?

"Yes, at least for right now." I pocket my keys and close the door behind us, locking the deadbolt into place. I don't think she is in any shape to run off, but it's better to be safe than sorry.

She turns to face me, and I can see she is nervous about being here. She is wringing her hands in front of her, swallowing repeatedly. The look in her eyes reminds me of a scared animal. I want to tell her she's safe with me, that no one will ever hurt her again, but then I'd be lying. Anyone could hurt her, including myself.

"Come on." I reach out and offer her my hand. She looks down at it for a moment, as if she's worried that taking it will harm her in some way. Then, as if she's made up her mind, she takes it.

I lead her into the bathroom, leaving her standing in front of the shower while I grab some towels. When I turn back around, I see her swaying and leaning against the wall for support.

She is so fucking weak, she can't even stand up for five minutes on her own. Damnit, this is my fucking fault. All mine.

How the fuck is she going to take a shower?

She's going to end up slipping and falling, probably breaking her damn neck in the process. I walk over to her and grab the hem of her shirt to pull it up and off her, but she stops me, grabbing me by the wrist, a quiet yelp of fear or maybe even shock falling from her lips.

"What are you doing?" She tries to make her voice sound strong, but she can't fool me.

"I'm helping you. I've already seen you mostly naked, remember? Plus, it's not like you're the first woman I've ever seen naked." I pause briefly, realizing maybe I shouldn't have said that.

"Look, you can't even stand up straight, so I'm not going to let you take a shower by yourself just so you can fall and break your neck."

She's looks so timid and completely unsure about all of this, but she lets go off my wrists and doesn't make another move to stop me.

Yet again, the way she blindly trusts me has my stomach in knots. She shouldn't trust me. If she was smart, she'd turn around and run out of this fucking room and back to her cell. She definitely wouldn't find comfort in my touch, that's for sure.

Gripping the hem, I pull the shirt up her body and over her head, and she lifts her arms a little bit so I can slip it off of her the rest of the way. I try not to let my gaze linger on her creamy white skin underneath and her small perky breasts, but I can't help it. It's been too fucking long since I took a woman, or at least that's what I tell myself as I continue to take in her body.

Even with her being a little too skinny for my liking, her body is undeniably beautiful, and I have the sudden urge to kiss her all over. To hear and feel her beneath me.

Fuck. No. I shake the thought away. Instead, I focus on turning the shower on. I adjust the temperature, waiting for the water to warm. The pipes squeak slightly, and once the water starts to fill the bathroom with steam, I turn toward her.

She takes an uncertain step toward the shower, and I start to peel my own clothing off. Since there is no fucking way I'm letting her shower alone, I might as well get my shower for the evening in, too. When I'm down to nothing but my boxers, I look up at her. It's then I realize just how different we look. She's all smooth creamy white skin, and I'm dark, with scars and tattoos.

Fear fills her gaze, and I realize that I probably should've told her I was going to be taking a shower with her. Gripping the edge of my boxers, I shove them down my muscled thighs.

If she's going to be afraid then she is, but either way, we're taking a shower.

"Take your underwear off," I order, stepping into the shower, extending a hand to her. She stands there frozen in place for a few seconds. Frustration fills my veins. Patience isn't something I have, not with my men, and not with anyone else in my life, but I know I have to be patient with her. At least a little bit. I give her a few more moments. I'm about to grab her and pull her in when she dips two fingers into her panties and pulls them down with shaking hands.

When she stands back up, she takes my hand and I gently tug her into the shower with me. The space is small, and suddenly, I'm aware of just how fucking bad of an idea this is.

5

Violet

He's huge. That's all I can think in that moment. Like huge, and I don't just mean his penis. I mean his body overall. How is it that he can seem bigger without any clothes on? I look him up and down. His eyes are an intense gray, a color that reminds me of the sky before a storm.

He's built, and I do mean built, like a tree standing thick and strong in the forest. A forest with tattoos. He has way more than the neck tattoo I have already seen. One arm is completely covered and the other one is half covered. There are two large ones on his chest and multiple pieces on his back. There are so many I can't take them all in.

His hair is a dark brown, almost the color of espresso, and I can't help but feel invaded by his body. His presence is intimidating and while I feel safe with him, I worry he may only see me as an object, rather than an actual human in this moment. After the way he looked at me when he took my shirt off, I wonder if he even cares about my feelings.

Another thought pops into my mind as the heated water beats down on us. Is he going to ask for his shirt back? Maybe he is going to send me back completely naked. A shudder of fear moves through my body.

"Can I still wear your shirt?" I ask as he squirts some shampoo into his hand. I try to keep my eyes trained to the floor rather than his body. There's only a foot of space between us and if I move even an inch, I'm going to be rubbing some part of my body against his.

"What?" he asks, as if I've asked him a stupid question.

"Your shirt, the one I've been wearing... can I keep it?"

He starts washing my hair without warning, his thick fingers threading through the strands with surprising tenderness.

"It's dirty... I'll give you something else to wear."

My mind relaxes at his words, and my body softens into his touch.

His large hands gently massage my scalp, and I find myself leaning into him as a low moan escapes my lips. I instantly regret making that noise and secretly hope he didn't hear it, though I know he did. When I open my eyes and peek up at him, his eyes are lustful. I worry for a moment he might try and have his way with me. After all, there isn't anyone who could stop him...

"Close your eyes." His voice is low and rougher than before, and fear sneaks up on me. My previous thoughts replay in my mind.

"W-Why?" I stutter, my body stiffening, making my muscles ache.

"So I can rinse out your hair." He takes the sprayer off the wall mount.

"Oh..." I mumble and close my eyes, feeling him run his fingers through my hair as he rinses it.

I let my head fall back and the position change has my head spinning. My stomach clenches, and I'm so overcome with dizziness that I think I might fall. Ivan must notice a change in my body because the next thing I know, his arm comes around my midsection, holding me flush to his chest with a steel grip.

"You okay?" he asks while holding me upright. My bare breasts rub against his muscled chest with every ragged breath I take, and I can't help the heat that creeps up my body.

"Yeah," I manage to say, but it comes out more like a breath than a word. "Just a little dizzy is all."

"I told you... you need to eat more. If you had finished that sandwich like I asked, you probably wouldn't be so weak." He attaches the sprayer back to the wall mount and takes a washcloth that's hanging on a hook, all while keeping a tight hold on me.

"Hold this," he says and hands me the washcloth. I take it from him, and he squeezes some soap onto it. It smells woodsy, like grass and the outdoors. He takes the washcloth back and starts to wash my back and my shoulders. My aching muscles relax at his touch, and I melt into him.

When he is done with that, he continues down my arms before suddenly spinning me around so that my back is against his chest. Another wave of dizziness hits me, but I press my hands to the wall and steady myself.

"Just lean against me. I'll hold you up."

I do as he says and lean into him. My breath hitches when I feel his erection pressed up against my ass. My heart beats furiously against my ribcage. I've never been so close to a man before.

He starts washing my stomach and my chest, moving gently across my skin. There's a kindness to his touch, one I don't understand.

How can his touch be so gentle, so kind, when he's doing all the bad things he is? He's a criminal... one who sells women. I should be running from his touch, not embracing it. He's the reason I'm here, isn't he? When the washrag moves lower, all my thoughts fly out the window.

"Spread your legs," he orders gruffly. I feel his chest heaving against my back. Against my better judgment, I do as he asks and spread my legs slightly... just enough for his hand to fit between them. When I feel his washcloth-covered fingers between my legs, I gasp, and my hands automatically grab onto his wrist to stop any further movements.

"I'm not going to hurt you, just relax."

I know I shouldn't trust him, but his words assure me and slowly I release my grip on his wrist once again, allowing him to clean me. I look down, watching as blood mixes in with the water swirling down the drain. Once he's finished washing me, he tosses the washcloth to the floor of the shower. I twist out of his grip and turn around to face him.

When I see the look in his gunmetal-gray eyes, I'm frozen into place. He looks so unhinged, so pent up with need or aggression or something I don't understand. Did I do something wrong?

"I promise, I'm not going to hurt you, but I want you to do something for me."

I blink slowly, my lashes fanning against my cheek. A nervous knot unravels in my belly.

Trusting his word blindly yet again, I nod my head, even though I know for certain that this is going to be something I don't want to do.

He looms above me for a moment, gauging my expression most likely, before he loops his arm around me again like he did earlier, holding me up to his left side. My right arm is dangling over his, while my left arm is in front of us. My gaze drops to his obscenely large penis.

"Give me your hand." His voice cracks, revealing a vulnerability I wouldn't have expected. I place my hand in his, and he guides me to his shaft.

"I want you to beat me off. Have you ever given a hand job before?"

I feel my cheeks heat at the word. *Hand job.*

"No," I whisper, feeling ashamed. I'm not sure why I feel the way I do, maybe because most eighteen-year-olds know more about sex and the male anatomy than I do.

A part of me wants to give back to him for being so kind to me, while the other part of me knows that being kind to one another is just plain human decency.

I look up at him, watching as his jaw clenches, the muscles jumping. *Is he angry?* He seems mad, and that only makes me more nervous. His grip tightens on mine, as he places our hands against his penis. I gasp at the simple touch. It's smooth and surprisingly soft beneath my hand.

"I'm going to guide you through it. I'm not going to hurt you or force you to do it, but I won't let you stop until I'm finished if you do this, okay?" I hear the want in his voice. He wants this, he wants *me*, and for some reason, that makes me happy.

"Okay," I whisper. I feel nervous but surprisingly I'm not really scared, not like I was with the guys who came into my cell. Ivan keeps saying that he won't hurt me, and I believe him. He doesn't want to hurt me, and he said he won't force me. He is giving me a choice, and I want to do this for him.

Within seconds of my response, he starts guiding my hand up and down his shaft with his hand still wrapped tightly around mine. He goes slow at first but I think that's just so he doesn't frighten me, and after a few strokes, he glances over at me to check if I'm okay, like he half expects me to starts screaming or crying.

I bite at my bottom lip nervously when he catches me looking down at where our hands meet. Heat creeps up my neck and onto my cheeks, and I wonder if I'm doing this right? I know he said he'd guide me, and he is, but I don't know if this is how it's done.

He starts picking up speed with each stroke, and a deep groan of pleasure vibrates from within his chest, slamming into me. I don't know what it is about that sound, but I suddenly want to hear it again, and I realize I want to be the one drawing that sound from deep within him.

"Can you do this by yourself?" he asks me with a near breathless voice.

I eagerly nod my head and see surprise flicker in his gaze. I want to please him. Right now, in this moment, I want nothing more, and it's not because I feel like I owe him, I just want to do it. I want to be close to someone, anyone. So, when he releases his hold on my hand, I do exactly as he was just doing, watching his facial expressions to determine if I'm doing it right or not.

He put his hand on the shower wall in front of us and lets his head hang down. I watch him closely as he closes his eyes, and his lips part, a growl emitting from his throat.

"Faster," he orders through clenched teeth. A heat settles between my thighs, his voice vibrating through me as I stroke him faster, my thumb rubbing over the slit at the head of his penis with each stroke. I squeeze him as hard as I can, my hand not quite big enough to wrap around him all the way. His eyes flicker open again, and he looks down at my body.

His arms tighten around me, pulling me close to his body as my hardened nipples rub against his heated skin and my bare pussy rubs against his leg. A number of sensations course through me, fear, excitement, pleasure. I refuse to cling to any one of them, afraid of what may come if I do. Instead, I focus on Ivan.

"Fuck... fuck..." he roars, his hand slamming against the tiled wall. The intensity of his pleasure pours out of him, and his hardened length throbs. My arm starts to grow tired, but I know he has to be close. I continue with the same rhythm until I hear him growl and watch eagerly as ropes of semen shoot from his penis and onto the tile in front of us. The sticky substance coats my palm and when I release my hold on him and pull my hand away, I stare down at it.

His eyes are closed, and his breathing is heavy. He leans against the wall as if he needs it to hold him up straight. It takes him a few moments to recover and when he opens his eyes again, he looks relaxed and satisfied. That is until his gaze meets mine and guilt starts to paint his features. I instantly have this irrational need to reassure him.

"It's okay... I didn't mind." I force a smile, but I know he can see right through it.

"I didn't plan this when I brought you up here. It wasn't my intention, I just..." I can tell he's sincere and means every word he says. He rinses us off one more time, never loosening his hold on me. I'm more than thankful for it, because I really don't think I could have stood up for much longer on my own. He has been carrying most of my weight this entire time, and I wonder how the hell he's still doing it. Then again, if I looked like him, I'm sure I could carry anything and everything around.

We get out together, and he releases me for a second to grab a towel.

He dries me off from head to toe before he wraps my body in a large towel and my hair in a smaller one. The way he does it with such ease has my mind kicking into overdrive. It seems like he has done this before and the thought of Ivan giving another woman a shower or bath like this has a lot of unwanted feelings settling into my gut. Curiosity gets the better of me and though I know I shouldn't, I ask anyway.

"Do you do this a lot? I'm only asking because it seems like you know what you are doing wrapping up my long hair in that towel."

"I haven't done this in a very long time, and I don't typically." Sadness coats his words. I'm relieved at his confession, and again, I don't understand why. It's not like he really cares about me. Not in a sense that he cares what will happen to me after I leave this place.

He wraps a towel around himself before leading me to his bedroom. Once there, he deposits me onto his bed. It's so soft underneath my legs, all I want to do is curl up and go to sleep on it.

Dread overcomes me like a wave when I remember what he said... I can shower and then I'm going back in the cell. I've been trying not to think about it, and I succeeded, but now that I remember what's going to happen, I'm on the verge of crying.

This is only a short vacation from my new reality. He is going to bring me back downstairs and leave me and then I might never see him again. My eyes burn with unshed tears. I don't know why but I don't want to cry in front of him right now. I watch him dig through his dresser, grabbing a few items and throwing them onto the bedside me.

He turns back around to face me, and I try to hide that I am on the verge of crying but, of course, he sees the unshed tears in my eyes.

"I told you... I can let you take a shower, but you have to go back to the cell now."

"I know. It's just... I'm always cold and alone. And scared that those guys will come back."

Ivan gives me a conflicted look, and I know I should be thankful for a shower and I am, but I don't want to be down there. I don't want to be away from him.

"I'll give you something warmer to wear and like I said before, they won't come back. They might be dumb but they know how to follow orders... they won't disobey me." His gaze flickers over my half-naked body like he might be tempted to want something more from me.

"I... that's all I can and will do for you. No one is going to mess with you while you're here." He doesn't apologize, and I don't expect him to. I just need to stop hoping for a miracle and realize that soon I'll be nothing but some rich man's toy. This is my new life...

"Here, put these on." He points at the clothes beside me. A thick gray sweatshirt that looks to be three times too big and a matching pair of sweatpants, with a black pair of boxers.

"Do you have some paper towels?" I feel my cheeks heat with embarrassment as soon as I ask the question. I'll take the embarrassment over bleeding all over myself.

"Yeah, why?" he asks as I watch him get dressed. His movements are effortless.

"For my... you know... period." I don't know what I'm more embarrassed about, talking about my period or the fact that I just watched him get dressed.

He doesn't seem to be embarrassed about either thing and walks out of the room, leaving me alone for few moments. I immediately start to panic.

Until this moment, I thought I just didn't want him to leave me in the cell by myself but now I realize I don't want him to leave me alone at all. I just want to be with him, near him. Maybe it's the constant being alone that scares me, or something else I don't really know, but the realization hits me hard because I know staying with him is never going to happen.

He comes back and hands me a roll of paper towels. I take it and pick up the clothes he's laid out for me. "Can I do this in your bathroom?"

"Go ahead." He nods toward the bathroom, and I get up and walk into the bathroom. I close the door behind me but don't lock it. I don't see the point. If he wants to come in here, I don't think the flimsy wooden door would stop him even if it was locked. That and if he wanted to hurt me, he already would've. I unwrap my towel and hang it on a hook before I unroll a few pieces of the paper towel and fold it into a pad.

I put it between my legs and pull the boxers on. I have to roll them up about ten time before they stay on, but this is much better than what I had before. I pick the bloody underwear up off the floor, cringing at the sight of them before tossing them into the waste basket under the sink.

Then I pull on the oversized sweatpants and sweatshirt, enjoying how heavy the thick material rests on my skin.

When I step back out moments later, Ivan is standing right in front of the door. He gives me a quick once-over and hands me a pair of socks. His face is void of all emotions and it's like he's slipped a mask on.

"Thank you." I sit back down on the bed and pull them on. The socks, just like everything else, are way too big on me, but I couldn't care less. Warmth is all that matters right now. Ivan is standing a few feet away, just watching me.

"It's time to go back downstairs." I nod, trying to be brave, but on the inside, I am so scared all I want to do is curl up in a ball and cry my eyes out.

We walk to the door together, and every step I take adds a two-pound rock to the contents of my stomach. Everything inside of me was screaming to beg and plead with him to stay.

"I'm going to carry you again. Keep your eyes closed," he warns before he bends down and picks me up just like before. I close my eyes and lean into him, determined to enjoy every last second of this.

6

Ivan

I PLACE her back on the filthy mattress in her cell, even though every fiber in my body doesn't want to. The thought of leaving her down her literally makes my chest hurt. She doesn't say anything, but her eyes tell me enough. She is begging me to take her back upstairs without a single word.

All she wants is for me to stay with her and if it wasn't for the way she was clinging onto me, I wouldn't even believe her.

How can she possibly feel safe with me?

Shaking my head, I turn around and walk toward the door. A quiet sob fills the room, and I can feel my heart crack wide open. Pushing through the expanding pain in my chest, I step out and shut the door behind me. I start walking away, thinking that I just need to get away and the need for her will fade. Instead, it gets stronger, like an invisible force pulling me backward, and I have to force my legs to move up the stairs.

Back at my apartment, I grab my jacket and my phone before I head back out. I need to get away from this place for a few hours to clear my head. It takes me ten minutes to walk through the heavily guarded compound and get to my car. It takes me another five minutes to make it through all the gates surrounding the building.

The whole time I can only think about one thing—the petite woman I left curled up on the mattress in that cell. I could never get her out of here unnoticed.

This place has more security than a level-five prison. The only way she is going to make it out of here is with a collar and a price tag around her neck—or in a body bag, but I refuse to let that happen.

That thought has me gripping onto the leather-wrapped steering wheel so tightly my knuckles turn white. I drive around aimlessly for a long time before I end up in front of some bar. I have every intention of getting so drunk that I forget my own name but after I down my second glass of whiskey, I realize that I can't bring myself to do it. I can't sit here and drink my sorrows away while she is scared and alone in that basement.

I throw some cash on the bar top and walk back out to my car, where I pass a couple on the way. They are holding hands, and she is leaning into him while giggling at something he said. And just like that, I find myself longing for something I have never wanted before... something I can never have, at least not with her.

Knowing that I can't save her from getting sold is eating me alive. It feels like someone poured acid into my gut. I can't change her fate but maybe I can at least keep her comfortable until the auction. I know it's a horrible idea and that it won't change anything in the end, but I just can't go on like it's not killing me to know she is down there. I could just go and sit with her... at least until she falls asleep.

On my way back to the compound, I pass a twenty-four hour pharmacy and decide to stop in. I suppose she could use some womanly stuff. I pull into the parking lot and park, exhaling deeply. What the hell am I doing? I don't even have a damn answer. Five minutes later, I stand in front of a shelf filled with tampons and pads.

What. The. Fuck.

Why are there so many different types of these things? How the fuck am I going to know what to get? Out of the corner of my eye, I see a middle-aged woman walk up to where I'm standing.

She grabs a pack of pads off the shelf and puts it in her shopping basket. Then she stops and looks up at me curiously. I look away before she sees me looking at her.

"There is no way in hell my husband would ever bring himself to buy me this. You look a little lost though."

Is it that obvious? Holy hell. Before I can get a word out, she turns and grabs another package off the shelf and hands it to me.

"Here, these are a good brand and they're a multipack for each kind of flow, so you can't go wrong."

What the fuck is flow? I hold the box of pads in my hand, looking down at them like they're going to grow a second head. The unknown lady gives me a soft smile, walking away before I can thank her. I toss the box into my little basket and look over the rest of the aisle.

Right next to the pads are condoms and a selection of lube. In an instant, my mind is filled with images of using both. Rolling a condom on my cock right before sliding into her. Rubbing lube all over her ass... maybe slipping a finger deep inside.. My dick is already pressing uncomfortably against my zipper, and I quickly turn to walk away before I get a raging hard on in the middle of this store.

I shake my head at myself... sex, with her? Not that it's a bad thought. The innocence she carries tells me she's a virgin. I mean, she had no idea how to give me a damn hand job. There's no way she's had sex and not given a hand job before. The problem with the thought is that sex is something I can never have with her. She must remain intact if she's to be sold to the highest bidder.

It's her owner's duty to strip her of her innocence to claim her, and I grit my fucking teeth at the thought. I hurry down the aisle and grab a pack of underwear hanging on one of the end caps. I check that they're a size small and then I rush down the next aisle and get a toothbrush and some toothpaste before I head to the register and pay for all of it.

The drive back to the compound only takes me a few minutes, and I park my car in the same spot as before and walk in with a bag full of stuff I never thought I would be carrying into this place... or carrying period. I walk straight downstairs, bypassing the guards, not stopping until I'm standing right in front of her cell, looking through the one-way mirror. If it wasn't for her blond hair, I would think there was just a pile of laundry laying on the bed.

I almost grin. She is curled in on herself, my clothes swallowing her tiny body. I stand there like an idiot watching her for a few minutes before I pull out my keys and unlock the door. As soon as she hears the door open, she sits up straight, her big blue eyes wide and alert.

I shouldn't be here; it becomes more apparent as a small smile pulls at her full lips. Clearly, she enjoys seeing me, probably looks forward to it. *Fuck.*

I cross the room and hold the grocery bag out to her.

"I got this stuff for you. I wasn't sure exactly what you needed so I got a multi pack."

She hesitantly takes the bag and looks inside it like something might jump out and bite her.

"Thank you." It's the most genuine thank you I've ever heard in my entire life, like I've just given her a bottle of water after a ten-mile walk in the desert. She takes the bag and carries it to the tiny bathroom.

"It's nothing." I shrug, playing it off when in reality it's huge. I've not only broken every one of my own rules by taking her out of her cell and giving her a shower, but now I've gone to the store and bought her a bunch of things.

This place isn't supposed to be a good, enjoyable, happy place.

It's not a vacation, it's a fucking death sentence, and I don't know why the hell I'm trying to make it seem like anything other than that. I see her wince as she hobbles back toward the mattress.

I clench my jaw. I shouldn't care if she's in pain. In fact, I don't… or at least I tell myself that, right up until I fucking open my mouth. "Are you okay?" I growl, simply because I don't want to ask the question but feel compelled to.

This woman represents everything I cannot have, everything that is bad about me and this damn world that I live in.

"Yes, I'm fine. It's just cramps; sometimes they're really bad." She sits back down while holding a hand to her stomach. "It should be better tomorrow. Usually the first and second day are the worst for me and today is my second."

"Where is that medicine I gave you?" My eyes scan the mattress, but I don't see the bottle. She reaches between the wall and the mattress and hands it to me. I open the bottle and let one pill fall into my hand.

"Take it," I order and hold it out to her.

"I really don't want to. I'll be fine, I swear. I have this every month, you know." Of course, I know she is right. This is nothing. She and every other woman on the planet deal with this every month. The problem is, none of my thoughts concerning her are rational.

"Take it and I stay until you go to sleep. Don't take it and I leave now."

She only thinks about it for two seconds before she takes the pill and washes it down with some water. I sit down next to her. She immediately scoots over to press her body against mine and leans her head against my arm. In a perfect world, someone like her would never look at someone like me to protect them, to save them.

"Why me?" she whispers. "Why did you have them kidnap me from that club?"

"I didn't. I don't know why they took you. I don't usually deal with this part of the business. The girls who get selected have nothing to do with me."

I don't know why I tell her this. I know I shouldn't. It doesn't change anything.

"They called you boss."

"I'm *their* boss... not *the* boss." I crack my knuckles, needing to do something with my hands before I run them through her silky hair.

She doesn't ask any more questions after that, and I'm so fucking glad that she doesn't. Silence settles over us and the room seems so quiet. I look at the four white walls. There is no sunlight or saving grace to this room. Everything about it makes me want to pick her up and carry her upstairs to my bedroom. She belongs in a bed. *My bed.*

No. The thought is irrational. She is not mine, and she never will be. There an internal battle taking place inside me and for once in my damn life, I want to do the right thing.

I couldn't save *her*... but I can save the tiny woman leaning against me. I listen, waiting for her breathing to even out and once it does, I listen a little longer before I get up very slowly, leaving her on the mattress. I walk to the door and unlock it. It creaks loudly when I open it, and I half expect her to wake back up at the noise, since it's so fucking loud. When she doesn't, I remember what she said to me before. If she takes the pills then someone could come into her cell and take advantage of her, and she wouldn't be able to defend herself.

The thought makes me furious. Jesus fucking Christ, I feel like it's a losing battle no matter what. I slam the door shut loudly while I'm still in the room and watch her closely.

Fucking great. Nothing. She doesn't even stir at the loud noise vibrating off the walls of her cell. I told the guys not to come near her again but what if one of my men is stupid enough to go against my orders? It wouldn't be the first fucking time. Every worst-case scenario possible pops into my head. What if someone comes in here, and she can't do anything? What if they steal from her the only thing she has left to give?

The only reason she got away last time is because she fought them, I remember Luca's face. He looked like a feral cat scratched his face... or a kitten. I look down at her motionless form. This time, with the pain pills in her system, there wouldn't be any fighting. She won't know what's happened until it's too late, and I won't be fucking responsible for that shit. I've got enough dark shit hanging over my head.

A surge of anger overcomes me, and I have to let it out. I'm so angry, furious. I need to break something but there is nothing in this fucking room, and that infuriates me even more. My hands are balled into tight fists, and I use one to punch the unforgiving concrete wall. It's a stupid choice, one I'm aware of as soon as my knuckles kiss the concrete. This just adds to the long list of stupid choices I've been making lately.

"Fuck," I bellow in pain, the sound of my voice loud in this piece of shit nothingness, and I grit my teeth, letting the pain fester inside of me. My hand throbs, and when I flex my fingers, more pain radiates from it, up and throughout my arm.

I know what I have to do, and I don't want to do it. I fucking don't, but I won't be able to live with myself if something happens to her while she is here. She's my responsibility now. I can't just forget about her.

I unlock the door once more before I pick up her limp body from the mattress and hold her to my chest. I carry her through the building and up to the third floor. As always, most of my men are either sleeping or doing other things. I somehow manage to unlock the door while holding her in my arms. Once inside, I take her to my bedroom and place her on the bed.

She looks like she belongs here. I shake my head and walk out of the bedroom.

Her earlier question rings loudly in my ears. *Why did they take her?* I know they write everything down about each woman they bring in and place the information into a file but typically, I don't read the whole thing. I just glimpse over it. Yet, now I have the urge to know how she got here and why she was taken.

I want to know everything about her. I clench my fists at my sides, I need to get her file, but the files are downstairs in my office. I walk back into the bedroom, telling myself I'm only doing it to check on her, when in reality I can't take my eyes off of her. I'm obsessed, my protective instincts overshadowing even my duty to the job.

She is completely out, having not even moved an inch. There is no way she is waking up any time soon, which is great because I need to go get that damn file. With one last fleeting look, I leave my apartment, locking the door behind me. I head down to my office to retrieve the file. The sound of laughter fills my ears. Sometimes, the men have card night, drinking and gambling.

I consider going down the hall to check on them but change my mind. I've got my hands fucking full as it is. As soon as I'm back in the apartment, I go and check on her just to find her in the same exact spot I left her in. With the file in hand, I sit down on the couch. For a long moment, I just stare at the brown folder, knowing that opening it will only make matters worse.

Knowing her name, how and why she was taken, is only going to act as gasoline on the already burning fury inside of me. Still... like the idiot I am, I open it. I swear I have a death fucking wish or something.

The first paper is the report that my men did on her when they brought her in. I read over it and my teeth grind together more with every word I read.

She was just too pretty to pass up.
Tiny. Five foot. 125 pounds. She looked like a virgin.

They weren't even there for her. They just took her because it was convenient. She was leaving the club early, and they just plucked her off the street and threw her into the van. I flip to the next page, damn near ripping the piece of paper in the process.

On the next page is a copy of her driver's license and a small background check that they ran. She smiles on the grainy black and white picture on the ID. She looks younger, happier, and I realize then that I've never actually seen her smile. Like actually smile, from pure joy. Yeah, she's given me a tiny smile, but nothing compared to the smile I'm looking at in front of me. I look over her ID, and all the info on the paper.

Violet Rivers, eighteen years old.

Shit. I knew she was young, but I didn't realize she was that fucking young. I continue reading; my eyes can't move fast enough. She just turned eighteen... I look at the date again and flip back to the first page.

Fuck. It was her birthday... she was taken on her fucking birthday.

I inhale a deep breath, but it doesn't feel like I'm getting enough air. I don't know why I do it, but I force myself to finish reading her background check.

Parents deceased. Only living relative... a sister, Ella Rivers. Violet just got out of high school, and she was enrolled in the local college, but the semester hadn't started yet. She didn't even have the chance to go to a single class... and now she never will. Now, she's on the road to being beaten, enslaved in a world full of hate and sex. Instead of going to college, she'll be used and abused, until they either kill her, or she kills herself.

"Fuck," I growl, wanting to scream. I shut the folder and toss it onto the table in front of me. I lean forward, holding my hands in my head, running my fingers through my hair. What the fuck am I supposed to do?

I can't let myself feel anything more for her then I already have. I can't let her in. Above all, I cannot save her from the monsters hidden in plain sight, not when I'm part of the reason she is here. I'm weak. I can't let her go. I can't save her, and it's killing me.

I scrub a hand down my face, and then shove from the couch, heading toward the kitchen. I open one of the cabinets that contain my favorite whiskeys. I grab the first one I see and open it, bringing the bottle to my lips.

She's nothing. Just another body, another job, another dollar bill. I tell myself this over and over again. I greedily drink from the bottle as if I'll find the answer to all my problems at the bottom of it. The whiskey coats my insides with warmth.

Why do I want to save her?

Because you couldn't save her.

I want to throw the bottle in my hands against the wall but instead, I continue drinking. I drink for hours, or at least I think it's hours. When I push up from the floor, my steps are unsteady, and I lean against the wall to stop myself from falling over.

Fuck. I squeeze my eyes shut to stop the world from spinning around me. I walk into my bedroom. I sound like a herd of elephants as I do, slamming into walls and knocking over some shit on one of my tables, I don't fucking know. Then I cross the threshold into my room and I see her.

Violet. My tiny kitten. So fucking perfect. So fucking beautiful. A temptress I'm willing to fucking risk everything for? I sag down onto the mattress beside her. The urge to hold her is so strong I grit my teeth and damn near sit on my hands to stop myself from doing so. Then, as if the universe is testing my control, Violet rolls over, snuggling into my side.

I press my nose into her hair. She smells like me, and roses, fucking roses. My mouth waters over roses, and I don't fucking understand this... her, me, what the plan is. I don't fucking get it but while I have her in my arms, I'm going to relish in her touch. I'm going to fucking hold her until I can't anymore, until the morning light enters the windows.

"Fuck, Kitten, what am I going to do with you?"

7

Violet

I'm warm. Overly warm. So warm it feels like the sun is beating down on me. I want to lean into the warmth, reach out and touch it. I groan into the soft sheets beneath my hands. *Soft sheets?* I don't know what it is yet, but something feels off... like I'm not waking up in the same place I went to sleep at.

"No. I'm sorry... I didn't..." a voice shouts beside me.

My eyes pop open, fear clinging to my insides like sticky honey. My gaze sweeps over the room, until they land on Ivan lying beside me. His face is scrunched up, pain and sadness painted on his features.

"No. No. No. It can't... she can't be gone..." Ivan roars, and I push off the mattress, gripping onto his thick shoulders. Is he having a nightmare? What's happening to him? I shake him or try to at least. His arms flail back and forth, his fists are clenched, and they land heavily against the mattress. He starts to toss and turn, and I worry he may roll over me and squish me.

"Ivan, wake up. Wake up." I shake his shoulders.

"I'm sorry, Mira. I'm so sorry." The anguish in his voice rips through me. *Mira? Who could she be?* I don't know what he's dreaming about, but something is haunting him, chasing him even in his dreams. I can't stand to hear him be so hurt.

"Ivan!" I yell this time. When he doesn't respond, I decide to slap him. Pulling my hand back, I slap him square across the face, my palm connecting with his heated cheek. The sting from the contact of my hand on his skin can still be felt when his eyes open, his hand coming up to grip my wrist as if out of reflex.

His grip is hard as steel, and I grimace at his touch. There's a feral look in his eyes, a deep fear. I only catch a glimpse of it before he blinks, and it's gone. Anger replaces those emotions and flares in his stone-gray eyes. A coldness sweeps through me as he sits up slightly. It's then that I catch a whiff of whiskey. It hangs in the air between us.

"Were you drinking?" I ask softly.

Ivan's eyes bleed into mine for a long moment, before he releases my wrist with a shove. I'm not sure what happened. When I fell asleep, everything was different. I was in my cell, but now I'm here, and I don't understand why. I don't understand why he's so angry with me.

"Why did you slap me?" His voice is gruff, and he sounds like he might've been swallowing gravel all night. I would assume so as well if he didn't smell like a distillery

"You were screaming. Did you have a nightmare?"

"That's none of your fucking business." His brash response surprises me. He's never talked to me with so much anger in his voice. Without even looking at me, he gets up from the bed.

"It's okay, Ivan. I'm sorry if she hurt you…"

As fast as Ivan got up from the bed, he's storming right back toward me, his eyes blazing with emotions I don't understand as, he puts his finger in my face.

"You don't fucking know anything. Nothing. You're lucky you've weaseled your way under my skin as far as you have, because otherwise, you'd be just like the nine other women downstairs."

I blink, his words like a punch to the gut. *Nine other women?* A sudden surge of anger grips onto me, refusing to let go. I'm angry because I'm here against my will. I'm angry for the other women also being held against their will, and I'm angry at this Mira for hurting Ivan, even though I obviously shouldn't be. I'm angry at the world and before I even realize it, I'm yelling back at him.

"I'm sorry... I didn't know, okay? I woke up and you were screaming in your sleep. I was scared. I didn't know what was happening, and I don't know who Mira is but—"

My words are cut off before they can even finish coming out. Ivan is on me in a flash, his hands gripping my arms so tightly I cry out in pain.

He starts to shake me, his face millimeters away from mine.

"Don't even fucking say her name. You don't fucking know anything!"

Tears fill my eyes. Why is he so angry?

I feel like I have whiplash when he releases my arms just to grip onto my waist with equal force. He picks me up and throws me over his shoulder, knocking the breath from my lungs in the process.

I just don't understand... I don't understand why he is so mad. Why is he suddenly treating me like this? Why did he even bring me up here? I don't know anything, and everything about this situation terrifies me. The only person I have is him, and he's angry with me, furious.

"Ivan," I whisper, needing him to tell me it's going to be okay.

"Shut up and keep your eyes closed," he orders as we walk out the front door and into the hall. I close my eyes and grip onto the fabric of his shirt, hoping that I didn't just make the biggest mistake ever. I should have kept my mouth shut. If I would have just stayed quiet, I would be still in Ivan's bed right now. I would be warm and tucked into his side. This is my fault. All mine. We walk down a flight of stairs, before turning to walk down another. Ivan's steps come to a sudden halt, his grip on me tightens and in turn, my finger nails dig into the cotton of his t-shirt.

"Ivan." An unfamiliar voice reaches my ears. It belongs to a dark sinister man. I know it even without seeing his face. It's merely his tone, and the reaction that Ivan has to his presence, that tells me all I need to know about him.

"Yulie," Ivan greets him.

"Is that one of the girls from downstairs?" Yulie's voice grows closer and heavy footsteps bounce of the walls. He's walking over to us. My body starts to shake, and I want to go back in time to change what I did. I want to apologize and beg and plead.

"Yeah, I don't like to fuck them down there. It's fucking filthy in those cells, and I don't want to catch some disease." Hearing Ivan talk so vulgarly about me only makes me more scared. I know he's lying to protect me but hearing him talk about me like I'm nothing more than something to fuck scares me and saddens me all at once.

"I hear ya. She does have a nice ass. I suppose she'd be worthy of fucking." I feel a hand grab my ass, but I don't know who's it is. I squeeze my eyes shut, wanting the moment to end as the same hand reaches between my legs. I feel him grip me there, between my legs, and I want to kick and scream, tell him to stop, but I know that would just make things worse.

It wouldn't just hurt me. It would hurt Ivan, too. It would make him have to hurt me and even though I know he's mad at me right now, I don't think that's something he'd really want to do.

"Too bad I have an early meeting to attend or I would take her off your hands for a few hours."

"She'll be in the auction if you want to have her all to yourself."

Bile rises in my throat, threatening to come out of my mouth if I don't get it under control.

"I thought we only sell virgins at the auction?" The man isn't asking, he's stating.

"That's why I only fuck them in the ass. Might as well use them while they're here. There isn't any harm in preparing them for the world that's to come."

The other man starts laughing, and I have to concentrate on not throwing up.

I wonder if Ivan's done this before? He's either a really good liar or he's done something like this before.

"I guess that's one way to get around it. You take care now."

Yulie's heavy footsteps move away from us, and Ivan continues walking down the stairs. Once we're back in the cell, he walks right up to the mattress and drops me onto it. I look up at him, but he's already turned his back to me and is halfway across the cell.

"Ivan?" My voice comes out small, and it trembles even though I try to stop it. He doesn't stop walking, or turn around, and he doesn't say anything either. He just walks out the door, slamming it shut behind him. The loud noise makes me flinch and a new set of tears make their way down my face. I feel sick and curl up into a tight ball in the center of the mattress, wishing more than ever that I would have just kept my mouth shut.

"I'm sorry..." I whisper to no one in particular. My chest heaves as I sob into the dirty mattress. I want to go home. I want to see my sister and go back to a normal life. I question what bad thing I've done in my life to deserve to be where I am right now.

I slam my fist into the mattress. I never should've gone to that club. I never should've listened to my friends. The tears keep coming, and I know there's no point in stopping them. My tears are the only thing I have left that are mine.

∼

Two days pass before I see Ivan again. I spend most of that time crying in a fetal position. My hopes that he's coming back to me are withering away with each passing hour.

The second meal of the day has already been served, so when I hear the door unlocking, I perk up. When I see his large body appear in the doorway, I almost jump up and run to him. Instead, I just sit there frozen in place, afraid to open my mouth. I don't know why he's here. Hell, he could be coming to get me to ship me away.

Without saying a word, he crosses the room, bends down, and picks me up, throwing me over his shoulder like he did last time.

"Keep your eyes closed," he says before walking out and slamming the heavy door shut behind us. He starts making his way upstairs, faster than normal, like he is in a hurry or maybe he just doesn't want to run into someone else. Then again, neither do I.

He doesn't stop until we are in his apartment and the door is shut behind us. I open my eyes and see he is walking into the bedroom.

"Ivan?" I whisper, but he doesn't answer. Instead, he swings me from his shoulder onto his bed, making me bounce on the soft mattress. I gaze up at him, confused and a little scared, but then I see his expression, and I know he didn't bring me up here to hurt me.

"I'm sorry," he tells me and gets on the bed with me, positioning himself on top of me. He is holding himself up on his elbows and his large body looms over my small one.

"I didn't mean to hurt you the other night. I lost control. But believe me, it was not intentional."

I know shouldn't trust him. Shouldn't just accept his apology. He's a criminal, probably a murderer, too, and he's selling me and other women for money. Still, I believe him.

He moves over me until his face hovers directly above my own. Then, without even an inkling of hesitation, his lips are on mine. He tastes like mint, and he kisses like me he's trying to remind me of the kind man he is.

I've kissed a couple guys; each occasion was sloppy and one I didn't want to revisit but none of them ever kissed me like this... like I was the air they needed to breathe. My breath hitches in my throat when his huge hand cups me by the cheek. His touch is tender, kind, and I melt into it.

I feel his tongue slip across my bottom lip, begging for entry. I've never French kissed before. It excites me, and I part my lips, moaning when his tongue touches mine.

The kiss deepens, and he strokes the inside of my mouth, leaving me feeling all warm and tingly inside. I lift my hands, pulling him down on top of me. I can feel his huge erection pressing into my belly, and panic shoots through me momentarily.

That panic quickly disappears when his warm body presses me into the soft mattress, making me feel safe and protected, as if he is guarding me from everything bad in the world with his body. I start to melt underneath his touch, and I revel in the feeling of his heavy body against mine.

My body seems to move on its own, as if it knows what to do, and I let it, because I've never felt the way I do right now. My fingers dive into his hair, tugging on the strands. While he cradles my head, kissing me with every ounce of who he is. I lift my hips and spread my legs wider, wanting more, needing more. Ivan grunts above me as if he's in pain before pulling away but only slightly.

His fingers roam down my body, his eyes remain on mine, pleading, questioning as he slips beneath the hem of the shirt I'm wearing. His thick fingers ghost over my skin, and I shiver. He touches me as if I'm going to break, like I'm a fragile piece of porcelain.

"I... I want you," I whisper, giving him permission but instead of touching me, instead of giving us both what we want, he pulls away.

"I want you, too, you don't even know how much, but we can't." He looks away as if he is trying to hide his face from me, as if he's ashamed. "Do you want to take a shower? You can go by yourself."

"What if I want you to come?" I ask, my teeth sinking into my bottom lip. I don't know what I'm doing or even what I'm asking for. All I know is that after being away from him for two days, I need to show him how valuable he is to me, how important his presence is, because then maybe he won't leave me all alone again.

"I don't think you know what you want, Kitten. If you knew

everything about me, about the things I've done, you wouldn't be wanting me to touch you, let alone take a shower with you."

His response hurts and feels a lot like rejection, but I've been hurt worse in my time here, and though I might be inexperienced and a bit naive, after the way he kissed me, I know he wants me. He can deny it all he wants, but his body proves otherwise.

"You're part of the reason I'm here, Ivan, and I still want you, so I think I know what I am asking for."

Nervous laughter spills from his throat. "No, you haven't the first clue what you're asking for, and I might be a bastard, but I'm not taking that from you, especially before the checking."

My brow furrows. "The checking?"

"Come take a shower, and I'll take one with you."

I oblige, springing from the bed. I walk into the bathroom and pull off all of my clothes, tossing them to the floor. I am not as timid as I was last time when I got naked in front of him. Ivan does the same, though his movements are slower and just like last time, I enjoy watching him strip. My eyes rake over the dark ink painted on his skin. He's toned and tan, and my mouth waters with every new inch of flesh I see.

"Are you still bleeding?" He turns the water on and steps into the shower, extending a hand outward to me.

"No." I take his hand and groan when the heated water lands against my back. When I look up at Ivan, there's a hunger reflecting in his gray eyes.

"I think you knew what you were doing when you asked me to take a shower with you, Kitten." His tone is playful and makes me smile.

I step closer and reach for his erection, but he snatches my wrist in an unbreakable hold.

"Not today, Kitten. I can't have sex with you, but I can give you pleasure." He grins before spinning me around and pulling me flush to his chest, so my back is pushed against his front. I feel his penis press into my lower back, right above my ass cheeks, and I wonder for a moment what he is doing. He said he can't have sex with me, because of the *checking*, whatever that is, but knowing what the future holds, that some rich man is going to take it, makes me want to give it to Ivan even more.

With that thought, I lean forward and push my ass back against his raging erection.

"Violet," he grits out, each finger on his hand wrapping around my hip, holding me in place. My name on his lips sounds strange, not to mention I didn't even know he knew my name.

"I want you to be my first. If I'm going to be sold anyway, why does it matter? If this is the only thing I have that's mine to give away then I want to give it to you." I peer at him over my shoulder. I can see the conflict in his eyes.

"No. I want you, fucking believe me, I do, but I can't. If they find out you aren't a virgin when the doctor checks you then it's procedure to give you to the men. The higher ups, then the lowers. Eventually, you'll be sent to the whorehouse, that's if you don't die first. I'm not going to let that happen to you because I wanted to get my dick wet."

I gulp at his confession. "Oh..." It's the only thing I can say. I'm a whole lot of shocked. Shocked that he would tell me these things, shocked that they would do that to someone. Overall, I'm just so fucking surprised at how cruel of a bitch the world is.

"But I can do other things to you. I can finger you." He releases my hip and trails his fingers down my lower back, over my ass, and between my legs. "I can eat you out. Feast on your pussy."

I shiver at his brash words.

"I've never done either of those things." My chest heaves at my admission.

"Don't say shit like that, Kitten, not when I'm already barely hanging on by a shred."

I shiver, feeling every word he said down to my core. He nudges my thighs apart with his hand and presses me against the tiled wall. I turn my head, placing my cheek against the cold surface.

My hardened nipples move over the damp tile, sending sparks of pleasure between my legs.

"I'm going to finger you, and then I'm going to taste you on my tongue. If you want me stop at any point, just say so but know I will not touch you again. Not even if you beg me, Kitten."

His body is big enough to loom over mine, and while I feel one of his hands between my thighs, the other grips onto my hip, guiding me to where he wants me. With my chest pressed against the wall and my ass jutted out, I feel exposed.

Our eyes connect, and I feel the heat of his body seeping into mine as he leans into me, all his hard edges touching my soft curves.

"Fuck, you're beautiful, Violet, so fucking beautiful." His breath fans against my ear, his teeth grazing the sensitive flesh.

"Please..." I whimper, unsure of what I am asking for. I feel his fingers spread my lips, and I gasp at the sensation. Another finger glides over my engorged clit and a shudder of pleasure moves through me.

"Have you ever played with yourself?" Every slip of his finger over my clit makes it harder to think, harder to breathe.

"Yes..." I admit.

"Did you ever come?" he asks, a small smile tugging at his lips. I remember the few times I made myself come with my clumsy fingers. I felt not even a fraction of what I'm feeling right now.

"Yes," I confess again

The movements of his finger halt, and I damn near scream in frustration.

"Please, don't stop..." I sound desperate and maybe I am. I want his touch, his kisses, the heat of his body on mine. I want to feel wanted and cared for. He leans his head down and nibbles on my shoulder. I let my head fall to the side to give him better access to my neck, and he takes full advantage of it, kissing, licking, and sucking on the sensitive flesh. My moans echo throughout the small shower stall and right back into my ears.

"Touch yourself, Kitten. Tease your clit like you would if you were alone. Pinch it and rub it, and I'll finger you."

I follow his command, wanting only the pleasure I know he can give me. My hand shakes nervously as I move it toward my pussy. I lick my lips, and my eyes flutter closed as I touch myself there just as he was. It doesn't feel the same... but then I feel him moving his fingers back toward my entrance. I spread my legs wider, giving myself to him completely.

"Mmm, I love that you're so eager for my touch, Kitten."

He circles my entrance with one thick finger, teasing it, massaging it, and then he dips in, just the fingertip. The feeling isn't completely foreign. In fact, it's enough to make me pant. He pulls out the tip of his finger and dips back inside, a little bit more than before. I don't think he is all the way in yet, but a delicious fullness fills my belly when he moves his finger around inside me.

"I'm not going to go real deep, just in case. But I'm going to keep my finger inside you until you come on my hand." His low raspy voice is right next to my ear, and I feel like his voice has a direct line to my pussy. Pleasure starts to build deep in my belly, the pressure of his finger inside me radiates pleasure outward.

"You stop touching yourself and I'll take my finger out," he warns.

I want to tell him I couldn't if I tried but the only thing leaving my mouth right now are moans and pants.

I rub my clit faster, pinching it between two fingers, while he moves his thick digit in and out of me. His movements are gentle and precise, and a coil of pleasure starts to unravel inside of me at the rhythm. I can feel him splayed out over my backside, his firm penis pressing against my leg. He's panting with need as much as I am, and all the sensations coupled together build deeper and deeper, pulling the typhoon of pleasure right out of me.

"Ivan... I'm going to..." I can't get anything else out because the pleasure flooding my veins takes my breath away. Every muscle in my body tightens, a euphoric fog clings to me and I end up on my tiptoes as the sensations overtake my body. Waves of pleasure float over me, and I cling to the tile. I can barely hold myself up. Only then does Ivan slip his finger out of me. My eyes feel heavy, and I let him sling both of his arms around me, carrying most of my weight. He gave me something I've never felt before, and I'll never forget that.

"Thank you," I murmur, leaning against his chest. I close my eyes, enjoying the aftermath of the endorphin rush, and though he doesn't say anything, I know he feels the same things I'm feeling. An invisible teether, pulling us together, bringing us closer and closer together.

8

Ivan

HER TINY BODY leans against mine, and I know if I wasn't holding her up right now, her knees would buckle. Her cheeks are flushed, and she's still trying to get her breathing under control. Then I realize... I am, too. Fuck, that was hot. Her pussy was so tight around my finger, clenching and squeezing the fucking life out of me. I want nothing more than to plunge my dick deep inside her, to feel her pussy squeeze my dick like she did with my finger moments ago.

My balls ache, and my cock is so hard I don't know if it will ever go down again. I groan, knowing that I can't have her. Not this way, not any way. She isn't mine to keep, mine to have.

I reach for the shampoo and squeeze some into her hair. With my free hand, I start washing her, massaging her scalp while moving the suds through her long hair. I wish more than ever that we were in another world where I could have her, make her mine.

"What's the checking thing you were talking about?"

I question for a moment if I should tell her or not. Would it be worse to know? If she knows and fights them, she could get hurt, but if she knows and is prepared, maybe it'll be easier for her.

Then again, she might be just as scared. I don't internally argue with myself until after I've rinsed out her hair. By that time, she's regained some strength and can stand on her own again. She turns to look at me, her big blue eyes pleading with me.

Fuck, I know then I'm going to tell her, even if I don't want to. She's got this pull on me, something about her makes me want to do the right thing. I hand her a washcloth after squirting some soap on it. She takes it and starts washing herself, while I start on myself.

"We have a doctor come and check out each of you to make sure you aren't sick and don't have any diseases that can be given to the buyer." I pause briefly, not wanting to say the rest. "They also check to make sure each of you are still virgins. We only sell virgins because they bring in the highest paying dollar and usually these things are checked when they bring you in, but this time around, the doctor wanted to wait."

Violet gives me a shocked expression. "So, they will just take me somewhere and force me to lay there while they inspect me?"

I gulp, "Yes. One of the guards will come and get you and take you down to the doctor's office. There you will strip and get into the chair."

"What happens if I don't want to do it?" she whispers. I think she already knows the answer, but I answer her anyway, just to prove how horribly dangerous this could be for her.

"If you don't do as they tell you, they'll hurt you. It will happen one way or another, Violet. And if you keep fighting them, they'll give you a sedative. If they do that then..."

"Then I can't protect myself," she finishes for me. The idea of one of the other men touching her makes me furious, makes me want to break bones, rip flesh, kill and destroy. Every instinct inside me tells me to claim her, but I can't, and it's fucking killing me. When all of this is over, I'll have to let her go. When it comes time for the auction, everything I did here won't matter, and I hate that.

Violet rinses all the suds off her body, and then I do the same. Once we're both clean, we step out and I dry her off, wrapping her hair up just like I did the other day.

She smiles up at me, but there is a sadness in those big blues. "I'm sorry about what happened the other night. About slapping you and yelling at you."

She has no reason to be sorry. I shouldn't have grabbed her, shook her, I shouldn't have hurt her over the memory of my sister.

"You have nothing to be sorry for." I wrap a towel around my middle, shielding my still rock-hard cock.

"I do though. I don't know who Mira is, and I shouldn't have assumed something." *Her* name being said out loud, especially from Violet's mouth, pisses me off. But I'm not angry at Violet. No, this anger is all mine.

"It's really okay. I shouldn't have lashed out over a nightmare."

Violet doesn't look like she believes me, and that's fine. I don't want to talk about my dead sister anymore, or how she came to be dead in the first place. Instead, I walk over to my dresser and pull out a t-shirt and a pair of boxers, tossing them to her. She pulls the boxers up and then pulls my t-shirt on over her head.

It swallows her slim body whole, and for the first time, I look at her, really look at her. She looks good in my clothes, and the comparison of my body to hers is yet another reminder of why I need to protect her. She's so small and delicate. I drop the towel wrapped around my middle without thought and pull on a pair of clean boxers.

"What's going to happen to me, Ivan? I've been here awhile. I don't know how long exactly, but I do know that this auction you keep talking about has to be coming up soon?"

She asks me questions she knows I shouldn't answer but ones I can't deny answering.

"I shouldn't really tell you," I mumble, heading toward the bed.

I'm exhausted, and after forcing myself to be away from her for two days, I miss her being here in my bed beside me.

"Please don't keep this from me. I need to know how much time I have left." She states matter-of-factly, talking like she is waiting for her death sentence... and maybe she is.

My chest hurts thinking about it, thinking about handing her over to some rich fuck so that he can violate her. I'm sending her to be broken in the worst ways.

"Ten days... you have ten days."

She shakes her head slowly as if she has to digest the information.

"Can I ask you something else?" She sounds unsure, and she looks up at me, almost embarrassed.

I nod.

"Why can't you keep me? Can't you just ask your boss if you can have me, or you buy me yourself? I could work off the money."

I walk up to her and kneel right in front of where she is sitting on the bed. I take both of her hands in mine and look at her. "Trust me, if I thought there was even a sliver of a chance that he would let me have you, I would do it in a heartbeat. But it just doesn't work like that. Rossi has a zero policy on weakness. If he were to find out that you mean anything to me, he would kill you with a smile on his face."

A small gasp escaped her lips. I know all of this probably scares her but everything I'm telling her is the truth. Maybe that makes me an asshole, but I'd rather her know than have her assume I don't want her at all.

"So, you would keep me if you could?"

I feel us moving closer and closer into uncharted waters. I've never wanted anything like I want Violet, but confessing it makes me feel weak. And claiming her is only going to prove that further.

"I would help you... but I wouldn't keep you even if I could." Regret fills my body as soon as the words leave my lips, and I see the pain of rejection in her eyes. I get up and turn away from her, unable to look at her despair any longer. Telling her how I feel about her... how I would keep her forever if I could would only make things worse. It would make this already complicated situation much more complicated.

"You can stay here at night, but you have to go back to your cell during the day." I hate it but this is the only thing I have left to offer her.

"Every night?" she asks, perking up a bit. I sit down next to her on the bed and we angle our bodies so we're looking at each other.

"If you want, yes." She nods furiously at my offer, her eyes lighting up.

"I can come and get you after they bring you food at night, but I have to take you back before anyone notices in the morning."

"Okay," she whispers and forces a smile. I don't know why I just now realize it, but she might be the bravest person I've ever known.

I have no doubt that she is scared shitless, and she has every right to be. I wouldn't hold it against her if she was screaming, kicking, and crying every time I left her in that cell, but she tries her very best to put on a brave face.

"Come on, let's get some sleep." I nudge her to scoot up and lie down but she stops me with a hand to the shoulder.

"What about you?" She looks down at the tent between my legs.

"Don't worry about me. You don't have to do anything," I try to assure her. I don't want to take anything else from her. She'll endure enough in the weeks to come.

"But... I want to. I can do it like I did it the other day."

I nearly lose it right then and there. I want her so fucking bad, it hurts. It literally makes my body ache.

"Did you not like it... last time in the shower?" There's a frown on her lips, and I want to kiss it away. I want to scream from the rooftops how much I fucking loved her tiny hand on my cock, stroking the life out of me.

"Of course, I did." I shake my head, and her brow furrows in confusion. I know I need to better explain myself simply from the look on her face, "I just don't want you to feel like you have to do something for me, like you're repaying me or something. You don't owe me anything. I would do this stuff for you even if you didn't give me a hand job or let me touch you."

"I really want to do it." Her voice is low but determined and then, as if she think she's strong, she takes her tiny hand and places it on my shoulder, pushing against me in a feeble attempt to get me to lie down. Her small attempt at making me do what she wants me to do has me chuckling.

"Please? I just want to make you feel as good as you made me feel." She peers up at me, her eyes wide, looking for acceptance. I lick my lips, knowing I'm going to tell her yes. It's a losing fucking battle when it comes to telling her no.

"Fine." I grit my teeth, scooting back up the mattress before lying down, with my hands behind my head. I feel her eyes move over me as she kneels beside me on the bed. She dips her fingers into the waistband of my boxers and pulls them down over my thighs. Once the fabric passes my cock, it springs free. Violet seems much surer of herself this time, and I want to tell her how sexy it is, how fucking happy I am that her perfect hands want to touch such a bad, fucked-up person like me.

Without any hesitation, she wraps her fingers around my swollen dick. A hiss escapes my lips, from the contact of her hand on my skin. She starts stroking me right away, up and down, up and down. I groan out in pleasure and she smiles at me, adding a little pressure. She's working me over so well that I have to force my hands to stay behind my head. I want to fucking touch her everywhere.

Using her other hand, she stacks it on top of the other to cover more of my length.

I look at her through hooded eyes and watch her stroke me. Her cheeks and neck are flushed, and her eyes are filled with lust. She wasn't lying. There's no fucking doubt about it. She wants this, she wants me, and that excites me. It makes me want things I have no business wanting.

It makes me want her even more.

"Faster, Kitten," I order, and she does. Her hands start moving faster, while she squeezes me more roughly than she had been before, and I'll bet if I slipped a hand down between her thighs, I'd find her soaked with need, ready for every inch of my cock.

Thinking about her tightness and how fucking good it would feel to be inside of her is what drives me over the edge. I knew I wouldn't last long but fuck, I feel like a teenager again. She only stroked me for a few minutes and the tingling in my spine turns into an explosion of pleasure raging throughout my body. I squeeze my eyes shut and throw my head back against the headboard. She keeps stroking me through my orgasm, and I feel my warm thick cum shoot out and onto my stomach.

"Fuck..." I huff, my chest rising and falling like I just sprinted the fucking mile.

When I open my eyes again, she is still kneeling beside me with her hands in her lap and an actual smile on her face. Not a forced or fake one. No, this is a genuine smile, and I don't fucking get it. How can she be so happy about doing something as mundane as beating me off?

I get up from the bed and clean myself off, pulling my boxers up in the process. When I come back to the bed, I rest my back against the headboard. She moves up toward me and leans in as if she wants to kiss me but is not sure if it's okay to do. She should know by now how much I want her lips on mine. Grabbing her, I pull her close. Our lip crash together, and she snakes her arms around my neck, pulling me in even closer until there is no space between us at all.

She's so perfect, and everything I can never have. I kiss her gently, like she's going to break if I don't and then I hold her in my arms. She starts to doze off, and I relish in the comfort of actually being able to hold her in my arms. I've held her in my arms before but never after something so domestic.

My eyes start to flutter closed, and I'm about to go to sleep when a loud knocking on my door has both of us on high alert. Immediately, Violet starts shaking. Her eyes are wild with fear and all I want to do is tell her that everything is going to be fine but even I know that'd be giving her a false sense of hope.

"Just a second," I yell to whoever is on the other side of the door. Violet looks at me as if I can save her but I'm sure she knows better by now.

"Hide in there," I whisper, pointing toward the small closet to the right of the room. She gets up, scurrying across the floor, her legs shaking. I get up as well and pull on a pair of flannel pjs. I wait until she's hidden inside the closet before I walk to the front door. I undo the locks, grip the knob, and suck in a deep breath. I make sure all emotions are void from my face before I twist the knob and pull the door open.

"Ivan," Yulie greets me, a sinister smile on his lips. Of course, he walks into my apartment without seeking permission, and I have no choice but to step aside and let him come in, that's just how this world works. I shouldn't have anything to hide, and I don't, minus the tiny woman hiding in my bedroom closet. I grind my teeth together, clenching my jaw to stop myself from saying something that will definitely get me in fucking trouble.

I wouldn't be surprised if I end up breaking a tooth tonight.

"Yulie, I didn't know you made late-night house calls." I joke, closing us inside.

"Well, there is a pressing matter that cannot wait until morning."

"Is that so?" I lift a brow curiously. Certainly, if there was a *real* pressing issue, Rossi would have called me, right?

"Yes, I just moved the doctor visit up. He'll be here first thing in the morning to check out all the girls." I didn't miss the way Yulie looked around the room, as if he was going to find something he shouldn't. He wasn't here just to tell me something... he was here to investigate.

"What's the rush?" I fold my arms across my bare chest. In a fight, I'd have Yulie beat ten to one. The fucker was a toothpick, a twig I could snap in half in a second.

"I need a new plaything sooner than expected. Mine... seems to have broken. Poor thing was beautiful as hell. I guess I'm just too hard on them." An evil smile spreads across his face, and I know exactly what he is saying. I force a smile, hoping he buys it.

"So that's why I want this done tomorrow, so I can have a new toy... or two. I really hope number five will be available. I'd love to have her as my new pet. Luca told me she's in need of breaking, and you know how good at that I am."

My self-restraint is being tested like never before. My hands twitch with a carnal need to rip his heart out of his chest and shove it down his throat. He wants Violet. *My Kitten. Mine.* The word didn't even exist in my mind before she came along, all I know is that I can't let it happen. I know what he does to his girls and they never last longer than a few weeks... some only a few days.

When she goes to the auction, I can at least hold on to the illusion that it's not going to be that bad for her. Maybe the guy will just be into control and not pain. Maybe she could actually have a decent life? I know it's a long shot, but I can't let myself think that there is no hope for her. I can't let her go unless there is a sliver of a chance that she could come out of this dark world alive.

If Yulie takes her, there is no such hope. He will use her and break her in every way imaginable until there is nothing more to break. Violet will never survive a man like him.

"So, you woke me up in the middle of the night to tell me you moved up the doctor coming in to tomorrow?"

"Yeah, I thought you'd be excited, too. Maybe we can both take number five for a spin. I could see if I can get one of the men to make sure she's used, before the check. Of course, we'd have to kill him afterward, but we don't have to tell him that," he snickers and slaps a hand on my back like we are old pals. All I want to do is smash his face against the wall.

"I guess I'm not that much in need." I shrug. "I'll make sure everything is running smoothly tomorrow, and I'll let you know which girls are available as soon as the doctor tells me." I already know which one won't be.

"All right, you have a good night then... or what's left of it." I walk him over to the door and open it for him. The asshole can't leave my place quick enough.

"We'll talk tomorrow then. Don't let me wait too long, Ivan."

"Of course, enjoy the rest of your night as well."

I shut the door behind him and lock the deadbolt into place. I walk back to the bedroom, wondering if Violet heard any of our conversation. As soon as I pull the closet door open and see her huddled up in the farthest corner, I know for a fact she heard at least some of it. She is making herself as small as she can with her arms wrapped around her. Light filters into the closet, and the look in her eyes reminds me of a feral cat.

"He is gone. Come here." I kneel and hold my arms out to her. She unfolds herself and scurries across the floor on her hands and knees, taking my hands. When I help her up, she looks around the room nervously.

"I won't let him hurt you. He won't touch you. Not unless he wants to die." I have no fucking clue where the words come from or how I'm going to stop him, but he won't touch her. I'll die before I let him get to her.

She steps closer and throws her arms around me. I let my own arms wrap around her body and pull her to my chest. My heated blood calms at the sound of her steady heartbeat. I pick her up and move her to the bed. Then I shut the lights off and climb into bed, pulling her close to my chest. This all feels normal, like we're a normal couple, but it's all too good to be true.

"I wish everyone here was like you," she murmurs into my neck.

I can hear her inhaling my scent. I calm her just as she calms me. We're so wrong for each other, and yet so right.

"I'm not a good man, but if there's is one good thing I'll do in this life, it's going to be for you."

Violet doesn't respond and eventually, I hear her breathing even out. I pull the comforter up and over us.

"If I could keep you, Kitten, I would. I'd keep you forever," I whisper into the nothingness, wishing more than anything I was a better man, and that she had never been brought here.

9

*V*iolet,

When I wake up, the sun is just coming up, filling the room with dim light. Ivan still has me pulled into his chest with his arm wrapped around my middle in an iron grip. I could stay like this forever... safe and secure in his embrace. I feel like as long as I'm with him, nothing can hurt me. I know it's only an illusion. He can't protect me from what's to come. Nevertheless, I like to hold on to that illusion as long as I can.

As is if he can sense that I'm awake, he stirs behind me, bringing his face close to my neck, inhaling me. When he breathes out, the air tickles my skin, releasing a set of shivers to run down my spine. As soon as I move, I feel his erection press into my ass.

He starts kissing my neck and the hand that was sprawled out against my stomach moves lower. My breath hitches when his fingers slip beneath the waistband of my panties. He finds my clit with ease and with skilled fingers, he starts to move in small circular motions. I can feel myself growing wetter and wetter with each stroke of his finger.

"I want to taste you," Ivan murmurs sleepily into my hair. *Taste me?*

"I want to have *you* for breakfast."

"Okay," I whisper without knowing exactly what he is talking about.

He pulls his hand out of my panties and grips onto the fabric at my hips, pulling them down in one swift movement. Moving away from behind, he makes me lie on my back so he can position himself in front of me.

He nudges my legs open, and I gladly let them fall apart. Kneeling in front of me, his eyes roam over my body like I'm some kind of priceless treasure. The need mixed with adoration I see in his gaze squeezes my heart tightly. Why can't it always be like this? I just want to stay with Ivan. I only want him to look at me... him to touch me and no one else.

"You are so beautiful," he says before pushing my shirt up. He starts peppering open-mouthed kisses over my stomach, leaving behind a trail of hot skin. I'm already panting by the time he moves lower down my body. His kisses end at the top of my mound, and I wonder what he's going to do next.

"Ivan..." His name falls from my lips as a moan. My hands find their way into his hair, and I grip onto the strands. Out of instinct, I spread my legs wider, the movement making cool air wash over my heated and already wet center.

"You're so responsive to my touch, Kitten," he growls against my clit before swiping his tongue against the swollen nub. The sensation is so strong I pull away by reflex, even though I don't want to. Ivan looks up at me over my mound, a mischievous grin on his lips, and grips onto my legs to hold me in place. He starts off licking my clit gently but quickly adds pressure as whimpers of pleasure slip from my lips.

He caresses, sucks, and nibbles on me like I'm his last meal, and he is thoroughly enjoying every last bite. When he closes his lips around my clit and starts to suck gently, my back arches off the bed and a loud moan rips from my throat.

I fold one of my arms over my face, covering my mouth to muffle my screams. Ivan doesn't seem to care about me being noisy, as he keeps working my clit with equal force, driving me closer and closer to the edge.

When he pulls away and drags his tongue down my slit, I almost lose it. He dips the tip of his tongue into my entrance and swirls it around, and from the sensations alone, I fall over the edge. Hot pleasure flows through me like lava erupting from a volcano, burning up my insides in the best possible way. Ivan growls between my folds, lapping up every drop of my release.

"You taste as delicious as you look, Kitten. And with your sweet cream coating my tongue, I'd love to do nothing more than to fuck you."

I can barely keep my eyes open while listening to him. The worst part is even though I know it would kill me, I'd love nothing more than to give Ivan that one piece of me. I'm going to die anyway. I know it. So, I should just give myself to him.

He gives me another lick before moving up my body, coming to press a kiss to my lips. I taste myself on his lips. His face moves away from mine and the smile on his lips fades and turns into a deep frown as if he just remembered something bad… and then I remember it, too.

"We need to get you down to your cell before breakfast." He looks away, at some random spot on the floor like anything else is better than looking into my eyes. "The doctor will get here right after breakfast. They're going to get you out of the cell one by one and take you to see the doctor. If the doctor clears you, you'll go back in the cell, if not… well, you don't have to worry about that."

"Okay." I nod, and he pushes off the bed and brings me a pair of sweatpants. For some reason, I feel like today might be my last time with him. I don't know why but it feels like it.

"I'll come and get you right after dinner, I promise. Don't fight them, Kitten. Keep your claws to yourself today. They won't hurt you unless you give them a reason to."

I want to tell him he's lying, they'll hurt me no matter what, but I don't.

Ivan brings me back to the cell just in time for breakfast. Dread sinks deep inside my belly like a ten-pound weight as I go back and forth between preparing myself for this checking thing and replaying in my mind what that Yulie guy said.

What if he still sends somebody for me? Or what if he himself ends up getting to me? I know Ivan said he wouldn't let him touch me, but how true is that? He doesn't stand outside my cell door all day. Anyone could come in here and get me at any point, and he'd never even know.

I pace the cold floor, unable to sit still. Every day the auction grows closer, and the fact that I'll have to leave Ivan and go with someone else sinks in. I'm terrified of the unknown, of what could happen tomorrow. I want this entire thing to be over. I want to wake up and realize this was nothing more than a nightmare.

When I hear people in the hallway, my steps falter and I almost lose it. My heart beats so furiously, my chest starts to ache. My body starts to shake uncontrollably, and a cold sweat breaks out over my skin. Male voices meet my ears, then the sound of doors opening, followed by the sound of women crying, and a few screaming.

The familiar sound of my door unlocking fills the room, but I know this time it won't be Ivan walking in. The door swings open and all air leaves my lungs.

"Hey, bitch, remember me? Big bad Ivan ain't here to save you this time." Luca grins at me, and I want nothing more than to fight him. I want to run straight into Ivan's arms all over again.

"It's time for you to see the doc. Time to see if you are really as innocent as you look." Moving impossibly fast, he grips onto my arm with bruising force.

"Let go of me," I snarl, wanting to fight him so badly it takes everything in me not to. The only thing holding me back is remembering Ivan's words. *Don't fight them, Kitten. Keep your claws to yourself.*

"No can do, baby. Let's go, or I'll drug you, and this time, I really will do whatever the hell I want to you." He looks over my body and even though I'm wearing Ivan's three times too big clothes, I feel exposed.

He pulls me out the cell door, and I try not to drag my feet as he leads me down the hallway and into a well-lit room on the left side of the hall. There is no door and no privacy whatsoever. It's mostly empty besides an examining chair in the center and a small table with medical trays next to it.

"Strip," Luca orders and releases me. His dark eyes rake over me, and he licks his lips, most likely enjoying this. "I'm going to get you ready for the doc. Get naked so I can put you on the chair."

I glare at him and then at the chair, which has stirrups to spread my legs. I grind my teeth together when I notice the restraints attached to the chair. The last thing I want is to be strapped down naked to a chair with this bastard in the room.

"Last chance before I get the sedative out and I'll just undress you myself." He chuckles like he said something funny.

"No. I'll do it." I force my voice to remain calm and start taking my clothes off. I shove Ivan's sweatpants and boxers down my legs. The cold chill of the air hits my skin and makes me feel nauseous. I pull the shirt off next, trying my best to ignore Luca being in the room altogether.

"Get on the table." I can hear the excitement in his voice, and it's making me sick beyond belief. I walk slowly over to the chair and sit in it with my legs closed.

"Legs up," he orders, and I put them up one at a time. His eyes move straight to between my legs as soon as they are up, and I'm completely exposed to him. I close my eyes for a moment, fighting back tears. I've never felt so dirty in my life. I feel like I could bathe in bleach after this and still not be clean.

He closes the restraints around my ankles first, slowly making his way upward. Every time his fingers make contact with my skin, I cringe as if his touch is tainting me.

"The things I could do to you..."

I try to think of Ivan, of my sister, of what the sun feels like against my skin. Anything but this sick fuck in front of me. My wrists are restrained next, and my pulse pounds loudly in my ears.

"I was kind of hoping you would fight me, but I guess this is nice, too." He moves right between my legs and touches my inner thigh, slowly dragging his finger closer to my center. I swallow back a scream when he is only a few inches away from the part that only Ivan ever touched when the door swings open and we both look up.

A gray-haired man with glasses walks in, carrying a medical bag. "Number Four in examining room two is ready to go. She isn't a virgin." His voice is flat like he couldn't care less about what's going to happen to any of us.

Luca sighs loudly, almost as if he's annoyed. "Maybe next time, sugar."

I watch him walk out the door and into the hall before my eyes move to the man who claims to be a doctor. I just can't bring myself to see him as such. Doctors are supposed to help people, heal them, and make them feel better. This man is doing none of those things. He pulls on a pair of latex gloves, not even looking at me.

"Do you know what they do to the girls after you examine them?"

He pulls a blood pressure cuff out of his bag and wraps it around my arm, ignoring me completely.

"How can you call yourself a doctor when you do this to women?" I'm angry, livid. He doesn't care, how can he not care?

He takes my blood pressure before checking my pulse, keeping his face completely void of any kind of emotion. His brown eyes are cold and lifeless as he looks over my body.

His fingers move to the side of my neck, feeling for my lymph nodes before moving down to push on my abdomen.

I watch him scribble something down on a piece of paper

before he pulls out a flashlight. I squeeze my eyes shut, trying to shut off my brain and be somewhere else at least mentally as he uses the flashlight to examine my vagina. When I feel him probe my entrance with his finger, I try and close my legs, and the restraints on my ankles bite into my flesh.

He doesn't go in far and it doesn't hurt but it's anything but comfortable. I feel violated by this man who calls himself a doctor.

Once done, he cleans my arm with some sterile wipes. His movements are slow but accurate. He doesn't hesitate or miss a beat, which isn't surprising, since I'm sure he does this all the time. The strong smell of disinfectant tickles my nostrils and my stomach starts doing somersaults when I feel the prick of a needle enter my arm. I look down and watch the vial fill with my blood.

"What are you going to do with that?" I gesture toward the vial.

"If you're smart, you'll stop asking questions and keep your mouth shut." He takes the vial from my arm and removes the needle before packing up everything and walking out of the room.

As if Luca was waiting outside the door, he walks in seconds after the doctor walks out. He undoes the restraints, not even looking at me before he jerks me off the table by my arm.

I barely get a chance to grab my clothing from the floor before he's pulling me down the hall and back toward my cell. He pushes me inside and slams the door shut behind me. When I hear the lock click, I exhale a breath I wasn't even aware I was holding and just stand there for a moment, thankful that this is over.

I get a new pair of panties from the bathroom and pull them on before I slip back into Ivan's sweatpants and shirt. Taking my normal seat in the center of the mattress, I wrap my arms around myself and wait. I listen to more doors open and closing, voices, cries, and screams for a while before the hallway returns to its normal silent state.

Unable to tell how much time has passed, I sit, waiting. I wish I had a watch. At least then I would have an idea on when it's close to dinner time.

All I can think of is Ivan and how he made me feel last night and this morning. I close my eyes and see his face. Lifting the shirt I'm wearing to my nose, I take in his lingering scent and imagine him being here, sitting next to me.

My daydream comes to an abrupt halt when I hear footsteps approaching. The sound of jingling keys fills the room, and then my door is being unlocked. I'm jittery with excitement. Ivan must have decided to come early. I almost jump up in glee but then the door opens and instead of happiness, I feel pure terror.

A man I've never seen before walks in, and one look at the evil grin on his face and my blood turns to ice. I scoot back to the end of the mattress until my back hits the wall. I realize then that I've backed myself into a corner and there is nowhere else for me to go.

"I was really hoping you wouldn't pass the test so I wouldn't have to pay for you. Turns out I'll just be changing the info on the doc's paperwork." When I hear his voice, I know exactly who he is.

Yulie.

Everything inside me is telling me to run, but it wouldn't matter. It won't change what's going to happen.

"Please... don't do this," I beg, even though I know a man like him is not going to listen. His eyes light up with unbridled desire when my plea meets his ears. He undoes his belt buckle and pulls his belt out with one tug.

"My plaything broke a few days ago so I have some pent-up aggression. You are going to help me loosen up." My chest heaves but I can't get any air into my lungs.

I look up at him, unable to move as I watch in horror as he swings the belt in the air. The leather lands against my face before I have a chance to move my arms to protect myself.

Pain explodes across the left side of my face and a scream rips from my throat. I manage to bring my arms up to my face before he strikes me again, this time hitting me across my shoulder.

I turn away from him as much as I can and the next one comes down on my back... then another and another. My skin is throbbing, and tears slip down my cold cheeks.

He stops for a brief moment, just long enough to rip the shirt off my body. I try and move away from him but I'm in so much pain, I know I wouldn't be able to fight him.

"Your skin looks beautiful covered in my marks." His words drip with venom.

As I lay in the fetal position, naked from the waist up, he continues whipping me with the belt. I lose count of how many times he's hit me, each strike hurting more than the next. I try to hold the pain in, biting the inside of my cheek until I taste blood. Then, as if someone heard my silent prayer, Yulie stops.

"What are you doing here?" Yulie growls, and that's when I realize that someone else has entered the room. I twist just enough so I can look over my shoulder. Ivan is standing right behind Yulie, and he is holding the end of the belt in his hand.

I look up to meet his eyes but what I find looking back at me is not Ivan... it's a wild animal about to go in for the kill.

10

Ivan

EVERY FIBER of my body vibrates in anger. Fury like I've never felt before consumes me as I look at Violet's body huddled on the mattress. Ugly welts mar her beautiful skin. I promised her I wouldn't let anyone hurt her and I failed. I failed her just like I failed my sister.

I feel something inside me snap. All thoughts but one leave my mind. One single thought that digs its claws deep into my skin.

Kill.

I pull the belt from Yulie's hand with one quick pull.

"What the fuck, Iv—" Before he has time to turn and face me, or even finish saying anything, I have it slung around his neck. His hands grip onto the belt, trying to loosen it, but I already have it tightened. Lifting my foot, I kick him in the lower back, and he falls to the floor with a grunt.

Once I have him where I want him, I move on top of him. Digging my knee between his shoulder blades, I grip the belt tighter, watching as the leather digs into his flesh. I lean into him so I can watch his ugly face start to turn blue. He's gasping for air and trying to say something, but I don't give a fuck about his words or excuses. In my eyes, he's already dead.

I've killed before, many times, but nothing ever felt this fucking satisfying. I smile, watching as his eyes bulge out of his head. I grip onto the belt, tightening it, enjoying every second of his feeble attempt to fight for his life. Power surges through my veins, a darkness filling my insides like a venomous bite.

His movements underneath me slow until they stop altogether. With one last pull, I release him, letting his face fall to the cold concrete. I exhale, taking a staggering step backward. I feel her beautiful blue eyes on me and when I turn to look at her, they're full of fright and terror. I'm afraid that I've put those emotions there.

"Kitten..." I call out to her like I'm trying to corral a scared animal.

She huddles deeper inside herself, and I feel my heart shatter. This is my fault. Had I come sooner, maybe he wouldn't have had the chance to hurt her so badly. I stare at her shaking body for a long moment. I've killed for her now... I've betrayed all I've ever known for her. I knew it before, but now I know without a doubt that I will not send her to the auction. She's mine. Mine to protect, mine to keep. I look over at Yulie's dead body... Once it's discovered that I killed him, I'm as good as dead.

I need a plan, and I need one fast if I want any chance of us coming out of this alive. I glance back at the body, then scan the room, trying to figure out what to do with this scumbag. A million scenarios rattle through my mind. Oh, how I would love to burn his fucking body or hang him from the ceiling. But none of those things will work. I continue to let my mind work until I think of something that's good and wouldn't have me leaving Violet in here the rest of the day. The thought alone is almost unbearable.

I look at her, as she is staring at dead Yulie. I lower myself next to her on the mattress, holding up my hands to show her that I won't hurt her. She doesn't move at all for a second but then her eyes gaze up to mine and the next moment, she is in my arms.

Her small hands grab onto my shirt and pull me as close as she can get me. She buries her face into my chest and starts crying. Her whole body is shaking, and I want nothing more than to wrap my arms around her tightly, but I'm scared of hurting her back. I gently cradle the back of her head and let her cry for a minute. I look past her next to the mattress and spot the pill bottle tucked in between the mattress and the wall.

"Kitten," I whisper in her ear. "Listen, I need to hide the body."

When she doesn't respond, I gently nudge her shoulders. Careful not to hurt her, I push her away from me so I can take her face in between my hands. I tilt her face up so she has to look into my eyes.

"Listen to me, Violet. I need you to trust me right now. I have a plan to get you out of here. I just need you to trust me... okay?"

"Okay." Her voice comes out low and raspy from crying.

I reach behind her to grab the pill bottle. "I need you to take one of these. I need you to stay here and go to sleep for a few hours. Kitten, I swear to you when you wake up, you will be in my bed and I will be right next to you."

I can tell she wants to object, and I don't blame her at all, but I can't take her with me yet, and still, I can't just leave her in here while she is in this state. I feel like a knife is twisting deep inside my chest. Then she nods her head slightly and takes a pill from my hand, and I just want to kiss the fuck out of her. She's so strong; she doesn't even see it. I hand her a water bottle off the floor and watch her take the pill. Her throat moves as she swallows it, her eyes remaining on mine.

"I'm scared, Ivan." Her lips tremble, and I vow from this moment on to protect her against everything bad in this world.

"I know." I pick up the ripped shirt and put it on her. She wraps her arms around herself and lies down on the mattress with her back facing the door. I lean over her shaking body and kiss her hair before getting up. "I'll be back," I whisper.

I stick my head out the door and look down both sides of the hallway. When I don't see or hear anything, I go back, and grab hold of Yulie's arm. I pull him into the hallway and kick the door shut on my way out. I drag his ass all the way into the examining room down the hall. I toss his lifeless body into the corner, wishing he would wake up just so I could kill him again.

No one should come in here anytime soon, since all the checks were done today but just in case, I lock the door behind me. I stand there for a long moment, letting myself digest everything that just happened. I squeeze my eyes shut, an image of my sister Mira dead in the road appears in my mind.

I fucking failed her and now I'm failing Violet, too.

I might have killed Yulie, but the marks on Violet's body will take time to heal, reminding me of how I wasn't there to protect her, how I lied to her. The need to punch something courses through my veins. I want to destroy, rip, tear, kill. I want to feel Yulie's warm blood coat my hands.

I want vengeance for Violet, something that I won't be able to give her since I had to make the bastard's death quick. Escaping this place should be easy but doing so with Violet and trying to remain hidden for however long is needed… that I'm not sure about. I run a hand through my hair. Is she even going to want to come with me after everything she just witnessed?

I don't know why I ask myself that. Of course, she is. The last place she wants to stay is here. But is she still going to want my hands on her? I've grown attached to her, and every single part of my body calls to her. I want her, completely, and enough to give everything up.

Walking back to her cell, I look through the one-way mirror. She is right where I left her, and I just stand there for a moment looking at her. The only way I'll get her out of this place is if I let her go to the auction, I'll just need to find a way to take her before she actually walks on that stage. I start pacing up and down the hallway. There is no way in hell I'm letting her cell door out of my sight. If someone happens to come down here other than Gabe to deliver food, I will not look too suspicious just walking down the hall. Every time I walk by her cell, I peek in just to make sure she is still sleeping and every time I see her body still on the mattress, I feel a sliver of relief enter my body.

After what seems like an eternity of pacing up and down the hall, Gabe finally comes around the corner, pushing a cart full of food trays.

When he looks up and spots me heading toward him, he flinches.

"Hey, boss... didn't expect to see you down here."

I just give him a brief nod. I don't have to explain myself to this guy and he knows that.

I walk past him and around the corner where he can't see me, but I can still hear him. I count him opening and closing six food slots. Four girls were sent out today. I know this because I gave Luca the okay to take them to Rossi and his friends.

When he is done and I hear him walking back down the hall, toward where I am standing. I walk back around the corner as if I'd just returned to speak to him.

"Hey, Gabe... tomorrow is my off day so I'm going to take number five upstairs to pass my time, if you know what I mean. So, don't worry about bringing her food again until Monday."

"Sure thing, boss." He scurries past me, pushing the cart in front of him, and I follow him to the elevator, pretending I'm taking the stairs back up. When the elevator doors close behind him, I turn around and head back to her cell.

I unlock it and step inside. She isn't moving, the pills having knocked her out good just as I had hoped they would. At least if she's knocked out, her body can heal, and she isn't in any pain.

I pick her up carefully, cradling her to my chest and make my way up to my apartment. I take the stairs up all four floors. I'm less likely to see someone on the staircase than on the elevator. No one takes the stairs in this place. They're all a bunch of lazy fucks.

When I finally make it to my place without running into a single soul, I sigh in relief. The less people know about me taking her to my room the better. I walk inside and close the door behind me. Then I head into the bedroom and gently sit Violet on the bed, rolling her body to the side. I don't want her lying on her back until I get to check on the marks on her back.

Peeling the shirt off her gently, I inspect her marred skin. I clench my jaw and force my hands to steady. Her whole back is covered in long, red, and swollen streaks. Some places are turning blue from bruising and in other places, the skin has actually broken. Her arms and shoulders are also marred, and there is one angry streak that crosses her beautiful face.

I've never felt this overwhelmed with guilt and fury in my life. I'm so fucking angry I want to kill everybody in this building. Everyone who ever touched her, scared her, or even looked at her. I want them all dead, every single person. I want to give her the vengeance that I know she deserves.

Pushing my anger aside, I get up and grab my little first aid kit out of the bathroom and start cleaning her broken skin before she wakes up.

Once I'm finished, I want nothing more than to get a whiskey from my office and drown myself in the entire bottle, but I promised her that I'd be here when she wakes up, so instead, I lay down next to her and watch her sleep.

I have no idea how much time passes until she wakes. It might have been hours or days. I don't know, nor do I care. All I know that I don't think I will ever get tired of just looking at her.

Even with her face bruised and swollen, she is still the most beautiful person I have ever laid eyes on. Her eyelids blink open slowly and for a moment, I have this fear in my chest that she is going to be scared of me... scared of my touch now that she has seen me kill, but then she smiles. It's a tiny one and it probably hurts like hell to do it, but it's the last thing I was expecting from her.

"You kept your promise." Her voice cracks.

"Of course, I did. I let you down once, and It's not going to happen again."

The smile wipes from her face, and a frown forms on her full lips. "You didn't let me down, Ivan."

I clench my jaw, holding back my anger. She has no idea of the raging war of insanity that's taking place inside my head.

"I did let you down. I told you I wouldn't let anyone hurt you and I broke that promise. I failed you, and that's not okay. It's just not."

She looks sad, and I don't want her to feel bad for me, not at fucking all. She just got whipped with a belt, for Christ sakes.

"Don't be sad." I rub a knuckle gently across her bruised cheek. "I don't want you to feel bad. None of this is your fault. You didn't ask to be brought here. I vowed to protect you until the auction, and I failed you. This is on me, and whatever misery I feel for failing you is my own. Let me feel bad, let me hate myself. I deserve to feel this way."

"Ivan." She pushes up onto her arms. I can see the pain in her features as she moves closer to me, her body hovering above mine. "I'm just lucky that I found you that night when I got out of my cell. If I didn't, I would already be dead, so while you're wallowing in your misery, just remember that you saved my life that night, just like you did tonight."

I know she's right. I fucking know it, but that doesn't mean I want to admit it. I open my mouth to respond but close it. There is nothing more for me to say. I would just have to keep a better eye on her, watch her cell at all times, unless... An idea enters my mind. I could get her a cell phone. Something she could keep just in case. I bet if I went down to my office, I could find a burner in one of my drawers. I usually always use one when contacting Rossi.

"I can't always be hanging around your cell, and I can't keep you up here with me all the time, even though I want to. I have some burner phones down in my office. I'm going to give you one and have you keep it with you during the day."

I see a spark of excitement in her eyes.

I pause, my eyes bleeding into hers. "Kitten, you have to promise you won't call anybody but me. You need to trust me on this, just like you trusted me earlier to take the pill. I have a plan to get you out of here, but if you do something that could compromise it, I will not be able to protect you, or get you out alive."

Her eyes light up, like I've never seen them before. "You can really get me out of here?"

"Yes, and I promise I will, but if someone finds out I gave you a phone, we are both as good as dead. This place is a fortress... a well-armed fortress. If someone alerted the police of this place, Rossi would know right away. He is connected, has people everywhere. He would burn this whole place down before the cops could get a strike team together. Do you understand me?" I can't even begin to explain the importance of this to her.

"Yes, I understand, but how are you going to get me out then?" She seems unsure, and she should be. I don't know yet how I'm going to do it, but I've already killed for her and once Rossi discovers what I've done, he'll have us both killed. There is no way around it.

"There is no way I can just walk you out of here, but the place the auction is at is not this heavily protected. They still have tight security, but I know some people there. I can pay some guys off, call in some favors to get you out quietly, and if that doesn't work, then I'll take you out by force. One way or another, I'll get you out of this mess and together, we will go into hiding."

"Together?" She sits up a little straighter, her eyes wide, like she doesn't believe what I'm saying. "You said..." She stumbles over her words. "Before, you said that you wouldn't want to... keep me, even if you could."

I clench my fists against the sheets. "I know I said that, and it's still true, partially."

She looks sad at my response, and I hate it. But she's also acting like she expected more, like maybe I'd want her forever and though the thought is appealing, I'm not so sure I could keep her. She deserves better, a life where she doesn't have to remain in the shadows.

"I can't keep you, Violet, and you wouldn't want me anyway. There are things about me that you wouldn't like and things I can't share. This is temporary. A means to an end. I will save you and then you'll be rid of me, free to do as you please."

"I just…" She averts her eyes down to the sheets. "Never mind, you're right." There's a bitterness to her tone but I can't force myself to think any further into it. I can't admit to her how I feel, or the things I want to do to her.

"Go take a shower, and I'll go downstairs to my office and find a phone, okay?" I give her a soft smile, but she doesn't look at me. She just moves away from the bed and toward the bathroom. All I can think as I watch her walk away is how if I could save her and keep her all to myself, I would.

But I won't subject her to a life on the run.

She's already broken enough, and the thought of hurting her, or putting her in a position where she could be hurt again, isn't something I will let happen.

11

Violet

I DON'T KNOW how to feel about what Ivan told me. Freedom. A life without him. It seems like those things can't coexist together... not anymore. Not after being locked inside this place for so many weeks. Weeks that feel like years. I try to imagine it. I couldn't go back to my old life. I couldn't just go home and put my sister in danger, pretending nothing happened. If I regain my freedom, I have to live somewhere else, far away from the only family I have left. I won't be Violet anymore but a shell of my old self.

I'll have to remain hidden just like Ivan will.

It should be easy for me to imagine being on my own, knowing Ivan doesn't want me, not like I want him. I try and analyze the reasons I want him the way I do and none of them make sense. I tell myself it's because he's been the only sliver of light in the darkness surrounding me that makes me want him, want him in a deeper way, but I'm not so sure. I think maybe it's the fact that deep down, I know he wants me, too. Though the circumstances of how we've come together are fucked up, I can see it, feel it in the way he touches me. But if he won't admit it to himself, what can I do?

I shake the thought away. If he didn't care, he wouldn't have trusted me to have a cell phone, knowing I could call anyone. He wouldn't have killed that horrible man, and he wouldn't bring me up to his room every night, holding me close to his body, telling me everything was going to be okay.

It's not that he doesn't want me, it's that he's afraid to admit it. He's afraid he's not good enough, but he has no idea how good he truly is. At least in my eyes and I plan to show that to him, tonight. I know I don't owe him anything for his kindness, but I do want to give him something that he'll always have as a reminder of me.

I sit in the cell alone, bored out of my mind, wondering if Ivan will take me up on my offer and what will happen if I actually do get out of this alive. Two days have passed since the checking, and I'm now back in my cell for the first time again. Ivan was able to keep me in his room all day yesterday and it was pure bliss, even after the conversation we had. He took care of me, making sure I was comfortable and had everything I needed. He even cooked for me.

It made coming back down here this morning dreadful. The last thing I want is to spend more time in this room, especially after everything that happened here, but he did as he said he would and got me a phone. I keep it hidden in the sweatpants I'm wearing just as he instructed.

It feels heavy in my pocket, giving me a sense of security. If someone comes in here to hurt me, I can call him. He set his number on up on speed dial and made me practice calling him, as if I didn't know how to use a cell phone or something. If I need to, I can have the phone unlocked and his number dialed blindly within three seconds while keeping it in my pocket.

The day seems to drag on as I wait for the last meal of the day. Thanks to the phone, I actually know what time it is. I go into the corner of the bathroom, where I know no one can see me and check the phone. It's nearly six and Ivan said food is delivered around six, which means I won't have to wait much longer to see him.

I feel like a little kid waiting impatiently for Christmas morning. The minutes tick by slowly when I'm away from him, but when I'm in his arms, it seems like they won't slow down. When I finally hear the food flap being opened and my tray being pushed through it, I almost tell the guy on the other side thank you. I take the tray and sit down on the mattress, chewing on the stale bread.

Besides what Ivan made me, I've only had less than appetizing sandwiches, and I'm sure it's starting to show. As soon as I get out of this place, I'm going to have a nice juicy burger. I visualize myself eating the burger and take a sip of water to wash it down.

It doesn't take long until the door opens once more, and Ivan's large frame appears. I jump up from the mattress and run straight into his arms. He hugs me briefly but then releases me, and I miss the warmth of his embrace with seconds.

"We can't linger, just in case someone comes down here for whatever reason. You know what to do, right?" He gives me a knowing look.

"Keep my eyes closed and my mouth shut," I confirm.

He nods and picks me up, throwing me over his right shoulder. I hold on to the back of his shirt as he hurries up the stairs, taking them two at a time. I have no idea how he does this while carrying me on his back, let alone without breaking out into sweat, but somehow, he does.

By the time we get to his place, I am dizzy from the fast movement while hanging upside down, but I could care less about my journey up here. All I care about is being here now... with him. Most of the marks on my back are nearly healed, the belt having not cut into my skin as badly as I thought.

I think back to my thoughts earlier, of how I planned to prove to him how deserving of me he really is. He denied me once before, but I won't let him deny me this time. If this is the only piece of myself I can give him, then I want him to have it.

"Ivan..." I nervously stand in the middle of the living room while he's in the kitchen getting me something to drink. "I want to... I mean..." I stumble over the words, unable to get them out. I'm a nervous wreck, wondering how he'll respond to my request.

Ivan returns from the kitchen and hands me a glass of orange juice. "What is it, Kitten?"

I take the glass from his hands, suck in a quick breath, and try again to get the words out. "I still want you to be my first. I know you don't think you deserve me, but you do. I want to have this experience together. I want to give that part of myself to you and not because I feel like I need to repay you, but because I want this. I want the choice. I want this memory."

Ivan shakes his head, taking a step backward. "You don't know what you want, Violet. You don't want me to be your first. You have no idea how stupid that sounds."

I should be angry at how harsh his words are but I'm not.

"We've done other things. Why can't we do this? Why can't I have this choice? I want you, Ivan. I want you and only you. It's only sex, right?"

He lets out a harsh laugh. "No, it's not just sex. It's your virginity, your first fucking time. It should mean something. It should be with someone important. Not me. I'm not important. I'm part of the reason you're in this place, the reason you've gotten hurt. This entire fucking ordeal leads back to me."

I place the cup he handed me on the table to my right and cross the space separating us. He wants me to see him as the devil, this evil man, but all he's doing is his job. Yes, he knows it's bad and wrong and yeah, that makes him fucked up, but it doesn't make him unworthy. It doesn't mean I can't give myself to him. I stand so close to him that I have to crane my neck up to see his face, and he has to look down to meet my eyes.

"Don't try and make me see you as something you aren't. The

real monsters were the three men who attacked me. You saved me, Ivan. You cared about me, when no one else did. You show me compassion and yeah, you can try and hide it from yourself, but you can't hide it from me. I know you care about me."

"Of course, I care about you, that's why I don't want to take this from you." His voice cracks, and I know he wants this... wants me. He just needs to be pushed, coaxed to the edge.

"You are not taking anything from me I don't want to give to you. Please... you said yourself that if someone finds out about us, find the phone, or finds Yulie, that we are as good as dead. We don't know what's going to happen in the next week, Ivan. I don't want to have any regrets, and I know I will regret it if I never have the chance to give this to you. I want you. No one else, regardless of any future. I want you."

Before he can answer, I grab the hem of my shirt and pull it over my head. I swallow nervously, watching as he clenches his fists, his eyes roaming over my chest. I'm so afraid he'll reject me that I start to shake. Like the knight he is, he's on me, pressing a hard kiss to my lips, owning every single piece of my heart.

He pulls away, and his lips ghost against mine.

"We'll do this, but only because you want it so badly. I'm not a good man and this part of you shouldn't belong to me, but whatever you're giving me, I'll take, because it comes from you."

I get up on my tiptoes so I can press another kiss to his lip. This time, he picks me up and I wrap my legs around his waist, letting him carry me to the bedroom. He doesn't let go of me as he kicks off his shoes and gets on the bed to lay me down as he hovers right above me. I pull on his shirt, urging him to take it off and he does, throwing it down to the floor. He lowers himself again, so that there is only an inch of space between our bodies, and I can feel the electric charge between us. Pulling us together like magnets.

He kisses my mouth sweetly before peppering kisses along my jawline, moving down my neck and over my collarbone, blazing a fiery path to my breasts.

Once there, he sucks the hardened nipple into his mouth, and I come unglued.

"Ivan," I call out, not knowing what I need but knowing I need more of it. He kneads my other breast with his huge hand, and I arch my back, pushing my breasts into his face.

"Fuck." He releases my nipple with a loud pop that resonates through the room. "I want you so bad it hurts." His lips move down my body, while both his hands hold onto my tits.

"Then have me... please have me..." I whimper, afraid that he may come to his senses and end this before it even has a chance to begin.

"Oh, I will, Kitten." He looks up at me just as he reaches my panty line; his eyes are dark and filled with need. My chest heaves, and heat spreads through my center and outward. I'm ready. I want him. I need him, like I need my next breath.

"Patience... I need you nice and wet so when I slip deep inside you, all you'll feel is inch upon glorious inch of pleasure."

"I'm ready now..." I pant as he releases my breasts and grabs onto the sweatpants and my panties at my hips, pulling them down my legs ever so slowly.

"Not ready enough. I need you soaked, drenched, Kitten. I need your sweet cream coating my hand and dripping down your thighs."

His dirty words make me moan, and I can't seem to get enough of him. I know after tonight, after this moment occurs between us, losing him will hurt like hell, but I'll take the pain for a small taste of pleasure. He nudges my legs apart and sits up, his body looming above mine.

I drink him in, every delicious inch of his muscled torso. I reach up, running my fingers over his slick abs, his muscles rippling beneath my fingers. Each beautiful muscle looks as if it's been cut from stone. My gaze drops to his stiffened cock, tenting his boxers.

"You're going to come on my hand before *he* comes anywhere

near you." His voice is thick with carnal need while his fingers trail over my mound and down between my wet folds.

"Please..." I look him straight in the eyes, sinking my nails into his flesh, leaving little half-moons behind. He smirks down at me, his thumb rubbing gently against my clit, teasing me. My eyes drift closed, and then I feel it. One thick digit slips inside. At first, he only goes knuckle deep, slowly plunging his finger in and out of my tightness. Coils of pleasure fill my belly and instantly, I want more, but of course, he is taking his time as if he is savoring every slip inside me.

My body squirms underneath his touch and a soft gasp falls from my lips when he thrusts his finger past the knuckle, sinking deeper inside my channel. I claw at his abs, needing more, so much more. I spread my legs wider and gnaw on my bottom lip, the burning pleasure inside me building with each stroke. An electric current shoots through my veins, and I lift my hips, trying to meet the thrust of his finger. I pout, my inexperienced thrust not helping me get him any deeper. A soft chuckle fills the air and my eyes pop open, finding Ivan's as if we're two magnets, completely drawn to each other.

We stare at each other for a long moment, the pressure builds deep inside me, and my chest rises and falls like I'm running in a marathon. He adds a second finger, moving the two in a scissoring motion, all while keeping eye contact with me.

I lick my lips and feel the heat of my orgasm wash over me. My insides quiver, and my pussy clenches tightly around his thick fingers.

"Ivan..." I scream his name, bucking my hips, grabbing onto his hand to hold it in my place. The pleasure is blinding, overtaking my heart, mind, body, and soul.

Ivan doesn't let up though; he keeps plunging deep inside me, stroking me until I start to feel a second orgasm build. He stretches my channel, preparing me for his thickness, and I watch through hooded eyes as he bites his bottom lip, watching his fingers dip in and out of me furiously.

"Come for me again, Kitten. Make that virgin pussy come all over my hand again." Ivan's words are crude, naughty, and downright delicious. I follow his orders, my womb tightening, unraveling at the seams as another orgasm slams into me. My channel gushes, and I feel my release do exactly as he asked, and just as he asked I come all over his hand.

I'm panting, my entire body shaking, a liquified mess when he pulls his fingers from my entrance and brings them to his lips. He licks the tips before plunging them deep inside his mouth.

"Fuck, Kitten, you're so damn tight and taste like something I don't fucking deserve, but damn, am I going to ravage you, like you're my last damn meal."

"Please, yes…" I claw at his chest like the kitten he claims me to be. He must enjoy this because he grins, moving from the bed for a moment to dispose of his boxers and grab a little foil packet from the nearby nightstand.

My eyes are glued to his incredibly stiff cock. It's huge, bigger than I remember it being. My insides tingle at the thought of his taking me, owning my body like no one else has before.

"It's now or never, Kitten. If you don't want this, say it, because once I enter you, it's going to be really fucking hard for me to stop."

I nibble on my bottom lip, lifting my eyes to his gray ones, not even contemplating my response. "You're it for me, Ivan. You're what I want."

"Good, because I want you, too," he murmurs, crawling back onto the bed. His huge body looming above mine makes me feel protected, secure, and I know I couldn't have chosen a better man to give myself to.

"Take me…" I want him so badly I can feel the need in every single pore of my skin. The air is electric between us and when he leans forward and presses his lips to mine, that electric current courses through my body, jolting it, restarting my heart.

He kisses me for a long moment, the sound of the foil packet opening meets my ears, and then he pulls away. He places the condom on the head of his swollen cock and rolls it down each glorious inch of stiffness.

"If I hurt you, tell me. I'll try not to, but there's no helping it on your first time. You're tight as hell, and there's no changing that, not that I would want to." He winks at me, and I melt, I actually melt into the sheets beneath me. Spreading my legs wide, he centers himself between them, his thickness probing my entrance.

Air stills in my lungs, and then I feel him moving. One of his hands moves to beneath my head, cradling it, while the other grips onto my hip, holding me in place while he moves forward. I nibble on my bottom lip. His body is strung tight, the muscles flex as he moves, and I lift my hands, touching every inch of his perfectly chiseled chest.

I hope this moment is as perfect for him as it is me. An unknown emotion flickers in his eyes, and then pain seems to contort his features, and I don't understand why. I almost ask him what's wrong but then I feel the head of his cock slip between my wet folds. He teases me, moving his thickness up and down over my overly sensitive clit.

"Ivan," I whimper, wanting him deep inside of me.

"Shhh..." he orders, with a pained smile, before bringing himself to my entrance. His hips thrust forward an inch, and the air in my lungs stills when I feel him enter me. I feel stretched and a burning sensation zings across my womb.

Ivan grits his teeth and flexes his hips forward another inch, slowly gaining entrance inside me. My heart squeezes inside my chest as he possesses my body with a gentleness that I never would've expected. I cling to his chest, wanting more, wanting him to own me completely.

Lifting my hips, even against his paw of a hand, I urge him forward, making him slip deeper into my channel. There's a sting of pain, but there's pleasure, too, and I want that pleasure. I want it so bad I can taste it.

"Slow down, Kitten," Ivan growls, and I sink my nails into his chest, lifting my hips again, stealing another greedy inch. A hiss escapes his lips as I do this a couple more times, enjoying the pleasure that courses through my veins and the rumble in Ivan's chest as he disapproves.

Once he's seated deep inside me, I moan. I feel impossibly full, my channel stretched and filled with every inch of Ivan. He stills, leaving me to adjust to his size but I don't need that. I just need him. Lifting my hips, I urge him forward, and this time, he doesn't fight it as if he, too, can't let a single inch of space separate us.

His head falls into the crook of my neck, and I feel his heated breath on my skin. He's panting, his muscles rippling underneath my hands. I can feel his cock twitch deep inside me. He's holding back, and I don't want him to. I want all of him, the dark beast he claims to be, the gentle giant he is. I want to see and feel each part of the man he is.

His fingers tighten in my hair, as he holds my head to his chest, and I can't take it anymore. I want more. I need more.

"Fuck me, Ivan. Take me how you want to. Own me," I whisper into his ear, I feel the tension in the air snap, and then he's doing just as I asked him to. He pulls all the way out of me, positioning his hips as he thrusts back in. Pain and pleasure consume me, coating me from the inside out.

"Is this what you want, Kitten?" He thrusts into me once more, grinding himself into my center, rubbing against my swollen clit.

The motion knocks the air from my lungs, and I sink my nails deeper into his back. He hisses out in maybe pain, maybe pleasure, I have no clue and pulls out of me completely, slamming into me to the hilt over and over again.

Each thrust breaks away the person I was before I came here, before I found him, before I started to fall in love with him.

"Damnit, Kitten, you're so tight, your pussy is swallowing my cock perfectly. Taking every inch of it like it was made for me."

"Yes," I gasp, letting him own me with every thrust. Tears spring from my eyes as he grunts, moving in and out of me at a treacherous pace. My chest expands as I inhale our mingled scents mixed with sex into my lungs. A tightness unravels in my lower belly, and I feel my orgasm building. I'm climbing higher and higher with every powerful stroke he gives me, his body moving against mine in a feverish way. I feel nothing but him in this moment. There's no one else but Ivan and me.

There's no bad, no good. No right or wrong. Just us, finding a means to an end. Seeking out what we both desperately want and need.

"I can't last much longer, Kitten. I need you to come..." Ivan's voice is rough, gravelly, and it makes me shiver, my hardened nipples rubbing against his muscled chest.

"I'm close," I whimper, and with uncanny strength, he holds himself up on one arm and maneuvers the other between our bodies, his fingers rubbing against my clit. That, coupled with the deep thrust of his cock, sends me flying over the edge, like a rocket soaring into the sky.

Every muscle inside my body tightens, and my head spins. I can't tell what's up or down and frankly, I couldn't care either way. My pussy strangles his length, quivering with aftershocks of pleasure. A few strokes later, I feel his body tense, his cock throbbing deep inside me, a roar of unbridled pleasure escaping his lips and filling my ears.

My whole body feels like air, as if I'm just floating into nothingness. My body and mind are sated, and my heart feels full, brimming with an emotion I can't explain.

Thoughts swirl inside my head about Ivan, about all he's done for me, about what he continues to do, and when I feel the tears slipping down my cheeks, I know I'm screwed. Before I can think about what I'm going to say, the words are coming out.

"I love you." It hangs in the air between us, and for a moment, I don't think that he's even heard it until I fell his body tense above mine. A coldness sweeps through me, and I wince as he pulls out, pushing off the bed and away from me.

"This is exactly why I didn't want to do this."

I blink, the euphoric pleasure easing from my veins, anger and sadness replacing it. His body is turned away from me, but I can still feel the anger and resentment radiating from him just because I said those three little words.

"It's not like I meant it. People say things in the moment all the time," I lie.

He turns on me, his face is a mask of anger now, and I see the guilt in his eyes.

God, why did I have to open my mouth?

He takes off the condom, tossing it into a trash can near the bed. Rivulets of blood smear against the latex and I know if I look down, I'll find the evidence of my lost virginity, at the hands of a man I know I truly want, that I truly love.

"You're a liar, Violet, and you're a bad one at that. I deal with liars every single fucking day. The worst kind of men you can think of. Don't lie to me."

His voice is stern, and I feel like I've ruined this entire moment. Maybe even more than this moment. What if I've ruined everything? What if he won't help me after this? He could leave me in the cell for the next eight days and let me go to the auction. There wouldn't be anything I could do on my own to get out of here. Without him, I'm completely alone and helpless. I wish I could take the words back.

"Feel however you want to feel but it changes nothing. Nothing we've done tonight changes anything. It was just sex, Violet. You asked me to do this for you and I did. I gave you what you wanted, and now this..." Ivan seems to grow more agitated as he slips into the bathroom. I hear the water turn on and a second later, he appears in the doorway, a washcloth in his hand, his eyes bleeding into mine.

"I didn't mean it, Ivan. I swear I didn't," I reply hoarsely, as he walks over to the bed and kneels down on it. I hiss at the contact of the warm washcloth against my overly sensitive pussy as he gently wipes away the blood and evidence of our sex.

"Stop," he orders, and I feel the fresh tears slipping down my cheeks. I'm an emotional mess right now, wearing every single feeling I have on my face. He only looks at my face briefly before he gets up and pulls on a pair of boxers. I watch him through my tears as he gets out some clean boxers and a shirt, tossing them in my direction.

"Get dressed."

Panic clings to me. Is he really going to send me back downstairs? "Please, Ivan, don't do this. I'm sorry. Please... don't bring me back downstairs. I'll sleep on the floor if you don't want me in the bed, just please don't make me sleep in the cell again." I might be pathetic sounding right now, but I don't care. The fear of being locked in that cell for the next week is so overwhelming that I would do about anything to avoid it.

He turns back to face me, and I try to blink the tears away, but all it does is makes some more roll down my face. His gaze softens, his anger level dropping from a nine to a seven.

"Just put some clothes on and lie down," he orders before walking out, slamming the door behind him, leaving me cold and alone.

I sob into the sheets, pain radiating out of my chest. I want this to be a lasting memory but all I can think about is forgetting this night, forgetting how I ruined us.

12

Ivan

THREE FUCKING WORDS. Three little words strung together. To some, they meant nothing, but they left me with a hole in my fucking chest. It wasn't the words that hurt me, it was the meaning behind them, and what they meant to *her* that bothered me.

I grit my teeth and clench my fists tightly, the muscles in my forearm burning with a need to destroy. *Why did she have to say those three fucking words?* I let the tension inside my body spiral out of control as I grab the bottle of whiskey from the counter and pop the cork off. With no care for a glass, I take a huge gulp straight from the bottle.

The amber liquid burns in the back of my throat, and I relish in that burn as it settles into my stomach. Warmth pools and spreads out across my insides, and I take another drink, and then another, drowning my pain, my past, and a future I'll never have in the warmth of whiskey.

It would be so much fucking easier if she saw me as a monster, as the fucking man giving her a death sentence, but I'm not even doing that. I'm saving her, setting her fucking free, and when all this is over, I'll be nothing but a black stain on her heart, a dark memory from her past that she doesn't want to remember. My grip on the bottle of whiskey is hard enough to shatter it, and I swallow around the bile that rises in my throat at the memory of losing my sister.

I saved Violet to make up for failing my sister, but I didn't really save Violet. I didn't fucking save anybody. She loves me. She fucking loves me, and that's not saving her, that's condemning her to a life she'll never be able to escape from. Everyone who ever loved me is either dead or wishes me dead. I destroy anyone who gets close to me, and I'll destroy her, too, if I don't let her go.

"Roman..." I called out for my brother, but he wouldn't look at me.

He hated me as much as I hated myself.

"You killed her, Ivan. You killed our sister." Tears filled his blue eyes, and I swallowed around the guilt and shame that coated my insides.

"I didn't mean for her to get hurt." I pleaded with him to understand, for anyone to understand. I was so alone, so broken, that parts of me wished it was me who had been struck by a car that day instead of Mira. I deserved to die, not her. She was young, beautiful, and had a long life ahead of her.

"All you had to do was be a brother." Roman shoved against my chest, and I let him. He pushed me, his fists slamming against my chest. We were both the same size now, and if I wanted to, I could probably stop him, but I didn't want to.

I wanted to die. I wanted him to hurt me.

"All you had to do was watch her, and you didn't. You let her die, you killed her..." Each word came with a punch, and I didn't even realize I was crying until the tears started to fall.

"It should have been me, Roman. It should have been." At my words, the punches stopped, and I blinked away the tears staining my vision. Roman looked me straight in the eyes, my little brother, the last person I had in my life to protect.

"I hate you, Ivan. I hate you," he snarled, and I knew he meant every single word he said.

When I come to, there are tears on my cheeks and my entire body shakes with anger and sadness. It's been years since I cried, since I fucking let the feelings unravel inside me, but vowing to help Violet, seeing her struggle and be attacked, brought those feelings closer to the surface.

"Fuck her," I growl, chugging the rest of the whiskey in the bottle. I'm angry... so fucking angry. I'm on the verge of exploding and even through the fucking haze, I know I still want her. Even when I shouldn't, I still want her. I want her to love me, because I want to love her, too... and maybe in some way, I fucking do.

I don't know. I let the whiskey burn me from the inside out, drowning out my emotions. Every single fucking thought fades as the alcohol takes over my body. I throw the bottle against the wall, listening as it hits, shattering into a million pieces in various directions. I grab the next thing I see and toss it against the wall...

I didn't save her... I didn't... Like a tornado ripping through a small town, I destroy my apartment. Nothing matters. Nothing. I grab a bottle of vodka and start chugging it. It burns my insides and makes my eyes water but I don't care. I just don't want to feel anymore.

A gasp fills the air... and I know who that gasp belongs to.

"Go the fuck away," I growl, keeping my back to her. I don't want to see her face, the pain in her eyes. She broke us. Ruined this fragile moment, a moment I gave her because she begged for it. I should have known better. I should have kept my dick in my pants.

"Ivan." Her voice cracks something inside of me, and I hear her small footfalls moving behind me. *What the fuck is she doing? Why isn't she listening to me?*

I whirl around, anger pouring out of me, like lava erupting from a volcano. She's picking up all the shit I've broken, the shit I wanted to break. She's trying to fix things that can't be fixed and for some reason, that makes me angrier.

"I said to fucking go away." I stumble over to her, feeling pieces of glass imbed into the bottoms of my feet. I feel the skin slice, but I don't feel pain. I feel nothing. I am numb. Broken.

Violet gazes up at me, her bottom lip trembling, fear taking root in those deep blues of hers. I can't image what she's thinking right now, how she's feeling?

I tell myself not to care when I grab her by the arm and force her to stand, failing to notice the broken glass shards in her hand. My movements jostle her, and when I hear the cry of pain fall from her lips, I stop, releasing her instantly. Our eyes meet, and we both look down to her hand at the same time where a piece of glass has pierced through her skin and is now sticking out.

"Shit..." Within half a second, I am completely sober. At the sight of her blood, anger is replaced with worry. Blood starts to drip from the cut, sliding down her wrist and onto the hardwood floor beneath our feet.

"I'm sorry," she barely gets out, her eyes misting over. Fuck, she's going to cry again. I'm such an asshole. She just wanted to help, and now she is sorry because I hurt her.

"No, Kitten, don't be sorry." Picking her up by the hips, I walk her to the kitchen. Shoving shit out of the way as I go, I sit her on the kitchen counter. Her fragile body starts to shake, and I know I have to do something. "I'm going to get the first aid kit. Please don't move."

I walk over the broken glass, not caring about anything but Violet in this moment. I walk into the bedroom and then the bathroom, grabbing the first aid kit. I jog back into the kitchen and see her body swaying, her head against the cupboard behind her.

"You still with me, Kitten?"

"Yes." Her eyes go wide as they drop back down to her hand. Her face is pale, and she looks like she might throw up. "Why did you destroy your house?"

I want to laugh. Even when she's hurting, she's still trying to figure me out, trying to piece me back together.

"Me destroying my house is the least of your worries right now. I need to get this glass out of your hand and stitch you up." I'm focused, determined. I've cleaned many wounds in my days. I've given many stitches; hell, I've stitched up myself, but I've never done this for a woman before.

"Stitches?" She starts shaking her head. "N-no, I don't like needles. I think it will be fine. I don't need stitches."

"Shhh, Kitten, calm down. It's going to be okay." I cup her by the cheek and look deep into her eyes. She's terrified, worried out of her damn mind, and I have to make her feel protected, secure.

"Breathe, just breathe with me and it'll be fine."

When she nods her head, to let me know she hears me, I release her and open the kit, pulling out everything I need.

"I'm going to pull out the glass and then I'm going to clean the cut. I want to see how deep it is before I start sewing you up. This isn't going to be like pulling a band aid off. I can't do this fast and quick or I might widen the cut." I hold onto her wrist with a death grip, afraid she may jump off the counter and run away. With a steady hand, I start to pull out the glass, slowly, very slowly.

"Close your eyes if you need to, it might help." I glance up at her, and she closes her eyes. Her tiny chest heaves beneath my shirt, and her skin is still a snowy white.

"Why did you do it?" she whispers.

"You're doing good, Kitten." I pull the glass out all the way and toss the shard into the sink, before I start to clean it with hydrogen peroxide, ignoring her question.

"Talk to me, Ivan," she cries, gripping onto my hand with her uninjured one.

I grit my teeth, not wanting to answer her, but knowing if I don't, she may just flip out more.

"I was angry, and I still am," I answer as I finish cleaning the cut, and then inspect the wound. It's not too deep... thank goodness.

"Why are you angry? Are you mad at me?" Her gaze widens when I release her hand and get the needle and thread ready.

"More myself than you, Kitten."

She visibly swallows.

"This is going to hurt. I wish I had something to give you for the pain, but I don't unless you want me to go get those pills from the cell."

She shakes her head without thinking about it.

"Just stay with me, and it'll be over soon, okay?"

"I'm sorry, Ivan," she apologizes yet-a-fucking-gain, and I have half a mind to tell her to shut up again. I'm tired of her being sorry, of apologizing for things that aren't her fault.

Instead, I start stitching her up. The needle pierces her creamy skin, and I realize then that she'll always have a stark reminder of me on her hand... a scar to remind her of the kind of mistake I was. Words land on the tip of my tongue, and I start speaking without thinking.

"I'm not who you think I am, Violet. Yes, I'm helping you, but I've hurt hundreds before you. A lot of people, a lot of women, died because of me, and some I've even killed myself. Me saving you doesn't change the things I've done. One good thing for all the bad doesn't make the bad disappear. It doesn't make me a good man for doing right by you."

"I know you aren't good, but you're good enough for me. There's light inside of you, and it's begging to be set free, beginning to shine bright. You're like a firefly trapped in a jar, and I want to set you free, Ivan."

My jaw tightens, and I steady my shaking hand as I pierce her skin once more.

"Stop trying to see the good in me, the good in everyone around you. We're all evil in some way shape or form. God didn't make us without flaws."

"What's my flaw then?"

"Loving me."

She quiets at my response, and I finish sewing her up. I clean up the blood off the side of her hand and toss all the bloody gauze into the trash. When I wrap the hand lightly, I can feel Violet's eyes on me, burning a hole through my body. I silently clean up all the glass off the floor, sweeping it up and tossing it into the trash.

A headache starts to pound directly behind my eyes.

"Let's go to bed," I order, picking her up from the counter by her hips, before placing her back down on her feet. She holds her hand to her chest and looks up at me, sadness in lingering in her eyes.

"Will you hold me?" The hopeful tone in her voice crushes me all over again. I press a hand to the small of her back and usher her forward. Things have changed between us, and I'm torn in half by the feelings accompanied with that change. I feel like I'm being pulled in two different directions. Part of me wants this, wants her so badly... while the other part despises the thought of it.

"Yes, Kitten, I'll hold you."

She lets me get her into bed, and I follow suit, settling onto the mattress, pulling out a few shards of glass that had embedded themselves into my feet. If Violet notices, she doesn't say anything, and I'm thankful. I don't have it in me to argue with her anymore tonight.

I turn the light off and pull her into my chest, inhaling her sweet scent into my lungs, wishing that her loving me didn't change things... that it didn't change us.

"Good night, Ivan," she murmurs into my chest.

"Good night, Kitten." I exhale, letting every inch of her surround me. She's the one thing I want, but the only thing completely out of reach.

∼

"Iᴠᴀɴ..." I hear someone calling my name, and my body shakes. I brush the hand away, rolling over. It's too early to get up.

"Ivan. It's past breakfast time." Violet's soft voice caresses my ears, pulling me out of my stupor. My eyes fly open and meet her worried ones. Her face is set in a frown, and I know something is wrong.

"What?"

"It's past breakfast time. You should have brought me down an hour ago."

"Fuck!" I get up from the bed, and she follows suit. I get us some clothes from the dresser, and we both start to get dressed.

I don't even have my boxers all the way pulled up when a loud knock on the front door has us both frozen in place. I glance at Violet over my shoulder, and she looks scared out of her mind.

"Don't worry, just... get naked and lay on the bed face down." She gives me a confused look, but I don't have time to explain.

"Just do it, Kitten, trust me."

I close the bedroom door behind me, hoping that she fucking listens. If someone comes in here looking for her, I can always say I have her up here for my entertainment, but it won't look real if she doesn't do what I fucking telling her to. Another loud knock echoes through my apartment before I can make it to the door.

"Hold on," I growl and pull the door open to find Gabe on the other side. *Fuck.* He must be here to tell me Violet is gone. It takes a lot out of me to keep an emotionless mask in place when I have the burning fear that someone is going to take Violet from me.

"Sorry to wake you, boss, but I guess you didn't get Rossi's message?"

"What message?"

"He is on his way here, and he called an emergency meeting. He is going to expect you to be in the conference room when he gets here."

"Shit, okay... I'll be down in a minute." I shut the door quickly and hold my ear to it, listening to

Gabe's footsteps disappear down the hall.

When I get back to the bedroom and find Violet naked, sprawled out on the bed, her head down and ass up in the air, my cock goes from limp to hard in zero point nine seconds. I have this primal urge to peel my boxers off and sink deep inside her. I step closer to the bed and notice she is shaking. That alone takes the edge off the need to fuck her right now, dousing my hardened cock with ice water.

"It's okay, Kitten. He wasn't here because of you, but I do need to get you back downstairs quickly."

She flips over, her soft sunshine-blond hair clings to parts of her face and when I catch sight of her perfectly shaped tits, flat stomach, and the beautiful valley between her legs, I almost forget what I just said and lose myself in her.

Tonight, I can have her again tonight. I remind myself. But right now, I need to get her to the cell and find out what the fuck Rossi wants. He hardly ever comes here, so some bad shit must have gone down for him to show up like this and call a meeting out of the blue.

For a moment, I think it might be because of Yulie's disappearance, but that's unlikely. That would be something to deal with quietly, not call a fucking meeting over.

"I would like nothing more than to pull of my boxers and climb in that bed with you, but we really need to go." I put on the rest of my clothes and look at my phone. *Fuck*, he did send me a message. I stuff both phones in my pocket.

"I heard, you have to go to a meeting?" she asks quietly, as if she is not sure if she is allowed to ask. I watch her pull her own clothes on and as soon as her skin is covered, I want to get her naked again.

"Yeah, Rossi is the... well, my boss. So, I really need to be there when he gets here." She pulls socks onto her small feet just as I tie the laces on my boots. "How is your hand?"

"It's fine," she murmurs right before I pick her up and throw her over my shoulder.

"We'll unwrap it and look at it later."

I carry her down to the basement, moving quickly down the stairs. She tries to hold on to my shirt to stop bouncing on my shoulder so much, but when I set her down in her cell, she still looks a little dizzy. I pull the burner phone from my pocket and hand it to her.

"I need to go." I'm trying to rush out, but Violet stops me.

"Wait, are you... are you coming back tonight?"

"Yes, Kitten, I'll come and get you after dinner."

A small smile tugs on her lips, and I almost kiss her, but then I remember that I really do have to go. Closing the heavy door behind me, I start to speed walk up to the first floor.

Thank fuck Rossi isn't there yet when I enter the room. Six guys are already sitting around the conference table as I take my usual chair, next to Rossi. I glance over across the table at the empty chair where Yulie usually sits and hope the fuck no one knows he was here last before he went missing.

Actually, I hope no one even knows yet that he went missing, though if they don't know by now, they will today.

"Anyone know what this is about?" I ask, breaking the heavy silence in the room.

All six guys either shake their head or murmur no. After my question, we resume to sit in uncomfortable silence. All the guys are clearly on edge, not knowing what is going on, myself included. I usually don't get worried about shit, not until now... not since I have her to worry about.

The door opens, and Rossi walks in with one of his personal guards.

"Hello, gentlemen." He takes a seat at the head of the table, a lit cigar in his hand.

"My bastard sons have finally figured out that I am not dead. They attacked my private estates last night, burning it to the ground, and I doubt they're going to stop until they find me. I called this meeting because I need everybody on high alert. Keep your ears to the ground and make sure my name is kept out of everything... as always." His eyes scan the room and land on Yulie's empty chair.

"Where the fuck is Yulie?" he booms, and a nervous sludge

coats my insides. When no one answers, he just shrugs as if he doesn't really care. "That cocksucker is probably passed out drunk in his sex dungeon," Rossi chuckles and half of the men in the room join in.

"All right then... I just wanted to let you know that I will be laying low for a few weeks and only a handful of people will know where I am. If you need anything, you'll need to ask Ivan or Yulie. I'll expect you all to treat them as if they were me. I've got a couple more rounds to do and then I'll be out of here. I have a plane to catch." Rossi gets up from his chair, buttoning his suit jacket up, flicking ashes of his cigar all over the table, while smoke billows in soft wisps through the air.

"Sorry your house burned down, boss," Derick calls from across the table.

"Don't be, the house didn't mean shit to me. I am, however, disappointed that I didn't have time to enjoy the virgin pussy I had tied up on my bed. It was truly a waste for such a fine piece of ass to die before being used. Any of you been down to see the girls going to auction yet?" He lifts his thick brows, his eyes piercing over each of the men, before meeting mine.

There isn't an ounce of emotion in my features.

"Of course, it's the only kind of window shopping I'll ever do," Derick snickers, and I have the urge to pick up the pencil in front of me and shove it into his eyeball.

"Well, if you've seen number five, you know what I had lying in my bed. It was her fucking sister."

If I hadn't trained myself for so many years to wear an emotionless mask, I would have looked shocked. I had a thousand and one questions, the biggest one being... how the hell did her sister end up in Rossi's twisted web?

"No shit?" Derick sounds interested, and I watch him rub his chin as if he is thinking about her right now... about *my* Kitten.

"Yes. A real fucking waste I didn't get to play with her for a bit before she burned to a crisp. Oh, well, the world is an oyster full of some of the finest pussy..." He laughs, but I can't muster up even a smile.

Fucking Christ.

I realize then exactly what he said... Violet's sister is dead. Rossi killed her. Well, he didn't kill her himself, but he left her to die. I want to shake my head, clench my fists, throw something. As if she doesn't have enough to deal with. Now this? It's like a bad hand of poker, and she just keeps drawing shitty cards. One shit card after the next.

How am I going to tell her? How am I going to explain to her that her sister got tangled up in Rossi's web, too? *Fuck!* No... telling her would just make everything worse for her. There is nothing anybody can do now to change what happened. Telling her would only cause her more pain, but the idea of not telling her, of breaking the fragile trust that's been built between us, angers me. The last thing I want to do is risk losing her, but if finding her sister after this is the only thing keeping her going, then telling her isn't going to help either of us.

I decide then I can't tell her... I won't.

"Ivan, walk out with me." Rossi's voice drags me out of my thoughts and as he makes his way toward the door.

I get up, shoving the chair away. I follow Rossi outside until we are in the hallway and out of earshot.

"Ivan, you're going to be one of the few people who actually knows where I'll be." His dark evil gaze pierces mine. A long time ago, I looked up to him, but since Violet, all I see him as is a vile monster... a man consumed with an uncanny need to destroy. "I hope I can trust you with this, Ivan."

"Of course, always... boss."

13

Violet

THE CUT on the palm of my hand throbs, and I have half a mind to take one of those knockout pills to ease some of the pain, but I remember how vulnerable that would make me, so I decide against it. I'll take the pain in my hand over being raped while unconscious any day. Yulie might be dead but that doesn't mean there aren't others who would try and get to me.

Only a few minutes until dinnertime... I smile in cheerful happiness.

Noises out in the hall reach my ears and have me sitting up a little straighter. Moments later, the food flap on my door opens and a tray is shoved inside. A sandwich. What a surprise, the same thing as always.

I sit down on my mattress and nibble on the stale bread that holds no flavor, even with the bologna smashed in between. Would it kill them to slap some mayo on here? I put the plate by side of the bed, hoping Ivan has something a little more edible at his place.

As if he hears me thinking of him, the jingle of keys followed by the door opening grabs my full attention. Ivan appears in the door, and I jump up from the mattress, running for the door. He carries me to his place as he always does and deposits me on the couch, closing and locking the door behind us. "I need to take a look at your hand, Kitten, since I didn't get to this morning."

Ivan's gray eyes seem darker than normal tonight, and I wonder what happened today, how his meeting went?

"Okay." I watch him get the first aid kit from the kitchen and my stomach growls, reminding me that I haven't really eaten.

"Do you have something I can eat? Turns out the bologna sandwiches aren't that good."

He grins at me. "Sure, I don't have a lot here. We have a small canteen downstairs where I usually eat, but I'll find you something when I'm done looking at your hand." He sits down next to me and unwraps my hand, shaking his head. "I'm sorry... I should have asked you if you were hungry."

"It's okay, you already do so much for me. It's not your job to ask me about things like when I last ate."

His angelic features turn into a frown. "It will never be enough, Kitten, never..." He cleans my cut again and smears some ointment on it but doesn't rewrap my hand.

"Come on, let's find you something to eat."

He leads me to the kitchen and makes me sit down on a chair. I watch him search through the cabinets and peek in the refrigerator before gazing at me over his shoulder.

"How about some oatmeal with apples?"

"That sounds amazing." I smile.

He makes me some oatmeal on the two-burner stovetop, and I can't keep my eyes off of him. Watching him do this mundane task is oddly comforting. Especially knowing that he is doing it for me. It gives me a sense of false hope that maybe someday we could actually be together, we could do this somewhere else, somewhere safe.

A few minutes later, he sits a bowl of warm oatmeal topped with cut-up apples in front of me. I dive in, shoving steaming hot spoonfuls into my mouth. Each bite lands heavily in my belly. I catch him looking at me as I vigorously eat the delicious meal. I feel like a slob, and embarrassment starts to heat my cheeks.

"Sorry." I try and eat a little slower, but he just smiles.

"Eat however you want, Kitten. You don't have to hide the fact that you're hungry." He takes the seat across the table, and I decide to change the subject.

"How was your meeting?" I curiously ask while finishing up my oatmeal at a much slower, far less sloppy pace.

Ivan shrugs. "It was what it always is. A bunch of full-grown men discussing illegal shit."

Irritation seems to drip from his words. He doesn't want to talk about it, and that's fine, I guess. It's not really my business anyway, and I don't care to know what they're doing next.

"I did want to talk to you about what's going to happen during the transport to Vegas. To prepare you, get you ready, since we're going to be leaving next week."

"Okay, what's going to happen?" I try to keep the fear out of my voice. All this time, I've had Ivan. With the auction fast approaching, I'm not sure how often I'll be coming up here, if at all, or spending time with him.

"I know you're worried and probably scared, but you need to make sure you do every single thing instructed of you between now and when we go into hiding."

I gulp, the oatmeal in my belly feeling like a ton of bricks. "You know I'll do whatever I have to." And I will. I want out of here. I want to escape this place so badly, I can almost taste the freedom on my tongue.

Ivan's gray eyes pierce mine. "A couple of days before the auction, they're going to come and get each of you. They'll bring you into a containment area, make you strip and hose you down. You'll be given a bar of soap and instructed to clean yourself."

"I'll get to see the other girls?" I ask, somewhat shocked. The entire time I've been here, I've not once seen another female, not that it's all that surprising.

Ivan nods. "Yes, but do not talk to them. Do not talk at all. I will be there. I'll be watching to make sure everything runs smoothly. If you or any of the other girls get out of line, they're going to hurt you, or I may have to hurt you myself."

My eyes go wide. "You would do that?" I don't know why I ask the question, but I can't truly fathom Ivan hurting someone who doesn't deserve it.

His jaw flexes. "It's not like I'd want to. It's not my normal job, but with Yulie gone, it falls into my hands. If I don't make sure the girls follow our orders, then they'll know something is up, and I can't risk any suspicions being raised this close to the auction. However, if you do as they tell you, then nothing bad will happen. I won't hurt you, Violet."

The worst thing of all is that I believe him, but that's not to say the other women won't get hurt or aren't hurt now. A part of me hates myself for being spared while they all suffer.

"And what about everyone else?"

Ivan looks away, shame filling his features. "There is nothing I can do, Kitten. All that matters is that I protect you. I vowed to get you out of this, and I'm not going to fail you again."

As much as I want to push him to help them, too, I understand he can't. He's already risked too much for me. If he risks any more, he might get caught, and if he gets caught, we're both as good as dead.

"What else?" I ask, knowing there is more. There has to be.

"The day of the auction, they'll give each of you a shot that will make you incoherent. You'll be awake and able to respond to things being asked of you, but you'll feel like you aren't in control of your body or your emotions. You're going to feel kind of numb. It is imperative that you don't try and run, that you keep your blindfold in place, and that you don't fight anyone, no matter what is asked of you. You will need to trust me completely because if you don't, then this will not work."

Worry coats my insides, but I nod.

"I will not let anyone hurt you, Violet."

I lick my lips, the urge to kiss him consuming me. He's protected me, guarded me in every sense, and he's everything I could ever want, even if he doesn't believe it.

"Can we talk about something else?" I don't know if I can handle anymore tonight. The thought of all of that happening within a week has my stomach doing somersaults.

"Maybe we could stop talking altogether?" I try to give him a seductive grin. I have no idea what I'm doing, but Ivan seems to know exactly what I'm up to.

"Kitten... stop." Ivan looks away to something behind me. "I'm not going to fuck you again."

My shoulders sag as his rejection sinks in. "Why not? Didn't you enjoy last night?"

He grins at me and shakes his head. "Silly little girl, you just have no fucking idea. You are sore, and I'm not going to hurt you. I only ever want you to feel pleasure with me."

"I'm fine, I promise." I make a little pouty face. "Please, I promise I'll tell you if it starts to hurt." I want to be with him. I need the physical connection, even if he refuses to give me anything emotional or admit there's more to us.

I want to forget everything and fall apart with him, just like I did for a moment last night. Afterward, I want to enjoy just lying in bed.

Getting up from my seat, I walk around the table to where Ivan is sitting. He follows my movements with his eyes, but his body is still as a statue. Not sure what to do, I just put my uninjured hand on his shoulder and run it down his arm, testing the waters.

When he doesn't resist my touch, I get more adventurous, moving my hand back up, around his chest and lower to trace his abdominal muscles.

I can feel them even through the layers of clothing. I move my hand even lower, but when I'm almost at my destination, he snatches my wrist so quickly I jump. I half expect him to shove me away or yell at me but instead, he gets up, the chair behind him tipping over and falling onto the floor.

He picks me up and throws me over his shoulder, making me panic. Is he going to bring me down to the cell for not listening?

"Ivan?" I open my eyes and turn my head to the side. When I see he is going in the direction of the bedroom and not heading toward the door, relief washes over me.

He flips me, tossing me over his shoulder, and I land on the bed, bouncing against the mattress.

I watch him pull his shirt off before he pulls my sweatpants and panties down in one swift move. His eyes are dark and blazing with lust.

Just seeing the way he is gazing down at me with such a primal need has my body on fire and moisture building between my legs.

My thighs rub together in anticipation as I watch him undo his belt and pants.

When he drops his pants and boxers, his erection springs free... and the thing makes my breath hitch. My legs part on instinct when he starts crawling onto the bed and over top of me.

He helps me out of my shirt, leaving me completely naked, just as he is. Lowering himself on his elbows until my nipples touch his chest, he takes my mouth and kisses me hard and passionately.

I feel like I'm melting away from his touch, so I entwine my fingers and place my arms around his neck to hold on to him, drawing him closer. His hardness presses against my inner thigh, and I try to adjust my hips to align him with my center.

He breaks the kiss and chuckles. "Are you that eager for my cock, Kitten?"

I should probably be embarrassed or offended by his crude words, but all I can think of is how bad I want him right now.

"Yes," I moan. "I want you. Please..." I'm panting with need. My center drips with arousal, and he grunts at my response, shifting on top of me.

"Are you wet enough for me, or do I need to make you come with my tongue first?"

I shake my head, reaching for him, but he moves out of my reach, and my fingers graze his heated skin.

"No... I want... you... I'm ready..." I whimper, afraid he may say no and deny me.

"I want you to ride me tonight." At his words, I move so he can climb onto the center of the bed. I wait, watching as he settles himself against the headboard. He strokes his thick cock up and down. Liquid beads at the tip, glistening in the light, and I want it... I want him.

Biting my lip, I crawl up over top of him, my eyes moving from his cock to his face. His gray eyes are full of hunger, and when his hands grip my hips, I lose it. I grab onto his thickness and center it at my entrance.

"Go slow, Kitten. Otherwise, it's going to hurt." There's a bite to his voice, and he doesn't realize it, but I want it to hurt. I want to remember him, and every moment we have together like this.

Staring into his eyes, I sink all way down onto his cock, letting the air in my lungs seep out. Ivan's head falls back against the headboard with a heavy thud, and a curse spills from his lips.

"Fuck, Kitten. I said slow." His fingers dig into my hips, and I smile, setting my hands on his shoulders before I move back up, dropping back down hard. The tip of his cock hits the back of my channel, and I release a hiss of pleasure and pain.

"I...." I stop the words from coming out, and instead, focus on drawing out the pleasure spiraling out of control inside of us.

"Shit," Ivan grits out, his eyes bright and pooling with need. I want to give to him like I never have before. I swivel my hips and watch as the pleasure courses through his features. Then I'm moving again, up and down, up and down, up and down, each stroke, each plunge onto his cock pushing me closer to the edge.

An electric current pulses between us, and I feel myself clench around his length. My nails dig into his flesh, and I move faster, feeling the impending orgasm just on the horizon. Ivan thrusts his hips upward, hitting a spot deep inside me, and I'm soaring... flying deep into the night sky. I sag against his body and let him take control, and he does. He owns my body as if it was made for him.

He holds me close and thrusts inside me until his cock starts to pulse, jets of hot semen filling my womb in seconds. As soon as the warmth seeps into my bones, I feel the need to sleep overtake me, and Ivan wraps me in his arms, leaving me to do just that... making me wish we could stay like this forever.

∽

I'M A NERVOUS WRECK, as the day before the auction comes. Thanks to Ivan, I know what is going to take place today, but I have no clue how I am going to get through it. Ivan brought me back to my cell before sunrise, like always, and I've been pacing the length of the room since then, afraid that if I stop moving, I may just lose my damn mind.

My fingernails are chewed down to the skin, and my hands won't stop shaking. I feel like I might puke, and my stomach throbs with nervous anxiety. When I hear a commotion outside the door, I know it's starting and all I can do is brace myself for what's to come.

In a matter of seconds, my cell door is being unlocked and opened. My heart shifts into overdrive when I see the man entering my cell.

"Hey, bitch, did you miss me?" Luca greets me with a sick grin. "Get out. It's time to clean you the fuck up."

I suck in a shaky breath and take a step toward him. He snatches my arm and holds it with an iron grip while dragging me from the cell. Cries and sobs echo down the hallway, filling me with even more anxiety. Ivan said nothing bad would happen to me, but I can't believe him. Not in this moment. Luca walks down the hallway and past the room where the doctor checked me. It isn't until we turn the corner and head down another hallway that I see other people. Another guy I've never seen before is dragging a crying girl down the hall and into a room all the way at the very end.

"Are you going to be a good girl and give me another show in there?" Luca snickers. "I'm going to need you to get in line and strip in the shower room. Don't talk, don't fight, just do as you're told or you're not going to like what happens."

I nod and he grins, showing off his crooked front teeth. As soon as Luca pushes me inside the room, I see Ivan. He is standing with his arms crossed next to the man who came in my cell with Luca that night. The sight of them standing together like they are old friends feels like a punch in the face.

The monster who tried to hurt me sees me first and winks at me. He fucking winks at me like this is all a fun joke for him. Ivan doesn't turn to look at me. He remains staring straight ahead at the two girls already lined up against the wall.

"Get in line," Ivan orders and the coldness of his voice turns the blood in my veins to ice. I do what he says and stand next to the other girl. When I finally get the courage, I look up and over at them. When my gaze reaches their faces, I almost fall to my knees.

They are both crying, their eyes red and filled with pure terror. One has a bruise on the side of her face, while the other looks as if she's been starved. My heart shatters inside my chest at the sight, and I don't know if I'll ever be able to put all the broken pieces back together again.

Shame courses through me. They have been locked up under horrible conditions for who knows how long, without anyone like Ivan helping them. They have no idea what's going to happen to them now, or in the future. The sudden guilt hits me like a ton of bricks. I've been sleeping in a warm bed every night, taking showers and having Ivan cook for me while these other girls are down here.

I knew this, but it was easier when I didn't have to see them, when I could forget they were here.

I chance a peek at Ivan and see him whispering something to the other man. Not once does he look at me or even notice that I'm here. I tell myself it's not because he doesn't really notice I'm here but that he's just trying to remain in character, but it hurts, it hurts bad, and I start crying in silence, closing my eyes and leaning against the wall behind me. I let one tear after another fall down my cheeks. I'm not so much crying for myself but for the other girls here. The ones that I have been too selfish to think about more than a few times.

I stand there and listen to the other girls being brought in, too ashamed to look at them and their tears. Every whimper and sob that reaches my ears is like another slice into my chest.

"Strip." Luca's booming voice fills the room, and my eyes pop open. Luca looks me straight in the eyes and smiles while Ivan and the third man just stand there looking at the other girls. Having lost my worry about modesty, I start undressing. Two out of the three men have already seen me naked anyway, and if I don't do it then I'll just be hurt anyway, and honestly, it's not worth it. I glance to my right and see the girl next to me frozen in place.

Ivan says something and when I look over, he's nodding in the direction of the girl beside me. He tells Luca something that makes him smile, and my insides coil with anxiety. Luca starts walking in her direction, and the girl next to me starts shaking so hard I think she might shatter the teeth in her head. Her skin is pale, and her face is hollow. She looks like she might puke at any second.

"You know what this is?" Luca holds up something that looks like a flashlight but instead of the light, it has two short metal pieces sticking out of the front.

When no one answers him, he continues, "This is a twelve-million-volt stun gun and if you don't get your fucking clothes off in the next few seconds, I'm going to light you up with it."

"P-Please," the girl starts begging, shaking her head back and forth as if she's trying to escape the nightmare before her. Her arms are wrapped around herself, and I want nothing more than to take her into my embrace and tell her everything is going to be alright. I want to do it so badly that I curl my hands into fists, afraid that I may just actually do it.

Luca shakes his head in disappointment. "Last chance, bitch."

I look over at Ivan, hoping, praying he will stop this, even though I know he can't. Then, for the first time since I entered the room, he looks at me. He looks me straight in the eyes, and I think my heart stops beating for a second. I've never seen him like this.

His gray eyes are cold, vacant, and unloving. Nothing but hate reflects back at me, and seeing him like this is tearing me apart. How can he be acting? Is this the man he's warned me about? Is this the real him? Would I have let him touch me had I see him as this man? Would I still love him? I don't really know.

Seconds later, I'm forced to watch Luca raise the stun gun and punch the metal tips into the girl's abdomen. The zinging sound of electricity fills the room the second before the girl's cries of pain drown out the noise. She falls to the ground on her knees in front of us, and I bite the inside of my cheek to stop myself from crying, to stop myself from telling him to stop.

"Get up and strip, you dumb bitch," Luca yells at the sobbing girl on the floor. When she doesn't get up, he raises the stick again, as if he's going to zap her. That's when something inside of me snaps. I can't stand here and do nothing. I can't watch them hurt her.

"Stop!" I lunge forward and try to slap the stick out of Luca's hand, but he is quicker and turns the stick on me instead, hitting me with the metal tips right in the arm. My skin burns, and it feels as if I've been electrocuted. Pain ripples through my entire body, locking up every muscle. Unable to control my movements and my breath, I fall to the ground just like the other girl had a moment ago.

I lift my head and my eyes collide with the other girl's. She's looking at me like I'm her hero, but she has no idea how wrong she is. "It's okay, just do what they say," I whisper breathlessly, desperately wanting to offer her my hand and help her up off the cold floor. She nods, and slowly shoves off the floor.

"Get the fuck up!" Another voice fills the air, making my body shake.

I try to push myself up but apparently, I'm not fast enough. I hear heavy footsteps coming in my direction, and when I see the boots in front of me, I know who they belong to. Before I can even look up to meet Ivan's gaze, he grabs me by one arm. His normally gentle touch is rough and cold as he yanks me harshly to my feet, releasing me with a shove. I cling to the wall behind me for support.

"Strip," Ivan orders without missing a beat, and I continue taking my clothes off while keeping eye contact with the girl beside me. I might not be able to hug her or even hold her hand, but at least I can let her know that I see her pain, that I am here with her and that she isn't alone.

When every one of the girls, including me, are completely naked, Luca comes around and hands each of us a bar of soap while Ivan and the other guy grab two hoses from the wall behind them and turn the water on. When Luca is done, he takes one of the hoses from Ivan and they start hosing us off with water while Ivan just stands there with his arms crossed over his muscled chest overseeing the entire event.

The water is ice cold, and I immediately shiver when the first spray lands against my skin.

"Start washing yourself with the soap," Luca yells over the noise of the water splashing against the walls and floor. "Make sure those pussies are all nice and clean for tomorrow. We don't like getting complaints from customers about smelly pussy, and if you don't get sold then... well, you don't want to know what happens to you," he laughs, spraying us all with a blast of ice cold water.

I grit my teeth, trying to push down the anger and hate growing inside me. I've never hated anyone this much in my life. I've never thought about killing someone until this day. If I had the chance right now, I would kill Luca, and I'd do it without a second thought.

After a few minutes, the water is turned off and we are left standing shivering in the center of the room. The sound of teeth chattering fills the air, and a minute later, Luca gets some old dirty towels from the corner of the room and tosses one at each of us.

The towels smell like mold, and I nearly barf into the fabric.

"Dry off, and then we'll be bringing you back to the cells," he yells.

I gaze down at the piles of wet clothing on the floor in front of each of us.

Are we supposed to stay naked until tomorrow?

"Time's up," Luca yells again, and they start hauling girls out of the room one by one. I lift my gaze from the floor and up to Ivan, who is standing in the room, most likely making sure none of us make even an attempt to run. I'm angry, so angry, that I want to slap him, tell him that I hate him, even when I don't. I could never hate him, not after all he's done for me, but that doesn't mean I'm not furious.

"Let's go." Luca appears directly in front of me, his hand reaching out, latching onto my arm. A squeak escapes my lips when I lose my footing and slip on the wet concrete floor. I barely get my footing before I slam into Luca's side.

"Learn how to fucking walk, and you won't fall." He laughs, tugging me along, out the door, and down the hall to my cell. He shoves me inside, his eyes roaming over my cold soaked body before he shuts the door, locking me inside.

I backpedal toward the bed, sinking down onto the filthy mattress. I wrap my arms around my middle and start to sob. Coldness seeps deep into my bones, and my teeth chatter together, the sound filling the silent room.

How could he do this? How could he let his men treat women

this way? How is he so kind and gentle with me but hateful and mean with them?

I wish like hell he was here right now so that I could scream at him, so I could tell him how angry I am with him for not saving them like he saved me. Parts of me knew my anger was irrational, but I didn't care, not in this moment, not after watching them hurt that girl. She looked younger than me and frightened beyond belief.

The food flap opens a little while later and something is shoved inside before it's quickly closed again. I get up on shaky legs and walk over to pick up a thin white cotton shift dress. I pull it on, even though I know it's not going to provide me with a lot of warmth. At least I won't be naked anymore. Sitting back down on the mattress, I curl up into a ball and for the first time since Ivan started getting me from my cell, I don't want to see him.

He's a reminder of what I have that those other girls here don't have.

I'm protected and cared for by the dark knight while they get nothing.

I should feel grateful, happy, but all I feel is guilt and shame.

14

Ivan

EACH STEP I take toward her cell is forced. I've never walked down to get her with such a pit of anguish in my stomach. Today was a fucking nightmare. The only reason I was able to hold back and not rip Luca's head off was the knowledge of saving her tomorrow. This is the only way, the only chance I have, and I knew there was no way I could let my emotions get involved.

As soon as I open the door to her cell, I know that everything is going to be different now. Things will change between us now that she has seen the darkness inside me. I've told her that I was a bad man, but she's never seen that part of me, never seen how cold and disconnected I can be. Instead of getting up and jumping into my arms, she remains curled up on the mattress, facing away from me.

I sigh and step into the cell, walking across the room. Kneeling down beside her, I gently touch her bare arm and cringe as she pulls away. Where she usually leans into my touch, she fucking pulls away, her body language telling me not to touch her ice-cold skin.

"It had to happen this way, Kitten. It was either protect you or them, and if I have to choose, I'm always going to choose you. You're my number one priority." I need her to understand this. Everything changed the day she collided with me. Something inside me broke lose when I saw her big blue eyes full of fright. I was looking for something without even knowing it... something more... and then she found me, she fucking found me.

"Come on, let me take you upstairs. You're freezing." I slide my arms underneath her and lift her up. She doesn't wrap her arm around me or hold on to my shirt like she usually does, but at least she isn't struggling to get away from me. I don't know what I would do if she was.

As I cradle her to my chest and carry her upstairs, her eyes remain closed, but I know she is not a sleep. Everywhere I touch, her skin is cold, and her body is slightly shaking in my hold.

When I get to my place, I lay her in my bed and cover her up with the comforter. Her eyes open to watch what I am doing, but she won't look me in the eyes.

"I want to sleep on the floor," she whispers, her voice raspy from crying.

"What... why?" I'm flabbergasted by her statement.

"I'm not going to be curled up in a warm bed when the other girls are alone and freezing downstairs." Her voice cracks at the end, and she tries to get off the bed. I touch her shoulders to push her back down, but she pulls away once more.

"Please don't touch me." Just like that, she rips my heart from my chest. I let her get up, but I keep her pinned between me and the bed. She leans away from me and all I want to do is hold her.

"I won't touch you, and I'll sleep on the couch if you sleep in the bed."

She nods and sits back down on the bed. When I step away, she lifts her legs and rolls onto her side. She doesn't get under the comforter, but at least I got her to lay in the bed. There's no way I could've handled having her sleep on the floor. It was enough having to put her back in that cell every day.

"Goodnight, Kitten," I murmur before leaving the room and closing the door halfway. I keep the door open so I can hear her if she starts crying, because if she does, I'm going in there to hold her, whether she likes it or not. I sit on the couch and listen for a long time, but she doesn't make a sound... at least nothing I can hear from this distance.

When I walk back into the bedroom as quietly as I can, I find her sleeping. Her face is relaxed, all the worry gone from her features and her breathing is slow and even. I pull the blanket over her barely dressed body before I return to the couch and try to get some sleep myself.

Unfortunately, everytime I close my eyes, images of today remain in my head. Violet having to strip in front of everyone, the other men's eyes and hands on her. Them seeing her, seeing what is mine, then getting tased. I can still hear her pained cry in my ears, and I don't think I will forget that sound... not ever.

∼

"Please, Kitten, do what I told you. I know you want to help the others, but we just can't." I keep my voice low, so no one from the hallway can hear. Her cell door is wide open, and Luca is already bringing some of the girls out. The last thing I need is for him to hear my plan.

She nods but doesn't say a single word to me. She hasn't talked to me since last night; hell, she's hardly even looked at me. It's killing me to see her like this but it's okay, or at least that's what I tell myself. I don't have a choice but to do the things I'm doing.

I'm trying to protect her and someday she'll realize that. Even if she has to hate me right now, it's all for a good cause.

"Give me your arm," I coax, and she holds her arm out to me

without objection. I stick the needle into her skin, injecting her with the drug. I let the drug spread through her veins before I help her up to her feet. I take out some cable ties and tie her hands behind her back. When I spin her around to look at me, our eyes finally meet. I know the drug is already affecting her as she blinks at me in confusion, her baby blues going in and out of focus. Her creamy white cheeks are pink, and her lips are absolutely kissable. Fuck, do I wish we didn't' have to do this right now.

"Ivan... I feel... funny." Her words come out slow, and even though I don't want to hear her speech slurred, I'm just glad to hear her fucking voice.

"I know, Kitten, you'll be fine though. Just relax and do what you are told. Soon, this will be all over, and you'll be free." I gently grab hold of her upper arm and start leading her out. I hear her naked feet slapping against the cold concrete, and I have to fight the urge to pick her up and carry her.

I walk her all the way outside to the van and guide her into the back where two other girls are already tied up and waiting to leave. They both look up at me with fear in their eyes. I hate that they have to see me the way they do, and that now Violet sees me the same.

I go back inside and get the last girl from her cell, passing Luca and Gabe, who have the other two with them. When I get back to the van, I help the last girl inside.

I sigh, closing up the back door. I hope after everything, Violet sees how much I've given up for her and how much I've cared for her through all of this.

"Gabe, you drive the van. I'll ride with you in case anything goes down." I point to Luca, who is waiting for me to give him an order. "Luca, you take the SUV and let me know if anything looks suspicious. We'll meet at the club."

Luca gives me a curt nod and then walks toward the blacked-out SUV. Everyone takes their spots at my orders, and we head out.

It takes us only an hour to get to Vegas, and when we pull into the club's parking lot, I damn near sag against the seat. Everything comes down to this. It's still early and the parking lot is mostly empty, thankfully. We drive up to the back door and get out of the van. One of the guards is waiting out back as usual and opens the door for us. Luca pulls up behind us just as I open the back of the van. Gabe takes one girl on each arm, while I take Violet and another. Luca exits the SUV and grabs the last two girls. I want to assure Violet one last time before everything goes down but there isn't any way to do so right now.

We walk the girls into the dressing room, where women with brushes and makeup are on hand waiting to get them ready for tonight. I sit Violet down on one of the chairs in front of the vanity mirror. Our eyes meet for a moment, and I see sadness and worry but also longing. She misses me, she wants me, and that's enough to keep me going. I blink and return my gaze to the floor before I turn around and walk through the dressing room toward Benny's office.

Benny's crooked smile greets me as soon as I walk into his office without knocking. "Ivan, good to see you, old friend."

"Everything set for tonight?" I'm not going to pretend that I like him or call him my friend. We are not, nor will we ever be, friends.

"Everything is set. I've got a replacement girl coming in. She'll be waiting outside in a car and you can switch her out with your girl right before the auction." This is the part Violet can never find out about. Benny found a replacement for Violet's spot; there was no other way around it. We promised them six girls and that means six girls need to be auctioned off tonight.

I remember Benny telling me it was some homeless girl he'd found on the Strip. She didn't really have a good life anyway, but that wouldn't matter to Violet if she found out. She would hate me and hate herself if she ever discovered the truth. But I will do whatever I have to, hurt anyone I need to in order for her to be free.

Maybe she is my biggest flaw, my biggest weakness, but she might also be my only chance of salvation.

"Great. As soon as I have them switched and her out of here, I'll send you the rest of the payment."

Benny gives me a nod, and that's the end of our conversation.

I walk out of the office and take my position at the entrance of the dressing room. We are not supposed to leave until their security is fully staffed and in place, which I'm hoping is soon. I want to get Violet out of here without a trace of evidence being left behind.

As soon as Rossi finds out what I'm doing tonight, he'll send someone out to kill us both. Plus, I need a head start to outrun him... because he will hunt us, and he won't stop.

Killing Yulie will be the least of my worries after I take Violet.

Minutes tick by, and I grow more and more impatient. The club is starting to fill up and the club's security is still understaffed. *What the fuck!*

When I notice how close we are to the time of the auction occurring, I walk back through the dressing room and into Benny's office. I only get a quick look at Violet as I race through the dressing room, but it's enough to piss me off. They put some skanky underwear on her and dolled her up while she is sitting in the chair looking lost as fuck.

I get to the office and there's a woman straddling his lap... but I don't give a fuck what I'm interrupting. "Benny, where the fuck is the rest of your security? Everyone is arriving and my men aren't on your payroll, so fucking get someone out here."

"Oh, shit, yeah..." He shoves the woman off his lap and reaches for his phone.

I roll my eyes, completely annoyed and fed up.

"We have three guys out; there was a fight a couple nights ago," Benny starts, his beady eyes bleeding into mine.

"I don't give a fuck what happened to them. Get someone out there. Otherwise, shit is going to get bad," I growl and turn on my heels. I head back to the door and wait for someone else to come and take my place. Thank fuck it doesn't take long for Benny to get someone out here. The guy smirks as he approaches me.

"Am I replacing you?"

I clench my jaw. "Yeah, you are. Guard this door like it's got a million fucking dollars inside of it. Do you understand me?" I grip him by the lapels of his jacket. His face pales, the smile slipping from his lips. He nods his head, and I release him with a shove.

I find Gabe and Luca talking to some assholes in the hallway leading outside. I exhale, trying my best to keep my composure. "You guys can go ahead and take the van back now. I'll talk to Benny one more time and then drive the SUV back to the compound. Good job, boys," I force out, praying that neither of them can tell something is off.

"Sure thing, boss." Luca hands me the keys to the SUV without thought and I watch them leave. I wait a few more minutes before I look out the back door, making sure the van is gone. When I find the spot empty, I march back inside, going straight into the dressing room.

Nervous anxiety courses through my veins. I need to get in and out as fast as I can.

But I stop dead in my tracks when I enter the dressing room and find Violet on the floor, palming her cheeks as if someone has just hit her. My blood turns to ice, and I clench my fist, ready to put it through some fucker's teeth. I watch the guy standing in front of her as he grabs her roughly by the arms, jerking her up into a standing position.

My lips curl into a snarl, and I'm across the room in an instant. Before the guy even sees me coming, my fist is flying into his face. I feel bone crack underneath my knuckles and watch his head snap back before he staggers backward, landing against the vanity.

My gaze drops to Violet, who is looking around the room with complete confusion, as if she has no idea where she is or what just happened.

"You're fucking lucky," I spit at him and gently pull Violet into my arms. She stands unsteadily on her feet, her hands clutching onto my shirt. The guy gives me a dirty look, wiping at the blood trickling down his nose. I want to stay here to kick this fucker's ass but getting Violet out of here is more important.

"Time to go, Kitten." I loop one arm around her and usher her out of the dressing room. Benny meets me in the hall, ready to bring the other girl in from the parking lot.

"Go ahead, Ivan. I'll get the replacement," Benny tells me while looking at some chick who's heading down the hall. I try to pull Violet to the back door, but she tries to pull away, attempting to walk in the opposite direction we need to go. Not having time to deal with her confusion, I just pick her up, tossing her over my shoulder before walking out the door.

Once outside, I head for the SUV. I unlock it and deposit Violet on the passenger seat and buckle her up. Her eyes are wide, and she looks like she's just seen a ghost. I hurry to the driver's seat and get inside, starting the damn thing. I squeal tires out of the parking lot and head toward the interstate.

Violet is sitting next to me in silence, which is not surprising, considering the drug she is on. She grabs my hand and squeezes it as if she wants to get my attention. I think she wants to tell me something but can't get the words out.

"Give it some time, Kitten. The drug will wear off, and you'll be back to normal. Close your eyes for a little bit and rest. You are safe now."

I glance over at her. She still looks frustrated and helpless, but she listens to me and closes her eyes. I keep her hand in mine and when I feel her grip loosen and see her head rest on her shoulder, I know she is asleep.

I don't let go of her hand the entire drive and when she wakes up about an hour later, we are almost at the safehouse. She straightens up in her seat and looks around with wide eyes like she is trying to figure out where she is.

"You are fine, Kitten, everything is fine."

She looks over at me and then back outside the window and into the night sky.

"We... we need to go back, Ivan," Violet whispers quietly. "We need to go back there, I saw my sister!" At first, I'm not sure I heard her correctly, and thus, she says it again. "That was my sister..."

"Who was your sister? What are you talking about, Kitten?" I didn't see anyone who could be her sister there, so I have no idea what she is talking about. It has to be the drugs talking. It has to be.

"My sister was there. I saw her."

"No, you didn't. It's the drugs in your system. I white knuckle the steering wheel. I don't need this right now. "Your sister is at home, in North Woods," I lie. "There is just no way she would have been at that place.

I need Violet with me, because I can't risk her trying to run away. That will get us both killed, and I didn't risk all of this just for us both to die. Violet pulls her hand from mine, and my hand suddenly feels empty after holding hers for so long, like it belongs there, and it just lost its home.

"She reached for me, she came for me, she wanted to save me..."

"Enough." I raise my voice, and Violet flinches as if I've just physically slapped her. "We will talk about it once the drugs wear off." I lower my voice and focus on driving.

Violet turns away from me and leans her head against the window. She'll be fine once the drugs are out of her system. She better be, because I'm not sure I have it in me to tell her that her sister is dead.

15

Violet

I SAW HER. I know I did. Strawberry-blond hair... blue eyes the color of the ocean. I saw Ella. She was there, reaching for me, and then she was gone. I try and tell myself it wasn't the drugs, that it wasn't all in my head, but I don't know for certain. If it was her, how did she get to the auction? How could she possibly know where I was? Ugh... nothing makes sense.

I catch Ivan white knuckling the steering wheel out of the corner of my eye. He seems angry, tense, and I'm scared to say anything else right now. Instead, I look around; we are in a nice car with leather seats, and we are driving down some interstate.

Suddenly, it hits me; we are driving down the interstate. I'm free, I'm out of the cell, away from that horrible place with those disgusting men. It is incredibly hard to be angry with Ivan at this moment when he is the one who freed me from that nightmare.

"Where are we going?" I murmur.

"I rented a small house, where we can lay low for a while. I used a fake name, paying cash. There is no way anyone could know we are here. It's safe. We'll be there in about ten minutes." He seems much calmer now that I've changed the subject, and I more than appreciate it. After everything that has happened to me, I don't know if I can handle angry Ivan right now.

We pull up to a small and rather secluded house a little while later. It's nothing overly lavish, more like an ornate cottage. He opens the garage with a code and pulls the car inside.

He cuts the engine and closes the garage door behind us. We both get out but once I'm on my feet, I realize that I am not fully in control of my body yet. My knees buckle beneath me, and I have to lean against the car and wait for Ivan to come around and get me. He picks me up and carries me inside as he always does.

"You think there will ever be a time where you don't have to carry me everywhere?"

"I hope not." A smile ghosts over his lips, giving me the urge to kiss him. I look around the house as Ivan walks through it and into to the bedroom.

"We should sleep. I haven't slept at all, and you've slept less than an hour."

I bite my bottom lip, trying to decide if I want to bring up my sister again. With each passing second, I know that I saw her.

"I want to call her," I say, just as he sets me on the comforter. "I want to call my sister, just to tell her that I'm okay."

"You can't, Violet. You can't call anybody; it's not safe. Don't you get that?" The harsh tone Ivan gives me is something I'm not used to, and I'm not sure what to make of it. I know he's stressed, on edge even, but he doesn't need to yell at me.

"I'm not going to tell her where I am, I'm just telling her that I'm okay. She's obviously been looking for me. She must be worried sick."

Ivan is listening to me, but I can see the anger building inside of him with each of my words. I just don't understand why this is making him so angry.

"Violet," he snaps, his voice raw, his eyes impossibly dark. "I said stop. I'm so fucking close to losing it right now, and I don't want to do that to you, but I don't have the patience to do this right now."

Tears well in my eyes. He's being so mean, and I'm confused and frustrated over his change in behavior, so much so that I shove at his chest with my hands.

"You don't own me, Ivan. I can do whatever I want, whenever I want."

The look on his face is one of pure rage and if I didn't know that he wouldn't hurt me, I would be cowering in the corner of the room.

He grabs onto my wrists, halting any future movements, before leaning into my face. He looks like a bull on the verge of charging. His nostrils flare, and the scent of danger permeates the air.

"Try to escape me, Kitten, and I'll drag you back here kicking and screaming. I might not own you, but I've risked everything to protect your pretty ass so stop fighting with me and fucking listen." He ends his sentence on a growl that vibrates through me. I tug my wrists from his grasp and curl my lip into a snarl. I've waited for this day since the night I was taken.

"One way or another, I'm going to call her," I growl, proving to him that I won't back down. My sister deserves to know I'm safe. I might not able to go home to her again, but she needs to know that I'm okay, that and I just want to hear her voice. She's all I have left and knowing she's okay, too, will ease the gaping wound that's formed in my chest.

Ivan stomps out of the room, and heavy footfalls echo through the house. Seconds later, he returns with a large box. He lets it fall onto the floor with a loud thud at the edge of the mattress and starts to open it, pulling back the sides to expose the contents.

"I ordered you some clothes and had them sent here." He hands me a pair of underwear, a shirt, and some cotton shorts all in my size.

"Thank you." I start to peel off the outfit they put me in at the club and put on the clothes Ivan gave me. Not wanting to fight anymore right now, I pull the comforter back and climb underneath it. The sheets are cold against my bare skin but I'm comfortable knowing I'll always be sleeping on a real bed every night. I pull the comforter back over my body and burrow into the pillows. I hear Ivan rustling with his clothing and then feel him climb into the bed, sliding under the blankets next to me.

It is not long before I hear his breathing even out and I'm certain he's asleep. I, however, am wide awake. I stare at the ceiling for a while before it occurs to me that I could just call her now while he is asleep. He'll never know... I can delete the call, slip back into bed, and all will be good in the world again. Nervously and oh-so-slowly, I carefully slip out of the bed and look around the room. I didn't see Ivan with his phone on him. I'm sure he got rid of it, but there must be one in here, or maybe even a computer. I could always send her a message from there or email.

On tiptoes, I sneak through the still-dark house, trying my best not to bump into anything. I find my way into the living room and turn on the lamp on the side table. As soon as the living room is illuminated with soft light, I spot it. A phone. There it is a phone sitting next to the TV. A landline. I grab it off the charging station and hold it to my ear until I hear the dial tone.

I sigh in relief and start to dial one of the few numbers I know by heart... my sister's. My hands shake as I hold the phone to my ear. This is it. In a few seconds, I will finally hear Ella's voice again. My heart stops beating in my chest when I hear someone else's voice come over the line.

"I'm sorry the number you have dialed has been temporarily disconnected. Please try your call again later," a computerized voice says on repeat. I shake my head and hang up just to dial once more. When I hear the same message as last time, I hang up and put the phone back on its station. I want to the throw the phone out into the yard, scream, maybe even punch something. I'm so angry, so upset.

I try to think of an explanation and find myself walking into the kitchen. I open a couple cabinets until I find the cups and then I get a glass of water. I try once more to digest my newest discovery. Why would she have her phone turned off? Nothing makes sense... nothing. Then suddenly, I get an idea. I could call her work.

Maybe they know where she is. I put the glass down and walk back into the living room and to the phone. Just as I pick it up and start dialing the number, I hear someone move behind me.

"What the fuck are you doing?" Ivan's loud voice makes my pulse race, and I jump a foot off the ground. My cheeks start to heat with embarrassment because I know I've been caught.

"I-I'm trying to call my sister, but her phone is disconnected." My voice is weak, and I hang my head in shame, knowing Ivan's going to lose it at any given second. I risked him getting angry and finding out I went against his word and for nothing.

"I told you not to call anybody! Do I need to tie you to the fucking bed? What do I need to do for you to grasp the seriousness of this situation?"

My eyes go wide with fear. He wouldn't do that... he wouldn't tie me up. I swallow, knowing that I'm wrong. Of course, he would tie me up.

"I didn't risk everything to save you just so you can do something stupid that gets you killed."

"You can tie me to the bed, but you can't keep me there forever." I shove past him and when I hear him hot on my heels, I start to run. I know there's no way I can overpower him, but I could make a run for it. Possibly escape. The thought makes my heart ache as I head down the hallway, still there is no way I'm going to let him tie me up. He didn't help me escape captivity to hold me captive himself, did he?

"Come on, Kitten. You know running from me is no good. I'm stronger and faster... then there's what will happen to you when I catch you. I can promise you it's going to include making you wish you hadn't picked up that phone."

I turn around and notice he's blocking any chance I have at running back down the hall. It doesn't help that it's impossibly dark, and my pulse is pounding in my ears making it hard for me to hear anything. I'm disoriented but I need to make a run for it.

I aim to move and duck past his side, but he steps forward, grabbing onto me. His fingers sink into my tender flesh before I have the chance to do anything. In an instant, he has my legs kicked out from underneath me. I fall to the ground with a gasp, landing with a hard thud.

I curse and thank him at the same time. If he didn't have a grip on my arm, I would have landed harshly against the wooden floor but, like always, he rescues me, pulling me up a little just before I land.

Still, the floor is cold and unforgiving. I gasp for air, and my teeth rattle. I try to get up, but he is already on top of me, pushing me to the floor face first. My head is turned to the side, while my cheek is pressed to the floor. He towers over me, placing his mouth at my ear.

"What to do with you now, Kitten?" Shivers ripple across my body. I feel his erection press against my ass as he leans down, pressing more weight into my backside. That combined with his hot breath on my skin has my inner walls clenching and my core tingling in excitement. Before I even know what I'm doing, I move my hips and push my ass against his cock.

He groans behind me, sending another delicious shiver of pleasure down my spine. "You like this, Kitten? You like me chasing you and holding you down? Do you want me to fuck you?"

I didn't realize how turned on by this I was until this moment. I never really thought about this before... thought about what turns me on. I never had the chance to explore my sexuality. However, right now, with Ivan pressing me to the floor, I realize that I do like this. I like this a lot. I'm so wet; I can feel my arousal through the thin material of my shorts.

Ivan grabs a fist full of my hair and pulls my head back slightly.

"I asked you a question," he growls, pulling harder on my hair. The pain on my scalp sends tingles of pleasure down my back and straight into my soaking core.

"Yes," I moan into the darkness. "I want you..."

"You want me to do what, Kitten?" There's a playfulness to his voice but also an edge. He wants me to tell him exactly what I want. I feel his fingers trail down my spine, blazing a path of pleasure and need. His touch is fire, and it's burning me alive.

"Fuck me... please." I barely get the words out before Ivan shifts on top of me and pulls my shorts down my legs. He keeps one hand on the back of my neck, securing me to the floor, while with his other he lifts up my hips until I'm on my knees. My legs are spread, and my bare ass is in the air.

"You're soaked... your pretty pink pussy is soaked, Kitten."

I mewl, wanting him, needing him like I need my next breath. We're both so pent up with emotions, with searing heat, that the only way to let it out is on each other. I know it's not Ivan's fault I can't call my sister or see her but I need... no, I *want* someone to blame.

"Being bad turns you on, I see. I'll remember that for later. Right now, though, I'm going to fuck you and depending on how good you are, I'll decide if you get to come."

The air in my lungs stills when I feel him center his cock at my entrance. He slides inside my wet channel with ease, stretching me to the point of pain. My mouth pops open when a hard slap radiates from my ass cheek down to my core. The foreign sensation gives me a new form of pleasure... one that I didn't even know existed.

Ivan starts moving, pumping in and out of me while holding me in place. He's like a crazed animal, pistoning his hips into mine. He isn't as gentle as he usually is, but I don't want him to be. There is something so primal about what we're doing and how were doing it. Him pinning me down, rendering me helpless, and using my body how he sees fit.

My pussy is drenched, my arousal trickles down my thighs, and I already feel the familiar tingling of an orgasm building deep in my womb, even though Ivan has only plunged into me a few times. I moan and claw against the hardwood floor as I meet Ivan's deep thrust. The head of his cock hits something deep inside me, each stroke bringing me closer and closer to the edge of insanity. I'm so close, so close, just a few more strokes. I can already feel the throbbing of my swollen clit, Ivan's heavy balls slapping against it.

The knot of pleasure unravels in my belly, and then, without warning, Ivan stops. He freezes mid-stroke, his hardened cock still planted deep inside me. I groan in frustration, slamming my palm against the floor, making him chuckle.

"Oh, Kitten, I'm nowhere close to letting you come. You disobeyed me and now you've got to be taught a lesson." He leans over me, and I can feel his muscled chest against my back, his hardness pressing into my softness. The he resumes moving, sliding in and out of me but at an excruciatingly slow pace. He's going to kill me, he's seriously going to kill me, but with pleasure...

"Please, Ivan," I whimper, but he continues to lazily move his hips, sliding in and out of me as if we have all night to do this.

"How does it feel to want, Kitten? I want you to listen to me. To trust me, to know that I care for only you... that everything I do..." He thrusts deep, his cock filling me to the hilt. "...is to protect you." He pulls damn near all the way out, leaving just the head inside my entrance. He slams into me again, and my knees give out on me with the force of the thrust. My hardened nipples rub against the wooden floor through my cotton t-shirt, heightening my pleasure.

I need more.

"More..." I beg, wanting more, needing more of him.

"On your knees, Kitten," Ivan gruffly orders and helps me to my knees, keeping his hand on the back of my neck to hold me in place. Once in position, he starts fucking me again, each thrust harder and deeper than the thrust before it, if that's even possible. I feel my chest constrict. It's hard to breathe, hard to do anything but take the pleasure he's giving me.

"Ivan," I cry out, as he bottoms out inside me, his thickness stretching me, owning me from the inside out.

"You want to come, don't you, Kitten? I can feel your little kitty purring, quivering, begging to gush all over my thick cock." His dirty words turn me on more, and I push back against him, meeting each thrust he gives me.

"Please..." I beg, my nails digging into the wooden floor. My knees throb, and my cheek aches, but I want this...I want it so bad.

"Are you going to be a good girl?" he asks, and I can hear the desire in his voice, hear how far gone and close to the edge he is, too. His entire body is braced against mine, his fingers dig into the flesh at my neck and at my hip, and it feels like he's embedding himself deep inside my skin.

"Yes... Yes..." I answer eagerly, praying he'll give me the release I've been chasing since he started fucking me.

"Beg," Ivan orders, his voice firm.

"Please, let me come, please, I'll be good. I'll listen." At my response, he releases the hold on my neck and snakes it beneath my belly, his fingers finding my swollen, wet clit.

"Come, Kitten, squeeze my cock tightly. Milk me, Kitten, make that pretty pink pussy quiver..." His fingers rub against my clit furiously, forcing me to climax. And I do, holy hell, do I. My legs shake, and light flashes before my eyes as I shudder beneath him. Every muscle in my body tenses and I'm soaring, flying through the air. The euphoric pleasure fills my veins, and I never want this moment to end.

I feel Ivan moving in and out of me, his thrusts are hard, his body tight and coiled with tension. I want him to come, too. I want to feel his release coat my insides.

"Come for me, Ivan." I gaze at him over my shoulder, and he turns to molten lava, his movements becoming jerky as he finally finds his own release. His cock seems to grow larger inside of me and then I feel the warmth of his release flood my womb.

My chest heaves as I try and get my bearings back.

What the hell did we just do?

"Did I hurt you?" Ivan questions after a few moments and trails his fingers down my spine. His touch makes me shiver, and I notice his flaccid cock is still inside me.

"No... I-I liked it... a lot." I'm shocked that I'm admitting it, but I did, and I'd be lying if I said I didn't want it to happen again.

"Good, I won't warn you again though. Your safety means everything to me, and even if you don't understand the importance of remaining hidden, I do, and I'll do whatever I can to make certain that we both come out of this alive. There are sacrifices that must be made, and I'm sorry if that upsets you, but I'm not just going to let you do whatever the hell you want without thinking about the consequences."

"Okay, I'll listen." I know deep down he is right, even if I don't want to admit it right in this moment. Everything he just said is true. I have no idea how to do this... no idea how to survive on my own. He knows how this all works, how to deal with these kinds of people and he's done nothing but try to protect me. He sacrificed his entire life to save me, and I need to trust him and do what he says even if it hurts like hell, even if all I want to do is call my sister and race home to her.

In the end, I don't want her to end up hurt either. She's all I have left, and if something happened to her because of me... I don't even want to think about it.

"Let's take a quick shower." Ivan gets up, pulling me to my feet with him. My knees shake like crazy as I try to walk, and Ivan wraps an arm around me, securing me to his body. I lean into him, and we walk to the bathroom together.

He turns on the shower, and the room starts to fill with steam. Without a word, he pulls my shirt off, and we step into the hot spray together. He washes my hair, his strong fingers massaging my scalp. He rinses my hair and moves on to wash the rest of my body, moving the soapy washcloth over every inch of my skin. I relish in the way he cares for me, showing me how much I matter to him.

When he is done rinsing me off, I take the washcloth and the soap from his hand and start washing him in return. I take care of every inch of his beautifully sculpted body, feeling his muscles flex under the washcloth as he moves.

With my other hand, I trace over his heated flesh, mapping out every inch of him, memorizing the way he looks and the way he feels because someday he won't be here. He can't stay forever, no matter how much I want him to. He doesn't want me the same way I want him, and he's already reminded me that this is temporary, and still, I can't help but wonder if it isn't.

If maybe it could be something more? I try not to dwell on the thought for long. Ivan and I will be here for a long while together, it seems. I'll just deal with whatever happens when it happens.

As we exit the shower and dry off, I realize how exhausted I am. Ivan was right, we both could use some sleep. I don't even bother putting any clothes back on and instead, I lie down in bed naked. I'm sure Ivan approves because he slips under the blankets behind me, pulling me to his chest. I feel every inch of his skin against mine, and I almost moan. His touch is comforting, his presence makes me feel safe, and it isn't long before sleep grabs me, dragging me into the darkness.

16

Ivan

I WAKE up blanketed in warmth. Violet's body is in my arms just as she has been for the last few weeks. Still, today is different. Today she is free... *we* are free. Today, I don't have to take her back to a cell and leave her there. I can hold her all fucking day if I want to, and no one is going to take her from me. Pulling her even closer, I bury my face in her hair and breathe her in. She wiggles in my arms as if she's trying to escape.

"That tickles," she giggles. The sound of her giggling fills the room and a warmth settles into my bones. *She is happy. I made her happy.* If I had any doubts before about all of this being worth it, they've vanished. I would do it all over again if I had to just to hear her giggle in my arms, just to see her fucking smile that beautiful smile of hers.

"Ivan?"

I close my eyes, enjoying the way she says me name. It sounds so familiar, so sweet... so loving. I want to hear her say it over and over again, especially when I'm seated deep inside her.

"What is it, Kitten?" I murmur into her hair.

"Why did you do all of this for me? Why did you risk everything to save me? You said you don't love me, and you don't want to be with me in the long run. If that's true, then why?"

I know she is hoping that I'll confess my love to her and maybe that would be easier than the actual truth, but I'm not ready to confess to loving her yet, even if I know I do. Right now, I just want to be honest with her. I don't know why, maybe because her body next to mine is like a drug. Her scent messing with my mind, loosening me up, making me want to tell her things that I've never told anyone else.

"That first night, when you ran into me in the hallway... you were so scared. You held on to me like your life depended on it, like you needed me to protect you. The way I held you... how you felt in my arms... how you looked at me with your big blue eyes... you reminded me of someone, someone I failed."

A long stretch of silence forms between us, and I wonder what Violet is thinking right now. Surely, this is not what she expected me to say.

"Mira?" she suddenly asks and a twinge of pain shoots through my heart, making it hard to breathe. Her memory still haunts me. I can still see her, feel her in my arms. My baby sister that I failed to protect, failed to keep alive.

"Yes, Mira... she was my sister. I was supposed to watch her, keep her safe... I didn't. I couldn't save her. She died in my arms, clinging on to my shirt with her small hands, looking up at me like I could save her. I lost everything that day... it was my job and I failed... So, seeing you clinging to me, looking for someone to protect you... begging me out of all people to help you. It reminded me of her, and I knew then that this was my second chance. There was no way I could fail you."

She turns in my arms to face me and snakes her thin arms

around my neck and all she does is hold me. And for the first time, I feel like our roles are reversed. I'm usually the one comforting her, and having her do this for me without asking, having her wash me in the shower last night, it all gives me something I didn't think I could ever have again... peace... love.

Not only was I able to protect her, but somewhere along the way, she started to give me more than she could ever take from me. Something about the way she does the things she does lets me know she does them simply because she wants to and not because she feels like she owes me something. We lay like this for a long while until I hear her belly rumbling.

"Time for breakfast, Kitten." I smile at her, pressing a tiny kiss to her button nose. She's so fucking adorable it hurts. She pouts but lets go of me and we get up and get dressed, before grabbing something for breakfast. What should be the most normal thing in the world is anything but for us. I enjoy every moment of these mundane tasks that we get to share together.

And I know I'm enjoying them the most because I'm doing them with her. As we clean up our breakfast dishes, I can tell Violet wants to ask me something. I pray it has nothing to do with her sister, because I don't have it in me to argue with her about that again, not right now.

"Ummm, Ivan?" Her voice sounds nervous, unsure. The way she is moving around in her chair, tucking strands of her soft blond hair behind her ears lets me know she is worried about asking me whatever it is that she wants...

"Yes, Kitten?" I lift a brow, waiting for her to speak.

She gives me a little grin. "Can we go on a walk?"

I swallow, not expecting that to be her question. "A walk?" I raise both eyebrows in shock.

"Yeah... just around the house. I mean, I don't really care where we go, even if we just walk around the backyard. It's just that I want to be outside, feel the sun on my face. I haven't been outside in so long." She's looking at me like I might tell her no, and there's no way I could do that to her. If she wants to go outside then she can go outside. We might be hiding but that doesn't mean the house we're in has to be seen in as a death sentence, as nothing more than a jail cell.

"Of course, Kitten, we can walk however long and far you want, so long as you stay close to me." I barely finish the sentence when she jumps up from the chair, her face alight with excitement, which in turn makes me excited and happy.

"Can we go now?" She acts as if she's a child who was just told she could go outside and play in the first snowfall of winter. I get up without realizing it, wanting to be close to her, to touch her.

"Sure. There should be some shoes, or sandals in that box I had shipped here." She takes off down the hall and I follow her into the bedroom, watching her dig around in the huge box.

I use that moment while she is distracted to grab the gun from the inside of my jacket. It's hanging on the chair next to the bed, where I placed it on purpose. I like to sleep with a gun close by just in case, and even more now that we're on the run.

I turn away from her and slide the gun into the back of my jeans beneath the shirt I'm wearing.

"Ha, found them!" she exclaims and pulls out some sneakers. She slips them on with ease and looks up at me with excitement dazzling in her blue eyes.

"Okay, my only rule is stay close and within my sight. I don't want you wandering too far off by yourself."

She smirks and rolls her eyes as I open the backdoor. "Okay, master," she murmurs beneath her breath and walks past me and out onto the porch. I watch her cautiously as she takes a deep breath, letting the fresh air fill her lungs. She tilts her face up toward the sun, letting her skin absorb the rays. She looks so different in the sunlight; it makes her hair shine as if gold has been spun into the long strands.

When she finally opens her eyes again, she turns to me, offering me a wide smile as if to say thank you and I forget how to breathe for a moment.

Her beauty literally steals the air from my lungs. Her eyes look different in the sun, brighter and bluer, her long blond lashes fanning against her cheeks as she blinks.

With the sun peering down on her skin, freckles I never noticed her having before are smeared across the bridge of her button nose. I have the urge to reach out and run my fingers across that smattering of beauty marks, to kiss each and every freckle on her skin.

"You coming?" She smiles at me again over her shoulder. I cross the distance separating us and take her hand in mine. It's something so simple, so easily done by normal couples, but it feels crazy to be doing it with her. We lazily stroll around the yard and down a little path leading away from the house and into an open clearing. There are some woods around the house, shielding it from anyone driving by, which is the primary reason I selected this place as our hideaway.

We walk for a long time, but I don't mind. I could do this all day with her. She is visibly enjoying being outside, her constant smile giving her away. I can barely keep my eyes off of her. My head is constantly turning toward her as we walk side by side, fingers intertwined as we hold hands. The longer we do this, the more I long for something more...something deeper. I can see myself being the man she needs, being her husband, being...

"It's beautiful out here." Her sing-song voice interrupts my thoughts.

I know she is talking about the scenery but all I see is her as I answer with a lazy, "Yeah."

"I'm getting kind of hungry though. Maybe next time we come out, we should pack a picnic or something?"

"That would be a great idea, actually." I smile, guiding her back up the trail and toward the house. Nothing could ruin this moment between us, nothing but...

As soon as we reach the end of the trail I can tell something is off. I have this deep gut-wrenching feeling that something bad is going to happen. I grip onto Violet's hand harder, and she looks up at me, concern filling her features.

"Are you okay, Ivan?" Her voice is loud, louder then I need it to be in this moment, and I press a finger against her plump lips.

"Something is off," I whisper, leaning into her body, my lips right beside her ear. At my words, she perks up, her eyes go wide, and I know she realizes exactly what I am saying. I guide us up the walkway some more and stay perched behind a set of trees, shielding Violet's body with my own. I release her hand and grab the gun from the back of my jeans.

"Ivan," she gasps softly when she sees it.

The air is thick with danger, and a soft wind blows across the yard, carrying with it two scents. The hairs in my nose tingle, and I know that smell... the cologne. I narrow my eyes to slits and shut every single thought off in my mind. Right now, my job is to protect myself and Violet.

My eyes move away from the house and down the driveway. There's an all-black SUV parked at the very end, blocking the only road out of this place, and I'm not dumb enough to assume that it's someone lost, looking for directions or something.

No, these are Rossi's men.

"What's going on, Ivan?" Violet asks, tugging on the back of my shirt.

"Kitten, I'm going to need you to go and hide." I twist around to look her straight in the eyes. "Do you understand? You need to hide, and you cannot come out until I come to get you. No matter what you hear, you don't come out."

"What are you going to do?" Her voice comes out frantic, as if she is scared of something may happen to me.

"Don't worry about me, Kitten, just make sure you're hidden." I quickly scan our surroundings, my eyes landing on a small shed half hidden behind a group of trees at the edge of the property.

"Just walk in that direction." I point in the way we just came.

"Keep walking until you see a shed. Get inside it, and close the door behind you."

She gives me a look that says she may fight me on this, but I have no time for that. I point her in the direction, and she hesitantly starts heading that way.

"Be careful, please," she whimpers, giving me one last fleeting look over her shoulder.

I watch her walk away, keeping my eyes on her until I can no longer see her. Once she's out of sight, I move closer to the house. I watch the idiots move around through the windows. They're tossing shit around, destroying the place as if they're looking for something.

Four... I see four bastards. They're loud, uncaring of the noise they're making. Stupid. So fucking stupid. I watch through the trees at the perimeter of the house as one of the fuckers lifts a pair of Violet's panties to his nose, inhaling them. Of course, Rossi would send these stupid assholes out to get me. As if I wasn't trained or skilled enough to kill them.

I wait until all of them are at the front of the house, before I make my way to the back door. I duck to the ground when I pass one of the windows, and I remain that way until I reach the back door. With the gun firmly in my hand, I slowly push down the handle.

I hold my breath at the creak the door makes, hoping they didn't hear it. Surprise gives me an upper hand against them. If I lose that, I might be in trouble, seeing that I'm outnumbered four to one. My thoughts shift to Violet for one fleeting moment.

Guard her. Make sure they don't get her.

I swallow, a lump of fear forming in my throat. I can't let her down. No, I *won't* let her down.

On light feet, I make my way to the hallway and stick my head out around the corner. I smile like a sick bastard. It must be my lucky fucking day. I watch for a moment as two of the goons are in the hallway facing away from me. I lift the gun in my hands, feeling how heavy it is. Then I'm moving... I don't waste any time, because time is my biggest enemy in this situation.

I step out of my hiding spot, aim the gun at one of the fuckers, and pull the trigger. The gun kicks back in my hand as the ear-piercing sound of the bullet leaving the barrel echoes throughout the house. I watch the lifeless body of the guy I just shot crumble to the floor just in time for his friend to turn and spot me. But that's not going to stop me.

I pull the trigger again, the bullet finding its target perfectly, taking the guy out before he even had a change to move his lips. Fuck, I've just lost the element of surprise, but in doing so, I took out half the fucking men, so there's that.

Moving backward with nimble feet and in the crouching position, I find myself in the kitchen hidden behind the heavy marble island.

"Oh, Ivan, that wasn't really nice of you," Luca's annoying voice coaxes as if he's trying to lure me out of hiding. "I just came to personally thank you for opening up a position for my promotion. That's not exactly a way to treat guests, now is it?"

Is he really that stupid to think that I'll talk to him and give up where I'm hiding?

"Where is that hot piece of ass you took? I planned to fuck her brains out, right after killing you... then depending on how good she was, I'd decide if she was worthy of a bullet or not." I hear him walking around. His footsteps are precise, quiet, but I need him to come closer, I need him to be within range so I can blow his fucking head off.

"You know, Ivan, I must tell you that I could barely contain myself having her naked and tied up to the chair before the check. I mean, I don't blame you for taking her. I've seen that pretty pussy up close. I may have even dipped a finger... or two."

I clench my jaw and grip onto the gun tighter. I'm not stupid, I know he is trying to make me mad, trying to get me to make a mistake, show myself or engage in shitty conversation with him.

Still, it's fucking impossibly hard to fight the urge to get up and bash his face in with my fist. The bastard needs to die a long painful death for talking about *my* Violet.

"And, of course, there was the time I brought her to the cell after the shower. Did she tell you about that? That I sunk my fingers into her wet cunt? She begged me to stop, but I just couldn't help myself. She was so fucking tight, so ready for me."

He is fucking lying, I know he is. Violet would have told me... She would have, wouldn't she? I try to push the anger away. I try to swallow it down. I can't let him win. I need my mind sharp. Violet wouldn't have let him touch her. She would've told me.

Closing my eyes, I listen to his footsteps approaching. He is close, but not close enough. I can feel the air shift in the room as his body continues to move closer to mine.

The need to kill pulses in my veins. I want to make this fucker bleed, and I will. I'll make him bleed all over this fucking house. I blink my eyes open. Adrenaline soaks into every pore on my body, making me see and hear everything in high definition.

I twist around the island with my gun raised to shoot. I pull the trigger, watching as the bullet rips through his shoulder. A groan falls from his lips, and he stumbles backward. I smile and take another step closer, raising the barrel of the gun to his head. Right as I do, I see something moving out of the corner of my eye. I turn to see what the fuck it is fully but I'm a second too late.

The fourth guy comes into view, standing a few feet away from me, with his gun raised. In that moment, I can't move fast enough to stop whatever is going to happen from happening, and I hear the gunshot before I feel any pain radiate from my stomach.

I grit my teeth, thinking of only Violet in this moment. If I die, she's as good as dead...

Don't let her down. Don't let her fucking down.

With my gun already raised, I point it at him and pull the trigger before he can fire another bullet into me. The side of his head explodes, blood and brain matter splattering against the pristine white kitchen, the same kitchen I shared breakfast with Violet in this morning. I hold a hand to my stomach and watch as his heavy body falls to the floor with a loud thud.

I look down at the wound and find my shirt is already soaked with blood. *Fuck!* I can feel the last bit of adrenaline draining out of me with every drop of blood that soaks my shirt.

Staggering backward, I grip onto the edge of the kitchen island and brace my body against it. That's when I hear it. Someone moving on the floor across the kitchen. My gaze swings frantically around the room, but it's to fucking late.

I've failed her...

I spot Luca, who has his gun raised at me, his face filled with pure rage, his finger on the trigger, a sinister grin pulling at his evil fucking lips.

"I'm going to enjoy fucking your bitch before I kill her. I'll make sure it hurts, too, then I'll plunge a knife into her heart for safe measure."

I raise my gun, my arm shaking, my hand sweaty, making the gun slip in my palm. I know I don't have a chance in hell but I'm not going out until every drop of blood leaves my body, until my lungs stop fucking sucking in air and my heart stops beating.

The sound of a gun being fired meets my ears, and I close my eyes, wishing I could have been better, better for Mira... better for Violet. I failed everyone I've ever loved and now I'm going to spend eternity in hell, wishing I was a better man for both of them.

17

Violet

I RUSH OVER to where Ivan is leaning against the kitchen island. T*here's so much blood*... It's dripping from a bullet hole in his stomach, soaking through the white cotton of his shirt. "Ivan," I beg him, my voice meek and quiet. I gaze down at the wound, afraid to even touch him... touch it.

"Ivan, please open your eyes." When he doesn't respond, I talk a little louder. "Damnit, do not die on me right now." I can't lose him, I just can't bear to lose him. We just got free, our life together is just beginning. It's not supposed to end now. We had hardly any time together. We haven't had enough time yet. *Please, open your eyes.*

As if he can hear my silent prayer, his eyes open. His gray eyes melt into mine with a look of shock.

"I shot him," I say quietly, the gun still heavy in my hand. "I shot Luca... I think I killed him." My eyes keep returning to his wound.

Blood... I can't unsee the things that I've seen. I can't undo the things I've done now. My eyes move back to Ivan.

"Oh, my god, we need to get you to a hospital. You're bleeding; there's blood everywhere." I'm panicking, the thought of possibly losing him all I can think about.

"No! No hospital," he groans. "They'll call... the cops."

"Ivan, you're bleeding out... and there is no way in hell I'm going to let you die because you don't want to go to the hospital."

"Just... get me... to the car."

Worry consumes me as I listen to how hard it is for him to talk. I wrap my arm around his midsection as he puts one arm around my shoulders. Using me as a crutch, he manages to walk to the garage. With every step we take, his breathing becomes more labored, and it gets harder for him to take another step.

"Almost... we are almost to the car," I exclaim. It gets harder for me to hold him up straight, and he slouches against my body more and more as we get closer to the car. *Shit, he is heavy.* When we finally reach the side of the car, I lean him against it, while I open the door and help him inside as best I can. He groans as he pulls himself into the car the rest of the way, using what looks like an enormous amount of effort. I can't even imagine the kind of pain he is in right now. He got shot... actually shot with a bullet.

I run around to the driver's side of the car, hitting the garage opener on the way before I jump into the driver's seat. *Keys?* I'm about to ask Ivan where the keys are when I see him trying to get something out of his pocket

"Are the keys in your pocket?" I question.

"Yeah," he moans painfully.

I lean over and move his blood-covered hand away to grab the keys myself. When I get them out, I hastily put the car key into the ignition and turn. The engine roars to life, and I throw it into reverse and back out of the garage. I grip the steering wheel, my palms sweaty, a nervous knot sits in the pit of my stomach.

"If you don't tell me where to go, I will take you to the hospital," I warn.

"Iron... Fist... Gym." He stumbles over the words, his fluttering closed as if he's trying to compose himself.

"A gym? You want me to drive you to a fucking gym? Right now isn't really a good time to work out, Ivan. In case you can't tell, you're bleeding out."

I shake my head. He can't be serious. Maybe he's lost too much blood and is delirious with pain.

"Please... just take... me there." He can barely get the words out and slumps over in the seat as if he doesn't have the strength to hold himself up any longer.

What the hell am I supposed to do? Worry courses through my veins. I want to take him to the hospital, but Ivan is right, they will call the cops, they'll ask questions we don't have answers to and then I remember something that Ivan told me, something about the connections Rossi has. If he has someone on payroll here then I'll have all but dug our graves, and even if he doesn't, what the hell am I supposed to tell the cops? If I tell them the truth, they'll lock Ivan up... and me for shooting Luca. I exhale a ragged breath, contemplating my next move.

"Please... trust me, Kitten." Ivan looks up at me, and the anguish and pain in his eyes makes me want to cry. He looks like he is dying with all the blood staining his shirt and his slouched over form. Still, I've always trusted him, and I know that he wouldn't be telling me to go somewhere if he thought it was a bad place to go.

"Okay, how do I get there?" I ask, driving through the grass and over the curb to get around the black SUV blocking the driveway. I drive out onto a side street and follow it before pulling out onto what looks to be a main road. Ivan doesn't respond to my question and instead, just points at the touch screen in the center console.

I narrow my eyes at the screen. One of the tabs reads *navigation*. I use the find destination tool and type in the name Ivan just gave me, while trying to stay in my lane on the road. I'm going slow as molasses and sigh loudly once it's finally done calculating the route.

Thirty minutes to your destination!?
No. No way.

"Ivan... are you aware this place is half an hour away? Are you gonna make it if I drive that far?" My voice cracks. I don't want to think about that, about losing him. I can't think about it, not if I want to get him somewhere that can fix him.

"Yeah... I'm good, Kitten, just drive and everything will be fine." He doesn't look good. His olive skin is coated in a sheen of sweat and his chest heaves as if breathing is taking every ounce of strength he has. I nod and follow the directions. Once I hit the highway, I floor it, making the engine roar. Going thirty miles over the speed limit might not be a great idea at this point, but I can't let him die.

Periodically, I gaze over at him, noticing how his eyes keep fluttering closed.

"Ivan, don't go to sleep. Talk to me... tell me something." I order.

"I'm sorry... I... it's this car. We need... to get rid of it." His body keeps sagging to the side until he's almost laying in my lap. I can hear how hard it is for him to breathe but I don't know what to do. I feel so fucking helpless right now.

"Why... what's wrong with this car?"

"Tracker... there has to be a tracker." Shit, Ivan is right. How else would they have found us so quickly? Rossi must have tagged this car somehow. I blink the tears away. This happened because he was saving me. I can't imagine what would've happened if I hadn't shot Luca when I did. I was so scared, so afraid but the thought of losing him terrified me, terrified me more than killing someone.

"Ivan, are you still with me?" I question, feeling the tears slide down my cheeks.

"Yeah." His voice comes out breathless.

"What do you want me to do when I get to the gym? Who am I looking for?" There must be a doctor at this place, why else would he have me go to a gym?

"Roman... ask for... Roman."

I glance from the road to Ivan and then down at the screen. Thanks to me driving well above the speed limit, we are only five minutes away. I white knuckle the steering wheel the rest of the way. The copper tang of blood meets my nostrils as I take the next exit with my tires squealing and follow the rest of the directions the navigation gives me.

"We are almost there, Ivan, just hang on a little longer."

A few minutes later, I pull up in front of a large white building with a small neon sign above the door. *Iron Fist Gym.* I put the car into park and run inside, nearly tripping over my feet. This is definitely not the kind of gym I was expecting to come to. When I walk in, I enter one large room. There's a boxing ring in the center with some gym equipment scattered around it. There are mats, and a bunch of guys working out. I panic for a moment, running a hand through my hair.

I have no idea how to find this doctor named Roman, or where to even start looking.

"Can I help you?" A female voice startles me, and I whirl around to find what looks like a teenage girl with pink hair standing a few feet away from me, eyeing me cautiously.

"Roman... Where is Roman?" My words are shaky and come out too fast.

She gives me a confused look. "Are you okay, lady?" The question is irritating, especially with Ivan damn near dead in the car outside.

"Just fucking tell me," I yell in her face. "Where is Roman?"

"Okay, okay, calm down" She holds her hands up like she is trying to calm me. "He is in the boxing ring over there, the one in the gray shorts."

I don't even thank her, I simply run over to the ring where the two guys are sparring. I don't how crazy I may seem in this moment. All I can think about is saving Ivan's life.

"Roman?" I call out, and the man in the gray shorts glances over at me with minimal interest. He must be Roman then.

"Who are you and what do you want?" he asks me without missing a beat, ducking when the guy in front of him throws a punch.

"Please, I need your help." My words come out as pleading, and he glances over at me again for a fraction of a second before he goes back to ignoring me. I don't know what to do... what to say. I'm so afraid that I'll lose Ivan that I'm ready to scream, beg and plead, cry.

"Ivan sent me. He said you could help."

As soon as the words are out, Roman stops, his movements halt completely and he waves the guy in front of him away. He turns on his heels and walks over to me and if I wasn't already scared out of my fucking mind, I would be right now. He is so big and muscular, just like Ivan, and he is stalking toward me like he is about to strangle me. He's intimidating as hell, and I want to take a step backward but I can't. I refuse to be afraid of this man when he's my only chance at saving Ivan.

"What does he want?" he sneers.

"He is outside, he needs..."

Roman cuts me off before I can even finish. "Why the fuck would my brother send in a little girl to get me?" He rolls his eyes as if he's annoyed. "Tell him to walk his fucking ass in here himself if he wants to talk."

I know I should be shocked by what he's said but I'm not.

"He is dying!" I blurt out.

It takes Roman about half a second to realize what I've said and then he's moving. He steps out of the ring and rushes past me, toward the front doors. I follow him out the door, suddenly realizing that Roman just called Ivan his brother.

"What the fuck happened to him?" Roman growls at me while opening the passenger door. His eyes are full of fury, and he looks like he might rip my head off.

"He was shot." I try to get my breathing under control, my pulse pounds in my ears, and all I want is for Roman to help him.

"I was going to take him to a hospital, but he insisted that I bring him here instead. Please tell me you can help him? He's lost so much blood, and I don't think that he would make it if I had to turn around and drive him to the hospital." Tears start falling from my eyes.

Roman ignores me and instead, grabs Ivan by the arms, pulling him into a sitting position. Ivan doesn't even say anything, nor does he look like he's breathing.

"Help me get this asshole inside." Cursing under his breath, Roman pulls his brother out of the car. A grunt of pain passes Ivan's lips while both of us slip under his arms and help him inside. His legs barely move and Roman carries most of his weight while I just help keep him balanced.

"Ivan also said that this car has a tracker on it and that we need to get rid of it."

Roman grunts as if he is annoyed by all of this as he kicks the door open with his foot and we carry Ivan inside.

"Devin... Mac," Roman booms through the large room, drawing attention. All heads turn in our direction but only two guys start to run toward us. I step away while one of the guys takes my place. The girl from earlier suddenly stands next to us, staring us down.

"Have some of the guys get rid of the car out front... immediately," Roman orders the girl, and she just nods before scurrying away.

I follow behind the three men as they carry Ivan down a long hall and into some back room. Once inside the room, I realize why Ivan wanted to come here. This place looks like a mixture between an operating room and a doctor's office.

I cautiously watch as the three guys place Ivan on the table in the center of the room and start moving around it like they're a well-trained team of doctors. Like they do this every single day.

"Lower the table as much as you can," Roman orders and to my confusion sticks a needle in his own arm. Puzzled, I don't realize what he is doing until the other guy sticks the same kind of needle into Ivan's arm and they attach the two with a clear tube. Bright red blood starts to flow through the tube from Roman's arm into Ivan's, and I realize then that Roman is giving his brother a blood transfusion.

"Can I help with anything?" I question, worrying my bottom lip while staring at Ivan's lifeless form. They're all working in sync with each other, and I have no idea what to do. I want to cry. I want to scream at the world for giving me this man only to take him away.

"Just stay out of the way, and you'll be fine," Roman growls, as they rip Ivan's shirt off his body. I gasp seeing the wound for the first time. Blood covers his skin, and all I want to do is run over to him and hold his hand and tell him everything is going to be okay, but I can't. Instead, I lean against the wall, feeling as useless as hell. All I can do is stay out of the way and watch as these three men save Ivan's life.

The guy who Roman called Mac puts a pair of latex gloves on and starts digging his fingers into Ivan's wound.

A pained cry rips from Ivan's throat as he thrashes against the table.

"Hold the fuck still," Mac growls and continues digging around until he pulls out a small silver bullet. He throws it into a metal bowl off to the side, and it lands with a loud clunk. Mac grabs some gauze and presses it into the wound, earning a loud growl of displeasure from Ivan.

"Pussy," I hear Roman say under his breath.

"Is he going to be okay?" I ask.

Roman's dark gaze swings to mine, and he looks me up and down, inspecting me with a fine-toothed comb. "Who are you again?"

His tone pisses me off, and I can't hold back the snarky response from slipping out. "Violet and I'm his... friend." I cross my arms over my chest and stare him down. It feels like he's judging me, and I don't like it. He doesn't know me or what Ivan and I have been through.

"That's what they call it now, huh?" he snorts.

"Roman," Ivan growls as if in warning, his eyes finally opening.

I rush over to his side and grab onto his clammy hand. He doesn't look at me and that's okay. I just want him to be okay.

"Don't *Roman* me. I have a right to know who the fuck she is. She's in my gym, and she brought your injured ass in here." Roman takes the needle out of his arm and pushes some gauze on the tiny wound while Mac starts to sew up Ivan.

"What kind of shit did you get yourself into anyway? Why didn't you just go to one of your people to get sewed up?"

Roman is clearly unhappy we are here but I don't care how unhappy he is so long as he keeps Ivan alive.

"They're not my people; they're Rossi's people… and they're the ones trying to kill me."

"Well, that's fucking great. What the hell did you do to piss him off?" Roman moves to the foot of the bed and crosses his arms over his chest. He's huge, just like Ivan. They share the same dark brooding features and olive colored skin. Roman's body is more muscular than Ivan's, more defined, like an athlete. In a fight, I'm sure they would be evenly matched.

"I took something of his," Ivan hisses, pain filling his features.

"Well, here's an idea… give it the fuck back." Roman stops talking and takes a step back, turning to his side. His line of vision following Ivan's.

I can tell the moment he pieces the puzzle together inside his head. Through clenched teeth, Roman speaks again, and his anger is damn near terrifying. "You took her, didn't you? You took one of his fucking whores? God, why am I so surprised? I should expect this shit from you by now."

"Shut the fuck up, Roman," Ivan growls, trying to sit up. His attempt is futile, since within a second, he's pushed back down on the table. "She isn't one of his whores. I took her before he could get his hands on her. I gave up everything for her. I brought her into hiding with me. I want more for us, more for her."

Roman rolls his eyes. "You must be fucking her then because no man I know is going to risk his life for a woman he ain't getting any pussy from." His remark makes my cheeks heat, he's crude, unapologetic, and completely different than Ivan in every single way other than physically.

"It doesn't matter what I'm doing. I don't owe you an explanation. Just leave her the fuck out of it." Ivan sounds annoyed, clearly not wanting to talk to his brother about our complicated relationship.

Roman laughs but it's humorless and makes his already dark features darker. "Then I guess I didn't need to save your fucking life, now did I?" Without another word, he storms from the room, slamming his fist into the drywall on the way out. The noise vibrates through me, but I don't even startle. I bite my tongue and tell myself it's not worth it to stick up for Ivan against his brother, but it is to me. I don't want him thinking that all of this is his brother's fault, not when almost all of it is mine. I release Ivan's warm hand from mine and start toward the door.

"What are you doing, Violet?" Ivan's voice is deeper than usual and stops me in my tracks. For a moment, I rethink talking to him. He's obviously angry, but I'm not scared of him. I've seen worse and had worse done to me by now.

"I'll be back," I throw over my shoulder, walking out of the room.

"Violet..." Ivan growls after me. "Fuck, Violet," he calls once more, frustration coating his words. I continue forward, ignoring him, and head down the hall and into the open gym. I notice instantly that almost all of the men who were here a short time earlier are gone now.

A grunt and the sound of something being hit draws my attention to the right corner of the room, where I see Roman landing some hard hits against heavy sandbags. Yet another difference between Ivan and him. Ivan isn't nearly as violent and angry as his brother is, and I wonder why? Why is this man is so angry at everything?

I walk over to him, stopping once I'm only a few feet away. I know he can see me, there's no way he can't, but that doesn't mean he has to pay me any attention and weirdly, that seems to make me angrier.

"I don't know what happened between you and your brother, but if you don't help us, he is as good as dead. They already found us once. They going to kill him and then..." I scowl, trailing off, as he lands another hard punch against the bag. With every hit, he grunts. Sweat drips down his face, soaking his thin cut-off cotton t-shirt.

"I don't owe you or him anything. He got himself into this mess, and it's not really any of your fucking business what happened between us. My anger with my brother is mine alone, and just because you're riding his dick doesn't mean I have to tell you a fucking thing," he snarls, not even looking up from the sandbag.

I blink, taken aback by his rudeness. I know I shouldn't be surprised, not after hearing him talk just a short time ago, but I am. He's so cruel, violent, and uncaring. It oozes from every pore of his body.

"Well, I don't care to know what happened between you two. I just wanted you to know that it wasn't your brother's fault. I begged him to help me get out of there, so if you're going to be mad at someone, then be mad at me."

I cross my arms over my chest as he lands another punch on the sandbag before stepping away from it and looking up at me. His eyes are a blue-gray that pierce straight through me, holding me in place. In a flash, he's in front of me, anger marring his features. He might be handsome if it weren't for the permanent scowl on his face.

"Hate to break it to you, sweetheart, but I was mad at my brother long before you came the fuck along, so while it's heart-warming that you give a shit about that bastard, don't try and fix something that was broken a long fucking time ago. This ain't about you, or what he did for you. This is about him." He turns, giving me his back, but I'm not done. Now that I know Ivan is going to be okay, I want to make sure everything else is, too. And that includes whatever is going on between the two of them.

"Is it about what happened to Mira?" As soon as the words leave my mouth, I regret speaking them.

Roman stops dead in his tracks and turns to look at me. Fury flickers in his eyes, and the hairs on the back of my neck stand up.

"What did you say?" He closes the distance between us with one large stride and before I have the chance to backpedal away from him, his hands are on me, his fingers biting into the flesh of my arms, holding me in place.

"Don't say her fucking name," he growls in my face so closely I can feel his hot breath on my skin. He's terrifying now, his body looming over mine, sucking the air straight from my lungs.

"I'm sorry," I whimper, and he releases me with a shove that sends me stumbling backward and away from him.

"Don't bring up shit you know nothing about. Now get the fuck out of my face before I do something my brother won't forgive me for."

I turn around and run back into the medical room with tears glistening in my eyes. I try and hold them back, but I can't. I can't believe this man is Ivan's brother. This cold-hearted bastard. Ivan is alone in the room when I enter, the other two guys having vanished. I walk over to the side of the bed and clutch onto his hand, needing his closeness. I never should've gone out there and tried to talk to Roman.

"What did Roman say to you?"

"Basically, he isn't going to help us. What are we going to do now? Where are we going to go? We don't even have a car anymore." Tears start to spill over my lids and run down my cheeks.

"I'll figure something out. Don't worry, Kitten. Just let me rest for a few more hours, and we'll go somewhere." His eyes drift closed, and I know he needs to sleep. There is no way he can get up and walk around right now, not after having a bullet taken out of him. I stand aimlessly beside the bed and hold onto his hand until my legs hurt, then I move and sit down on the floor next to the bed. I can only assume it's late outside. Ivan hasn't woken up again, thankfully, because god knows he needs to rest. I wring my hands together, thinking of what is going to happen next. We've survived all of this, which is better than being dead. My thoughts are interrupted, and my head snaps up when a large figure suddenly appears in the doorway. My heart races impossibly fast in my chest. What is he doing here? Did he come back to argue? To hurt me?

"Time to go," Roman barks. "I'm closing up the gym, and I need you out of here like five minutes ago."

Ivan stirs beside me, and I get to my feet quickly. His eyes blink open slowly and a small smile tugs at his lips when he sees me. I want to return the smile but can't manage to even make one with Roman in the room.

"I don't have all night." Roman sounds inpatient and unsympathetic.

Ivan sits up with a pained grunt, holding his stomach. I try to help him up as much as I can, but he is just too fucking heavy. He's like moving a brick building. It takes him a minute, but he finally gets on his feet, steadier than I expected him to be. He starts walking out the door, pulling me into his side. Roman follows behind us and once we are out the front door, he closes it and takes out a pair of keys, locking the doors.

"Well, now that I've saved your life yet-a-fucking-again, you can be on your merry way. I don't really give a fuck what you plan to do. Just don't die in front of my gym. It's bad for business," Roman says without a trace of emotion. He starts to walk away from us. He's just walking away. I can't believe him.

How can you be so cold toward your own family?

The way he's acting toward Ivan right now really makes me miss my sister. We'd never treat each other this way, no matter how angry we were at each other.

"There is a little motel not far from here, let's just go there," Ivan whispers down at me and starts walking. I wrap an arm around him and attempt to hold some of his weight but he's heavy, too heavy for my weak body. We only take about three more steps before he starts to sway, his body leaning into mine more. I'm trying my best to hold him up, but his strength is withering away with each step.

He leans off of me and against the building. His chest heaves, and his eyes drift closed for a second. I wish I could help him more, I wish I was stronger, and that we were back at our little house, and that he never got shot.

A car passes us and then suddenly stops a little way down the road. Ivan's leaning against the wall, with his eyes closed, so he probably doesn't see it, but panic pulses in my veins when the car makes a full U-turn in the middle of the road and starts heading back our way again. It's a blacked-out SUV, and I can't see who is inside because of the heavily tinted windows.

Oh, god, more of Rossi's men.

I'm damn near hyperventilating when the car pulls up right next to us on the curb. I put Ivan's arm around my shoulder and try to get him to walk away with me, but he just grunts. His eyes are still closed, and he's not moving. Oh, god... we're going to die. Ivan's going to die, and all of this is going to have been for nothing. Air fills my lungs, but I forget to exhale...

The driver's side door opens a moment later, and Roman's brooding face appears in front of us.

"Fucking Christ, get in the damn car," he grumbles, pulling me away from Ivan by the arm. Then he starts to half carry his brother to the back seat, leaving me standing there, still recovering from the panic attack he just gave me.

"Get in or I'll leave your ass here," Roman yells, and my heart jumpstarts, pounding furiously against my ribcage. Not wanting to test him, and knowing he most likely will leave me here, I run around the car and get into the back seat on the driver's side. Ivan is already laying across the bench, and I lift his head, slipping into the seat, resting it against my thigh.

Roman slips into the front seat and turns around in his seat. "Don't do anything stupid, keep your mouth shut, and don't ask any questions. You do those things and we won't have any problems."

I gulp and nod, running my fingers through Ivan's thick unruly locks to calm myself. I've met a lot of scary men in the last month or so, but Roman is probably the scariest in my book, and all because I don't know what he will do next. He's hot and cold. He says one thing and does another. At least with the other bad men, I knew they were mad and always would be.

He's Ivan's opposite in every way possible, and I wonder how that happened? Is Ivan really this dark and moody? Or is there something deeper going on inside Roman? When the SUV starts moving, Ivan groans, holding a hand to the wound on his stomach.

I barely look out the window to see where we are driving. Instead, I keep my eyes on Ivan, making sure he is okay. Only when we come to a stop do I look up and realize we are in front of a house. No, not a house, a fucking mansion. Even in the dark, I can see how huge the place is.

"Is this your..." I get out before Roman twists around in his seat, his glare stopping the rest of the words from escaping my lips. I'm reminded of the no question rule then and I squeeze my lips together tightly. I don't want to find out what he will do if I don't listen to him. With Ivan injured and barely clinging to life, all I have is Roman and the help he's offering me.

We get out of the car in silence. Roman helps Ivan out of the car and up the walkway, into the house. I follow behind them like a lost puppy. I can't stop my eyes taking in the house. It's simple, but unlike anything I've seen before. Sleek and manly.

He takes us down a long hall with numerous doors and stops at one at the very end of the hall. He opens the door with the flick of his wrist and deposits Ivan on the king-sized bed.

Then he turns around to face me. "You can stay here until he is healed up enough to move around on his own but then I want you two out of my house and out of my fucking life. Got it?" The look in Roman's eyes tells me not to test him. He's like a feral dog, ready to bite at any given second.

I just respond with a nod, too scared that talking may set him off. A thank you sits on the tip of my tongue, but I keep it there. There isn't any point in thanking him, not when it's obvious he doesn't want us here. He leaves the room a moment later, slamming the door closed behind him.

I slip out of my shoes and then pull Ivan's boots off of him. Exhausted from everything that has happened today, I lay down on the bed next to him and let my eyes drift closed. I take one of Ivan's hands into mine and cuddle into his side. I don't know what we are going to do next but at least we are safe, and at least we have each other.

That's all that matters now.

18

Ivan

I BLINK my eyes open slowly. It's hard, really fucking hard, but I do it. My lungs burn and my body aches like I got hit with a goddamn truck as I try and sit up. Fuck, Luca really got a good shot on me. At least the fucker is dead now. All I need is this fucking bullet wound to heal, and I'll be back to my normal self and out of my brother's hair.

A thought slams into my gut and instantly, I'm on high alert.

Violet. Where is my Violet?

Blood pounds in my ears as I sit up faster than necessary. I feel the wound in my side throbbing, but I don't care. The only thing that matters is *my* Violet. As my gaze sweeps around the room, I notice the tiny sleeping body next to me, and the even tinier hand in mine. *Sleeping.* Beside me. She's sleeping, and she's safe.

Thank fuck. I stare down at her sleeping form, her beautiful face painted in peace, her soft blond hair half covering her face, hiding her angelic features. She's so fucking perfect, too perfect even. My cock hardens as I stare at her. Shit, the last thing I need to be doing right now is screwing her.

I sigh, leaning back against the headboard, moving my eyes to anything else in the room to distract myself. This was the last fucking place I wanted to bring her. I shake my head, thinking of the way Roman treated her last night. I can't imagine what he said to her when I was in and out of consciousness. He's an asshole, an epic one. His anger and hate for me radiates over into everything in his life.

He's just never faced the anger, found someone to push him over the edge. Someday, he'll fall in love and find someone to make all that pain go away. I know it. He's still worthy of something good in life.

I release Violet's hand and scoot toward the edge of the bed, hissing through my teeth as pain radiates throughout my body. I'm at the very edge of the bed when the bedroom door bursts open, slamming against the wall behind it.

Roman's eyes are filled to the brim with fury. Does he eat fucking fire for breakfast or something? Why the hell is he so angry all the time?

You, I remind myself. I am the reason he is angry all the time.

"One fucking time. One fucking time I help you and you pull me into this shit storm of your life." He clenches his fists at his sides, standing just inside the bedroom. My own anger starts to take root hearing how loud and uncaring he is to Violet, who is still sleeping.

"Can you be quiet? She's still sleeping."

Roman's eyes move to Violet's sleeping form behind me, a snarl pulling at his lips, his voice still loud and ringing throughout the room.

"You think saving her made up for what you did?"

I roll my eyes, attempting to get out of the bed. This is the last thing I want to be discussing with him right now. When I don't say anything else, that seems to egg him on more.

He huffs out a laugh, looking as if he's ready to slug me in the face, "Saving her didn't fucking bring our sister back. It didn't make me forget what a piece of shit you were for leaving me behind while you went and did some illegal shit. Not that it matters anyway." He smiles. "I've got my own illegal business going on, all without you. I've made a name for myself all on my own."

I sigh, the sting of pain in my side subsiding when I finally land both feet on the floor. I remind myself that I need to go slow. I need this bastard of a wound to heal so I can protect Violet and get us out of here.

"Good, I'm happy for you. As soon as I'm healed up, I'll be out of your hair, and you can go back to hating me."

Roman doesn't like my response and crowds me, his chest pushing against mine. He wants to fight me, he wants to show me every single ounce of anger inside of him, but he won't, because that'd be showing me emotion. If I know anything about my brother, it's that he doesn't want anyone to know what's going on inside of his fucked-up head.

"Looks like you are well enough to stand, so why don't you take your bitch and leave now?"

Forgetting the bullet wound that's throbbing in my side, I shove Roman backward and out of the room until we are in the hallway. Pain shoots through me with every move I make but instead of trying to tolerate it, trying to push it down, I let it fuel me. Fuel the anger vibrating deep inside of me.

"Listen very carefully, Roman, because I'm only going to say this once to you." I step into his space, snarling, "You can hate me all you want, you can even fight me if it makes you feel better, but you will not talk to her the way you want to, like she's some piece of garbage. You are not going to scare her or make her feel like shit either. You have no fucking idea what she's been through. You can't imagine the shit show I got her out of. You're going to treat her with fucking respect. Are we clear?"

A smile forms on his thin lips. "I think it's hilarious you think you can come into my fucking house and tell me what I'm going to do and not going to do."

He's pushing me, wanting to see how far I'll go for her.

"Roman..." I exhale a ragged breath. "Please, just fucking do this for me... for Mira." Saying her name hurts, it hurts really fucking bad, and I know hearing her name hurts Roman.

"She is not Mira. She's not our fucking sister and saving her doesn't bring Mira back. And none of this matters anyway, because I don't give a fuck about her, or her happiness. I came down here to tell you that I'm not getting involved in your shit. Tell your fucking people to leave me alone. I answer to no one. I'm my own boss, Ivan."

"What the fuck are you talking about? I have no people anymore. It's just me now."

"Really? Does Xander Rossi know that?" He cocks a brow.

"Xander? I have nothing to do with him. I worked for his father, not him, and up until a week ago, Xander didn't even know his father was alive."

"Well, he's been asking around for you since yesterday." *Shit. What the hell does he want? Isn't it enough have one criminal organization looking for me?*

"Does anyone know I'm here?"

"Of course not. Do you think I'm stupid? I don't want a fucking target on my back. I trust everybody who was at the gym yesterday. No one is going to say a fucking word, not unless they want to die." A darkness cloaks his face.

With Xander and his father both looking for me, and a wound that's still seeping blood, staying here is our only chance at making it out of this alive. I need to protect Violet above all.

"If you kick us out, we're as good as dead, and we both know it." I pause, gauging his facial expression. "If something happens, you're not only going to have my life on your conscious, but hers too, and she's done nothing to you. Fuck, she's done nothing to anybody. They just plucked her off the street for no other reason than her being in the wrong place at the wrong time. She is innocent in all of this shit."

I can see Roman's struggling with this decision. He looks conflicted but I know he'll make the right choice. Violet might not be Mira, but he, too, sees the connection. Mira was just as innocent. She had done nothing to deserve to die, and neither has Violet. I might have cost us Mira, but I'm not going to fuck Violet over. Not after all I've done to save her life.

"Fuck," Roman finally huffs out. "Stay, if you must, but stay out of my way." He storms off, a warning hanging in the air. As soon as he's out of sight, I immediately grip onto the wall to steady myself. I stand there for a moment, catching my breath, when I hear a quiet sob come from the other side of the bedroom door. I walk back into the room and find Violet crying on the bed. She looks up at me, her blues rimmed red with tears.

"It's all my fault. It's all because of me," she whimpers.

"No, Kitten, none of this is your fault," I assure her.

"If you didn't help me, no one would be after you right now, and you would not have gotten shot. Now, I've put even more people in danger. I'm just going to leave. You'll be better off without me."

I sit down on the bed next to her and cradle her cheek against my hand. She has no idea what she is saying. How much saving her saved me.

"Don't say that, Kitten, I'll never be better off without you. I needed this. I needed to break free from the hold they all had on me. You stumbling into my life just placed everything together perfectly. Saving you helped me save myself."

"I mean it, Ivan. You said so yourself, you don't want this to last... you don't love me. I can leave now and stop being a burden to you and Roman. I can stop hurting everyone, causing more problems." Her words sting; they rip me apart from the inside out.

"Kitten, do you really think I would have done all of this if I wasn't in love with you? If I didn't fucking love you all long?"

"You love me?" Her eyes light up, and she nuzzles into my hand, but I can still see doubt flicker in those blue depths of hers. A part of her doesn't believe me, believes it might be too good to be true.

"Yes, I love you. I couldn't admit it before, not to you... or to myself, but that's because I wanted to think that I was doing this for you. I didn't want to return the feelings because I was afraid of what it would mean. You're going nowhere unless I'm by your side."

She crawls into my lap and melts into my chest, her tiny hands pressing against my muscles, and strangely, I wish we were naked right now, her pretty pussy swallowing my cock.

"I love you, too, more than you could ever know, but I think your brother hates me," she admits shamefully, as if she has a reason to be shameful over my brother hating her. It's not her fault he's a prick.

"Roman hates everybody, and I mean everybody, so don't take it personally."

I barely finish speaking when Roman appears back in the doorway.

"Doc said to take this," he growls, throwing a pill bottle at me.

"What are these?" I ask, grabbing the pill bottle off the bed. There isn't a label on it, and I know how my brother is. He's been known to take some shit, shit that fucks with his head, and his mood. The last thing I want is to take something and put Violet in danger.

"Antibiotics." He rolls his eyes. "Worried I'd give you something else? Swap out some of the pills? Give you something that would make you lose control?"

Violet gasps in my arms as she buries her face into my chest. Roman's dark gaze roams over her body for a second longer than acceptable, and I find a growl escaping my lips.

She's mine. All fucking mine. Every single inch of her creamy body belongs to me, as well as her fucking heart.

"I have a fight next week. You should come. Check out what it's all about. If you're going to be staying awhile, you might as well get acquainted with the shit that goes down around here."

I clench my jaw, I thought maybe when he said *illegal shit* he was slinging drugs, prostitution at best. But of course not. He's running in the underground fighting circles. Knowing him, he is into the most dangerous ones... the ones where the only way out is death.

"I don't know if that's safe for Violet, plus I need to figure out a way to get rid of the bodies over at the rental."

Roman laughs. "Well, keeping her here at the house isn't going to be safe either. Everyone comes back here for a gigantic party at the end of the night. And I already sent some men over to dispose of the fuckers' bodies." He smiles, and it's a downright serial killer looking. "Let's just say no one will ever find them."

I sigh in relief. Yes, Roman is an asshole, a prick, but when he does shit, he gets it done, never half assing it. He might still hate me, hold a grudge, but he's not going to leave me in the dark. At the end of the day, we're family, and family is all that matters in this fucked up world.

"Thank you," I mumble.

"Don't mention it, and I do mean it. Don't mention it. I didn't do it for you. Like you said, as soon as all is well, we can go back to hating each other like we always have."

I roll my eyes at his dramatic tone. He leaves the room without another word, and I take the moment of silence to hold Violet's fragile body tighter to my chest. Everything is going to be fine. She'll be protected, secure by my side, and no one will hurt her or us.

She's safe... safe in my arms.

"I love you," I whisper into her hair, wanting to say the words over and over again, knowing I shouldn't have waited so long to say them. I'd been guarding my heart for so long, I failed to see what was right in front of me. I failed to see the love that poured from deep within her but there was no missing it now, and if I had to, I'd kill everyone and do anything to make sure she remained mine.

Mine and safe.

19

Violet

A LITTLE OVER a week had passed since Roman rescued us and helped patch up Ivan's wound, which was finally healing. I knew this because he kept trying to get me to have sex with him while I kept denying him, even though I wanted him just as badly. He needed to be healing, letting the wound close completely, but all he really wanted was for me to be wrapped around him.

I'm sitting in one of the many living rooms this place has, reading a book that we had gotten when we went on a grocery run. I don't particularly like being here, and I don't really like Roman, but I'm happy he and Ivan are finally getting along better. Roman still hardly interacts with me. Most of the time, he pretends I'm not here, and I am fine with that. I would much rather him not look at me than give me the death stare he gave me at the gym the first night I met him.

I started seeing a change between Roman and Ivan a few days after we got here. Roman seemed to have warmed up to Ivan being here. Maybe he remembered that he is still his brother after all. I see them joke and laugh more often and that makes some of the coldness Roman gives me bearable. I tell myself he's misunderstood, heartbroken over the loss of their sister, but I'm sure there is something deeper going on.

"Come here, Kitten," Ivan calls from the kitchen just on the other side of the room. I hear male laughter and hushed voices. I don't like when he uses my nickname in front of all the men who live here. I don't want them to know what he calls me. I just want it to stay between us, as our own little thing.

Placing the book down on the table in front of me, I get up and pad into the kitchen, noticing that everyone is occupying the space. I feel exposed with everyone's eyes on me.

Mac and Devin greet me with smiles. Roman completely ignores me, as he always does. He doesn't even look up at me when I enter the room.

Ivan reaches for me, pulling me into his side, a smile creeping onto his lips. "We're going to order pizza before the fight tonight. What kind do you want?"

I can see the disgust fill Roman's features, and I don't understand why he dislikes me so much.

"Cheese is fine." I shrug. I don't tell Ivan I'm not hungry, or that I haven't been feeling good lately. If I do, he'll worry, and I don't want him worrying about me when there are lots of other things going on right now. This Xander guy has been calling Roman to get ahold of Ivan. The fear of something bad happening to Ivan again consumes me. Maybe he should just call him, telling him he doesn't want to be a part of whatever it is he's calling about.

"On it, *Kitten,*" Devin jokes, and I smile at him. Devin and Mac have grown on me. They're nicer and far easier going than Roman.

"Tonight at nine is the fight. It's invite only, but since you're arriving with me, you should be fine." Roman is speaking directly to Ivan, and I turn my face into Ivan's shirt, inhaling his deep scent, trying to calm the chaos coursing through my veins. "As long as you keep her at your side at all times, then everything should be fine. If you lose her in the crowd though..." Roman's voice trails off, the warning not missed, not at all.

"I won't let her out of my sight, so we don't have shit to worry about." Ivan's voice is strong, deep, and he pulls me closer, making it hard for me to breathe.

"Good, because if something goes down, I can't help you. I'm there to fucking fight and earn a paycheck. Not to babysit you or her." I feel Roman's eyes on me, they burn into my skin, making me feel as if he can see deep inside me.

Devin calls to order the food, and not shortly after is it delivered. After we eat, we get ready for the fight. I have half a mind to ask Ivan if I can just stay home, but I know he'd say no. He never goes anywhere without me. I slip on a pair of skinny jeans and a sweatshirt.

"Are you okay?" Ivan asks, cupping me by the cheek, forcing me to look at him.

I don't want to lie to him, but I also don't want to give him any more reason to worry about me, since that's all he seems to do.

"I'm fine. Just nervous about the fight is all."

"Are you still scared of Roman? You hardly talk when he's in the room." His gray eyes peer into mine, and it's so hard to keep in the words that I want to say.

"Stop worrying about me and worry about yourself. You've still got some healing to do."

His thumb swipes across my bottom lip and then he's leaning into me, taking my mouth, kissing me feverishly. I grip onto his shirt, feeling all his hardness, wanting to strip him bare and touch every inch of his beautiful body.

"Are you lovebirds ready to fucking go?" Roman's voice carries down the hall, interrupting our conversation, which I'm thankful for. If he asked me one more time if I was okay, or if something was wrong, I was going to break down.

"Yeah, we're ready." Ivan pulls away, leaving me whimpering

and breathless. Taking my hand into his, he pulls me downstairs and then outside to Roman's car. Everyone piles in... and I'm squished in the back seat between Ivan and Devin.

Ivan's muscled arm wrapped protectively around me, pulling me into his side. The drive isn't long, and Roman drives us in complete silence. He white knuckles the steering wheel as if he's pent up with aggression. We drive for a little while longer and end up at some old abandoned warehouse out in the middle of nowhere. Roman parks in the back, driving past the full parking lot in front of the building. He exits the car and we hear the back hatch open and notice him pulling out a black duffel bag. I wonder what's inside of it for a moment but assume it's just his fighting stuff. It has to be... unless he's bringing weapons? I guess I never cared to ask Ivan what kind of fights they do here.

Ivan helps me from the car, and we walk up to the building together. Roman guides us around a corner to some side entrance, where four large guys are manning the door. They're huge, their arms as thick as tree branches, permanent scowls on their face. Their bodies tower above mine, and I shrink into Ivan's side more.

"Don't be scared, Kitten," Ivan whispers, leaning down to press a kiss against my head.

"Roman." One of the guys nods at us as we get closer. "They're all with you?"

"Yeah, they're good," Roman replies nonchalantly. Then, without question, the doors are being opened for us. Ivan maintains a tight grip on me as we walk into the building together with Roman leading the way. I hear the roar of a crowd somewhere off in the distance, but the noise is more a whisper then an actual roar until Roman opens a door leading us into a dark stairwell.

Two things hit me when as we're walking down the stairs into the basement. One, a strong smell permeates the air down here. It's a mixture of beer, the sourness of sweat, and the coppery tang of blood. The second thing is the sound. There must be hundreds of people down here. Some are cheering while others are booing. One way or another, everybody is just being loud, and the noise makes my head pound. I can barely hear myself think, let alone hear if Ivan is talking to me.

When we reach the bottom of the stairs, I see that there is already a fight taking place. I hold back a gasp when I catch a glimpse of the guys in the center of the ring, if you could even call it a ring. It's just a slab of concrete with tape borders. They're covered in blood, with bruises already forming against their skin. I'm half shocked to see that they're still fighting; shouldn't someone be stopping them? How do they know if someone is a winner?

"Don't worry, I won't look like this at the end of my fight," Roman chuckles, and it takes me a moment to realize that he was talking to me. "Stay together; we are going to the locker room."

Ivan and I make our way through the crowd until we get to the side of the ring while Roman, Mac, and Devin disappear into a hallway. Ivan keeps his arm around me, and I take full advantage of his protection, leaning into him even more.

"These fights are just to warm up the crowd," Ivan tells me, leaning down and talking into my ear so I can hear him over the crowd. "Roman's fight is the main event."

"What makes these fights different from Roman's fight?" I ask curiously.

Ivan's mood darkens in an instant, as if I've just reminded him of something bad. "In those warm-up fights no one usually dies." He frowns.

"What are you saying?" I must have misunderstood him. Ivan's frown deepens. "Are you saying the fight Roman's going to be in will be one... to the death?" The confusion fades away as I grasp the concept completely now.

"Yes, Kitten, that's exactly what I'm saying," Ivan confirms, and I have no response to what he's just told me.

What is this, the Middle Ages? I don't understand the intrigue. Who would want to actually watch someone be beaten to death? A knot of worry fills my belly. I don't care if Roman likes me or not, I don't want him to die. He's Ivan's brother and even if I don't want to admit it, he's cared for both of us, giving us somewhere to stay, making sure we were both safe.

"Don't worry, Kitten. Roman won't lose. He never does... obviously. He'd rather kill himself then let someone else do it for him."

I nod, gulping around the fear that's lodged itself in my throat. I don't like this place... or anything about it, for that matter.

My thoughts are interrupted by the loud cheering of the crowd and when I look to the ring, I see one of the guys on the floor and the other one has his arms raised. A mixture of blood and sweat coats his muscled chest and when he smiles, all I see is blood. With his raised hand in the air, I notice that these guys are not even wearing boxing gloves; all they have is some kind of tape wrapped around their knuckles, as if that's going to protect their skin or bones from breaking.

I watch as the two men leave the ring and people around start to exchange cash. I see at least three guys calling out to the crowd, taking bets on the next fight like they're auctioning something off. Shortly after that, a big man with an even bigger stomach makes his way to the center of the ring. He grabs a microphone someone hands him.

"Five minutes. That's all you got, ladies and gentlemen. Get those bets in and you could be walking away with a pretty penny tonight." The man's slimy voice rubs me the wrong way, and I tighten my hold on Ivan's hand.

I grit my teeth and breathe through my mouth, feeling a bout of nausea grip me. Something about all of this makes me uneasy, and that uneasiness is only mounting with each passing minute. When they finally call the next fight, the crowd goes crazy, hoots and hollers vibrate through the space.

Then Roman appears, stepping into the right corner of the ring. He's got a smile on his face and a smug look in his eyes. His muscles ripple as he bounces on his feet. At that same moment, another guy comes out, going to the opposite corner of the ring. I stare at

Roman, who looks completely relaxed, as if this is just another day at the office for him.

The bell rings and both men walk into the center of the ring with their fists raised. Part of me wants to look away, but I can't bring myself to do it. It's like watching a car accident take place in front of you.

I watch eagerly as Roman's opponent throws a few punches but not one of them hits its target. For being such a burly man, Roman moves incredibly fast. He dodges at least five hits before he starts throwing punches himself. I've never seen Roman fight, but I have seen him go at the punching bag in the gym and in comparison to that, I feel like he is holding back.

The other guy growls like an animal, his movements becoming more aggressive as he lands punch upon punch against Roman's face and head. I chew on the inside of my cheek to stop myself from yelling, from telling them to stop. I squeeze Ivan's large hand in mine impossibly hard, my gaze shooting up to Ivan. When I see the same fear I'm feeling in his eyes, I know I should be scared.

Time seems to drag on as the fight goes on minute after minute, the crowd becoming more and more restless.

For a while, it looks pretty even, then things change as Roman remains standing there in the center of the ring with his hands covering his face, taking one punch after the next. For a moment, I wonder if this is what Roman wants. If he enjoys the pain being inflicted on him. He doesn't seem to care that his opponent is kicking his ass and that scares me. I want to do something, anything. We can't just stand here and watch him die.

When I turn to Ivan, expecting him to be just as worried, he shocks me by grinning down at me. Either he has lost his damn mind, or he knows something that I don't.

Confused, I turn my attention back to the fight. Roman's opponent gets two more punches in before things take a sudden turn.

Without hesitation, Roman starts to throw punches... real punches. He hits his opponent so fast and with such force that I can almost hear the bones crack from across the ring. I cringe, my heart pounding in my chest.

I watch as he continues hitting him, jab after jab, in the lungs, face, head, no spot is unclaimed by Roman. He's like an animal claiming its prize. Nothing stops him or slows his movements, and I watch the darkness consume him. I see blood on his hands; the man is now on the cold hard floor. Roman keeps hitting him, even though the guy is clearly unconscious.

I can't watch anymore, I can't. Ivan must know this because he pulls me into his chest.

"It's okay, Kitten. I got you," he whispers into my ear over the screams of the crowd. I bury my face deeply into Ivan's shirt, inhaling his unique scent. I may not be watching, but I know Roman is killing that man, beating his head into the concrete.

A short time later, Roman is announced as the winner and the crowd goes wild. Everybody is screaming Roman's name and cheering him on. As the crowd moves, Ivan and I are jostled around. I look up into the crowd, pulling away from Ivan and see large stacks of money being handed over.

I take a deep breath, trying to calm myself and my erratic heartbeat. At least it's over now and Roman is alive. For a second there, I was worried. Just when I get my erratic heartbeat under control, I hear someone screaming a few feet away from us. I furrow my brows in confusion because it doesn't sound like the other screams around us. This one is filled with terror, not excitement. I look over to see what's happening when the sound of a gun going off echoes through the basement and the crowd erupts into a frenzy of panic.

Everything happens so fast I can't even digest what is taking place. People are screaming and trying to get away and then more shots are fired, making the blood in my veins turn to ice. I didn't escape the cell and all those evil men just to die in this place tonight.

Ivan holds my hand impossibly tight as things around us go from frantic to pure chaos. Together, we are pushed away from the ring as a tidal wave of out of control people try to escape. He starts to pull me off to the side and away from the insanity but there are just too many people trying to go the same way. I try to hold on to Ivan's hand, but someone pumps into my arm. A sharp pain radiates from the limb, and I lose my grip on his hold.

I look around helplessly, the crowd jostling me back and forth as I'm trying to push through. I'm almost at the stairs when someone slams into me from behind, shoving me to the side. In an instant, I lose my footing and fall into the crowd, landing painfully on my knees. The impact is jarring and makes my teeth rattle. I try to push up off the floor but there are just too many people moving around me. Every time I gain an inch, someone pushes me back down, immobilizing me to the floor.

I squeeze my eyes shut, wishing for Ivan to find me, and hopefully before I'm trampled.

Then, as if my silent prayers are heard, someone grabs me by the arm and pulls me up off the floor. *Ivan.* Before I know it, strong arms are lifting me up. Instinctively, I throw my arms around his neck and wrap my legs around him, burying my face into the crook of his neck, holding onto him like a monkey.

"Calm down, *Kitten,* or Ivan is going to get jealous."

My eyes fly open when I hear Roman's deep voice next to my ear instead of his brother's.

With one arm around my waist, he uses the other to push people out of the way, working his way through the crowd and in the direction of the locker room. My chest heaves, oxygen barely entering my lungs as we fight the crowd. I watch as Roman grits his teeth, pushing and shoving, using his strength and body to get us where he wants. Once we reach the entrance to the locker room, he settles me onto my feet. I lean against the wall, my knees damn near buckling beneath me.

"Stay here while I find Ivan and Devin." Roman looks at me for a moment with something that looks a lot like concern before walking away.

"I got her." Mac startles me, coming up to my side. "Let me see your arm," he orders. I don't know what he is talking about or why he's asking for my arm until I look down and see rivulets of blood dripping down my arm from a scratch. "Come on, I have a first aid kit in here."

He leads me into the locker room and while my mind is still reeling from what just occurred, Mac starts cleaning the scratch. Just as he places a band aid over the scratch, the door flies open and a very terrified Ivan bursts in. He gives me a quick once over before taking me into his arms.

"Are you okay?" He presses his nose into my neck. He squeezes me to his chest for a long second, his entire body shaking. I don't know if it's the adrenaline, or the fear of possibly losing me that has him shaking, but I'm feeling the same thing.

"Yes, thanks to Roman... only a small scratch on my arm," I squeak, just barely getting the words out. I suck in a precious gulp of oxygen, my hands are shaking, and I feel tears prick my eyes. I came so close to dying again, to losing Ivan again.

"Everybody good?" Roman asks, stepping into the room. "Because the party at my house is still on, which means we need to get fucking going."

By the time we leave the locker room and head upstairs, the crowd has cleared out. Ivan has an iron grip on me the whole way to the car and when we get in, he pulls me into his lap instead of letting me sit beside him.

"I'm fine. Really," I try to assure him, but he never loosens his grip. When we get to Roman's house, people are already waiting in the front yard for us. Roman gets out of the car and people start cheering and whistling; a few even slap a hand on his back, congratulating him. Roman smiles and opens the front door, allowing everybody to pile into the house. As we walk inside, I see more cars pulling up the driveway and within minutes, a full-blown party is taking place in the living room and slowly spreading throughout the house. Roman seems to be in an unusually good mood, laughing and joking with everyone. I remain seated on Ivan's lap while he sits on the couch.

Devin walks up to us and hands Ivan a bottle of beer.

"You want one, Violet?" he asks me. I'm not really sure. I've never gotten drunk and the last time I tried the whole partying thing, it was anything but good, but last time I wasn't with Ivan, and I know no one is going to hurt me here. Not with Ivan looking after me, or Roman. I know no one is going to hurt me with them both here.

"Sure, I don't know what I like though. I've never tried anything with alcohol," I admit shamefully.

"Hold on, I've got you." He walks to the kitchen and returns a moment later, handing me a bottle with a liquid in it that looks the color of beer. "Here." He hands it to me. "All the girls like this."

"Thanks." I look at the bottle in my hand, the label has an apple on it, and it reads hard cider. I take a sip and a sweet, bubbly liquid hits my tongue. It's different but not in a bad way, more like something I'm not quite used to yet. I take bigger sip the next time, enjoying the sweetness of the liquid and the coolness of it as it slips down my throat.

I remain seated in Ivan's lap, drinking my drink and watching the rest of the party goers. I go to take another drink and realize the bottle's empty. I frown, tipping it back against my tongue, but Devin's already on it. In seconds, he's got me a second one, and I give him a shy smile, feeling bad that he went all the way into the kitchen to get me another drink. I'm sure if I asked Ivan, he'd had gone, but it just shows how much Devin cares about making me feel welcome in the group.

"Are you enjoying your drinks, Kitten?" Ivan askes as he, too, watches the other party goers.

"They're good. I've never really got drunk before," I admit with a giggle.

Ivan chuckles. "It's not really anything fun. You might feel good now, but by morning, you'll be hating yourself."

"I hope not," I whine. "I really like these." I wave the bottle in front of his face. I'm pretty sure I'm on my third bottle now. I've been feeling a little funny since my last one, but a good kind of funny. It feels as if my worries have been lifted off my shoulders.

Without reason, Ivan's hold on my hips tighten and his finger dig into my skin almost painfully. I turn to look at him and when I see the look on his face, the good mood I saw there just a few minutes ago vanishes. I follow his death stare across the room to Roman, who is snorting some white powder into his nose off the kitchen table.

"I'll be right back," Ivan growls and pushes me off his lap and onto the couch. I frown, knowing that there is most likely going to be a fight. I watch him stalk over to Roman, grab him by the arm, and drag him out into the hallway. I can hear Roman's loud voice booming through the crowd, but I don't know what he's saying and honestly, I don't care.

I sit there by myself for a few minutes, feeling awkward without Ivan with me. All of this is so new to me, I don't know what I should do. I finish yet another bottle of the delicious beverage, but Devin is nowhere to be seen. I suppose I'll just go and get myself one then. I move to the couch, but as soon as I'm standing on my feet, I realize that my steps are unsure and a bit wobbly.

Maybe another bottle isn't such a good idea. The buzz I have right now is good enough for me. Maybe if it wears off a little bit, I'll have another one. I turn to make my way back to the couch, half leaning against the wall and find myself face to face with some guy who was apparently standing behind me this whole time. A tiny squeal escapes me, and I almost drop the empty bottle to the floor.

Thank goodness my hand-eye coordination is on point even with me drinking. The last thing I need is to get another cut.

"Sorry." The nameless man holds up his hands. "Didn't mean to startle you."

"It's okay." I catch my breath. "I just wasn't expecting anyone to be directly behind me." I give him a smile. I cover my mouth with a hand as a hiccup slips past my lips.

Another man comes up to us, slapping the guy I almost ran into on his back. "Hey, buddy, haven't see you in a while." Then his gaze swings directly to me the moment he notices I'm standing in front of them. "Who's your friend?" He wiggles his eyebrows playfully. Neither of the men seems harmful and for once, I feel like I can move out of my comfort zone, maybe even make some friends?

No one's going to hurt me, I repeat to myself, letting the alcohol in my veins calm me.

"We actually just met... I'm Violet," I tell them and hold out my hand.

"Oliver." The guy I ran into takes my hand first, shaking it gently. I smile and turn my attention to the second guy. I'm just about to shake his hand when Ivan appears beside me. His gray eyes are darker than I've ever seen them before, and I even feel a bit taken back by his presence.

"She's taken," he growls, dismissing the two men beside me, not even looking at them.

"Ivan." I scold, as he picks me up and tosses me over his shoulder caveman style. His grip is tight, and I grab onto the back of his shirt as he moves us through the house.

"Just like old times, Kitten." He slaps a hand to my denim-covered ass cheek, making me squeal with pleasure and pain. "Except this time, you're mine, all fucking mine, and no one can take you away from me. Not Rossi, not his fucking men... not even you could escape me if you tried."

"You don't own me," I respond, feeling my insides turn to mush. My response earns me another hard smack and my pussy throbs. I want him... I want him so badly.

"Oh, but I do, Kitten. I own every single fucking inch of you and if you ever try and leave or escape me, I'll find you and tie you to our bed."

I squirm in his hold, realizing we're moving farther away from the party. Obviously, he wants me just as badly as I want him.

"Show me. Show me that you own me," I challenge. I want him to lose control, and I want him to let it out on me. I want to feel him in every single pore of my skin. Thinking about how he pushed me down in the hallway and fucked me on the floor from behind, how he dominated my body and made me work for the pleasure he was giving me, has me wiggling in his arms with need. I can feel how wet I am already, and I want to show him, prove to him how much I want and need him.

"You don't know what you're asking for, Kitten. Such a tiny little thing like you couldn't handle the big beast inside of me."

"I'm stronger than you think, and I want you," I whimper as Ivan comes to a stop, opening our bedroom. He walks inside, tosses me on the bed, and slams the door shut behind him, twisting the lock into place. Darkness blankets the room, and then he flicks on the lamp beside the bed.

It emits a soft glow, and before I can take my next breath, Ivan is on me. He rips at my clothing without care, and I do the same, my hands unable to keep up with his. Peeling my jeans down my legs, I'm panting with need once the fabric hits the floor. He's got me melting into a pool of molten lava, and he hasn't even really touched me yet.

"Are you strong enough to handle what I want, Kitten? How deep can your claws sink into my skin? Deep enough to draw blood?" He rocks his hardness against me a few times before he unbuttons the button on his jeans.

"I've been gentle with you, and I always will be if that's what you want, but I've been holding back and there are things I want to do to you...Very bad things, things that might hurt a little before they give you pleasure. Are you sure you want me to let go?"

My womb pulses, and I feel the wetness between my thighs dripping. Is it possible to come from just words alone? My nipples harden, and I roll my hips against him, showing him that this is exactly what I want.

That I want him to do bad things to me, to use my body for pleasure.

I want him to mark me, to be his completely.

"Yes, please," I whimper, reaching for him, my fingers sliding across his bare abs and the still healing scar. "Please?"

He smirks, his eyes full of mischief. "Better get used to that, Kitten, because you're going to be doing a lot of begging tonight." He leans into me, his lips so close to mine that I can almost taste him, I nip at his bottom lip, feeling an electrical charge in the air.

Something's changed between us; it's almost like a power exchange is taken place. I trust Ivan with my heart, my mind, body, and soul, and I know he'd never hurt me. And now I'm giving myself to him completely, giving him *all* the power.

This is what I want…what I've always needed. For my white knight to show me what it's like feel both pleasure and pain at the same time.

20

Ivan

FUCK. Her tiny whimpers and pleas set me off. I don't think I have ever been so hard in my entire life. My sweet little Kitten is sprawled out on the bed in front of me like a sacrificial fucking offering. Her big blue eyes plead with me to give her more and though I'm riding the edge, I wonder if falling may hurt her. I've never let go with her. I've never just given into the primal need that surfaces inside me when she's near.

"I want to claim you where I've never claimed you before," I growl, kissing her fiercely. She tastes like tart apples and cinnamon, and I want to devour her mouth.

"Take me, wherever you want." She spreads her thighs wide, offering her pretty pink pussy to me. I almost chuckle at how giving she is, and I wonder if she knows what I have in mind.

"Are you sure?" I slip out of my jeans and grip the hem of her panties, ripping them from her body. She licks her lips seductively and reaches for me again, most likely wanting me to comfort her, but that's not what I want from her tonight. No, I love my Kitten, I love her sweet, gentle, kind as fuck soul, but tonight, I want something deeper from her.

"Please..." she says once more with pleading eyes, and my resolve breaks. With nothing more than the flick of my wrist, I flip her over onto her belly. I listen to the swoosh of air as it leaves her lungs and watch as peers over her shoulder at me. Not an ounce of worry in her blue orbs.

"I've had your pussy, Kitten, but I want something else now." My fingers trail up her back side, and I listen as her breathing turns to heavy pants.

"My ass..." she whispers, and I grin like the bastard that I am.

"Yes, Kitten. I want your puckered little asshole. I want to sink deep inside of it...but before I can do that, I'm going to make you come. I'm going to make you come so hard you'll beg me to stop."

And she will, because for this to work perfectly, for her to enjoy this the first time, she's going to need to be drenched and hanging right on the edge of insanity. Her legs shake as she moves onto her knees, showing her slick slit.

God, she's fucking dripping with need, and I want to taste her sweet honey so badly. I grip onto the sheets in an effort to control my need, but I don't need to control myself... not right now.

Releasing the sheets, I move onto the bed, laying down on my back, and smirk as she gives me a confused expression.

"Come here, Kitten." I grab onto her arm and tug her forward. "I want you to ride my face. Sit that pretty pink slit down on my face and let me eat what is mine."

Violet visibly gulps but moves over me until her pussy is centered over my face. I lick my lips and grab onto her hips, pulling her down. Holding her in place, I slip my tongue between her folds and flick it against her tight bundle of nerves.

"Oh, god..." she gasps, when I suck her engorged clit into my mouth. I alternate between sucking and flicking my tongue against the little nub. Violet moans, tossing her head back, attempting to grind her hips into my face. I smirk, and then nip at her sensitive clit with my teeth, making her yelp.

"You want to come, you've got to beg. Beg me to let that pretty pussy gush all over my face."

I growl into her folds, and she leans forward, her eyes closed, her hands clenched.

"Please..." There's a desperation to her voice that sticks to my insides. "Please let me come all over your face."

I lick her slowly, feasting on her like it's my last meal. Violet lets out a frustrated moan and pushes her center into my face, making me chuckle against her folds.

"Please, Ivan," she begs, grinding against my face for even an ounce of friction. She is so eager and the stark contrast between her sweet nature and the dirty little girl she is in bed is the biggest fucking turn on ever. Only I know this about her. Only I get to see her let go, to become wild with need and stop being the sweet innocent girl she is to everybody else.

I loosen my grip on her thighs, letting her move more on top of me while I keep licking and sucking on her clit at an increased pace. I move her up a few inches so I can swirl my tongue around her entrance. I dip inside as deep as I can, and I shudder when I feel her walls clenching around me.

When I see her arch her back, I use that opportunity to hold her hips up more and lick right over that puckered little asshole of hers. She moans as I start swirling my tongue around it, and I already know she is going to enjoy this.

I move back down to her slit, teasing her entrance. By now, she's a melting mess of need, and I can't fucking wait to take her tight little ass much longer, but I need her to orgasm first. I move back to her clit and continue to work her there. I snake one of my hands around to her ass, splay my fingers across her smooth skin, and slip between her ass cheeks, finding her tight hole with one of my fingers.

Violet tenses slightly, but she doesn't stop me, nor does she stop moving her pussy against my face. Her sweet honey drips from her entrance, and I swallow every drop she gives me. With my hand between her ass cheeks, I gently massage her asshole, swirling around the entrance. While I bring her to an orgasm, when her hips start to move uncontrollably, I ease a finger into her ass. I keep my finger there for a moment and then I start to move in and out of her, very slowly, very gently. At the same time, I suck and nip on her clit until she comes hard. I can taste her juices on my tongue and savor every last drop of it.

"Ivan," she whispers, and I look up at her over her mound. Her eyes are wide, and bright, and she's taking from me every single thing I give her. She wants this, she wants me, and that makes my fucking heart explode. It makes me crazy with need, with love.

I finger her ass until every last ripple of orgasm has gone through her body. Then I pull out my finger, moving out from underneath her. She whimpers at the loss of contact, and I crawl up onto the bed, centering myself behind her. I nudge her forward, pushing her head down, and her ass up.

"I want you, Kitten. I want you so badly it fucking hurts me." I take my swollen length into my hand and fist it, stroking it a couple times before I bring it to her pussy. With a growl, I slam into her to the hilt, listening as a hiss of pleasure and pain slips past her lips.

Her pussy quivers around my length as if it knows what's to come. Dipping a hand between her slick folds, I let her arousal coat my fingers and then I bring them up to her asshole, starting all over again. I massage the tight muscles, moving in and out of her pussy until I feel her legs shaking and her pussy tightening around me.

With two fingers, I move inside her tight ass. She moans, pushing back against my hand as if she's begging me for more. I smile and stretch her as best I can to accommodate my length. Then I pull completely out of her and bring the head of my swollen cock to her ass.

I nudge her legs further apart and ease forward, gritting my teeth to stop myself from slamming into her. I want her ass, her pussy, her mouth. I want to claim every single part of her with my cock.

"Ivan," she whimpers just as I slip the head of my cock inside her tight ass.

"Breathe through it, Kitten, nice and deep breaths," I assure her, running a hand down her spine. Her tiny body shakes, her hands fist the sheets, but she doesn't ask me to stop, and thank fuck, because I'm not sure I could even if I wanted to.

"Just relax that asshole for me, don't fight it, just relax and let me in."

Snaking a hand beneath her, I rub gentle circles against her clit, slipping in another inch.

"Fuck, Kitten, your ass is swallowing every last inch of my cock. How does it feel? How does it feel to be claimed here?"

A deep moan of pleasure rips from her throat, urging me forward and before I realize it, I'm seated deep inside her ass. She squirms against the sheets as if it's all too much for her tiny body, but I'm not done yet, not even close.

"You're going to come for me, Kitten, again and again." I pull out and thrust back into her, making her whimper against the sheets. The sound is music to my ears, and I do it again, this time rougher than the last. When she pushes back against me, I grip onto her hips and fuck her like I want to.

I thrust deep and hard inside her, finding a rhythm that leaves us both breathless.

"Fuck... I'm coming..." Violet moans, and I wish I could see her fucking face right now. See the pleasure wash over her angelic features, see her pink lips part, her eyes close.

"Yes, come for me, Kitten. Give it to me." I slam my hips against her, crushing our bodies together. She owns me; she fucking owns me. Her body shakes, and I force her to stay on her knees with one of my hands as I move in and out of her relentlessly, pushing us both to the brink. Her whole body tightens as she peaks again, squeezing my cock with her tight asshole.

"Shit..." I pant, feeling my balls draw up and a tingling of pleasure shoot down my spine. "Fuck, Kitten...fuck..." I thrust harder and harder, my grip on her bruising as I fill her tight little asshole with every single drop of sticky cum inside of me. I come for what seems like an eternity, my body going rigid against hers as I hold her in place. I don't want this moment between us to ever fucking end. I just want to hold her in my arms, her body connected to mine for the rest of our lives.

"I love you," she whispers into the sheets, and I know she means the words. She fucking means them deep down to the depths of her soul. I ease out of her and pull her into my arms, needing to hold her until she is embedded deep inside me.

"I love you, too, Kitten, so fucking much."

She peers up at me, her eyes dazzling, and when her lips press against mine the rest of the world falls away. When I pull away, her eyes start to drift closed.

"Did I hurt you at all?" The idea of doing so kills me inside. I want her to experience pleasure, and only a little bit of pain.

"No. It was..." She trails off a little bit. "It was actually really pleasurable." Her pink cheeks give away her embarrassment, but she doesn't need to be embarrassed, not with me.

"We'll do it again and each time will be better than the last," I assure her, holding her as tightly to my chest as I can. The only thing in this world that matters to me is the one person I have cradled in my arms, as long as she's happy and content I know I will be.

When I look at her, I think of a new beginning. A brand-new chapter, in a completely different book, one I want to write with memories of the two of us.

∼

THREE WEEKS PASS IN A BLUR, with Roman doing fights every weekend and the parties, it's hard to remember that we're in hiding, running from a man who would easily kill us if he got his hands on either of us. Roman and I have only grown closer with the passing days. I don't think he will ever completely forgive me for what happened with Mira but at least we have a relationship again, other than the one where he hated me, if you could call it a relationship.

I look over at Violet, who is napping beside me on the couch. Having her by my side every day has been amazing and unlike anything I could've ever imagined. I hold her when we go to sleep at night, and she is in my arms with me when I wake up. The sex we share seems to bring us closer, strengthening our newfound love.

And while having her and my brother back in my life makes everything seem perfect, it isn't. Xander Rossi is still breathing down my neck, wanting something. I don't know exactly what he wants yet, but I am not fond of the thought of giving him anything at all. If he's anything like his father, it won't be just a simple exchange.

Violet keeps asking about her sister. She wants to call her or send her some kind of message to let her know that she is okay. I have been trying to avoid the subject at all costs, but she is getting more insistent every day and I don't know how much longer I can keep up the act.

I sigh heavily staring down at her, thinking of the way her face will look when I tell her that her sister is gone. That Rossi killed her. I don't want to hurt her. Fuck, it's the very last thing I want to do. I don't want to ruin how happy we are right now, but there's no way around it, she's going to force my hand. She's going to make me tell her and there won't be anything I can do to stop the hurt from taking up space in her fragile heart.

Roman walks into the living room, his eyes moving from me and then to Violet as he takes a bite of his sandwich. At first, I worried that Violet and Roman would continue to butt heads, but after he saved her life that night, something changed inside him. It was almost like he saw her as a little sister.

"You can't avoid Xander forever. He's not the kind of man you want to cross."

I roll my eyes at his words. "You say that like you've met his father." I cock a brow.

"I haven't, no, but I can tell you that Xander's been far more patient with you than he has with anyone else I know. He's given you time but if you don't talk to him, he will come for you, and that's not something you want to happen."

Roman doesn't seem scared, or even concerned really. He just kind of acts nonchalant about the whole thing, like it's just another damn day in the office when really, it's not.

"I know," I growl under my breath. "I just... I need to protect her and getting involved with Xander is going to put her right in the line of gunfire."

Roman nods as if he understands but he's never been in love before, he's never carried his heart in someone else's body, praying nothing happens to them.

"I don't even know what exactly he fucking wants from me." I'm guessing he wants information on his father, since they have been actively trying to kill him for a while, but I don't know Xander and I'd rather not deal with him at all.

"Only one way to find out, I guess." Roman shrugs and takes another bite of his sandwich before he strolls out of the room.

Violet stirs beside me and stretches her body with a quiet moan just like a kitten. *My Kitten.*

"Hey, Sleeping Beauty," I murmur.

She smiles, crawling over to me, before settling into my lap. "I don't know why I've been so lazy lately. I'm always tired." She yawns directly in my face, and it's adorable as hell.

"Don't worry about it. Sleep all you want as long as you are next to me...or on top of me...or under me, or I'm inside you." I wiggle my eyebrows at her, feeling my cock harden. I want her, but who am I kidding? I always fucking want her.

"I'm sensing a pattern," she giggles. "Or maybe I feel lazy

because I'm actually being lazy. I really haven't left the house much, not unless it's to go to the gym with you and Roman or grocery shopping. It's been a month of hiding. Do you really think they are still looking for us?"

"I don't know, Kitten. Rossi really isn't the kind of man to just let stuff go. Taking you put a target on my back. He lost money because of me, and then there's the fact that I betrayed him and all of his men. No amount of time is ever going to make him forget what I did. The only way he'll forget is when he dies, and even then, his men will seek out revenge."

I already know where Violet is going to go with this, and my mood darkens accordingly. She still doesn't fucking get it. She doesn't understand, and I don't know how to explain it to her without hurting her, without destroying everything we have built.

She sticks her chin out, and her blue eyes flicker with defiance. "I won't stay here in this house forever, Ivan. I want to be a normal person, start school like I was supposed to, maybe even get a job and I want to talk to my sister."

There it is. No matter how much I push the subject away, she always brings it back up. Everything starts and ends with her sister. I can't take it any longer. I can't continue to lie to her.

"Violet, let it go... please." I pick her up and place her onto the couch and stand, feeling too much tension to remain sitting.

"Ivan, I just want to talk to her. I'm not asking to drive up to her place and ring the doorbell. I just want to talk. I could call from a payphone or something if that makes it any better. I mean, you act like you're hiding something. Are you hiding something?" Her eyes pierce mine, judgment and uncertainty reflecting back at me. Lying to her is killing me, eating away at my heart.

"Violet, you can't call her, okay? I'm not going to have this fucking conversation with you every day." I try to ignore her questioning me, procrastinating the inevitable, but I know she is not stupid. God, no, she is so fucking smart and kind, and every day I'm reminded of how she couldn't belong to me.

"Why not? Ivan, tell me! Why can't I call her? You obviously know something I don't, so spill, tell me, because all you do is tell me no, you can't, but you never really give me a real reason. So, tell me, Ivan. Why can't I call her?" She pushes from the couch and presses a finger into my chest. She's angry, and me being here, telling her what I'm about to tell her, is only going to be gasoline on an already burning inferno. My nostrils flare, and I clench my fists at my sides. I want to destroy this fucking room.

"You can't fucking call her because there is no one to call."

She gives me a confused look. "What do you mean, there is no one to call? She's my fucking sister, Ivan. She'll answer if I call her. She's all I have left."

I clench my jaw, really, really, really not wanting to tell her what I'm about to.

"Don't make me do this, Violet."

"Do what? Tell me the truth. Make you actually come clean about whatever it is you know?" She's seething now, and I so badly want to go back to how we were just a short time ago, with her in my lap, that sweet smile on her plump lips.

"Tell me." She slaps a hand to my chest, making the organ inside ache.

"Violet," I warn.

"Tell me, Ivan. Tell me now." She speaks through clenched teeth, and I can't stop the pain. I can't stop the words from coming out.

"She's dead, Violet. She's fucking dead, are you happy now?" My words are coated in venom. I'm angry, angry that she made me tell her, made me hurt her.

Violet stills. She doesn't look shocked or sad or even mad at me. She just looks like she is frozen in time. She is so still, I don't think she is even breathing. The silence between us stretches on, and I worry that she may be having some kind of mental breakdown.

"You are lying," she says, her voice flat and without emotion.

"It's not true. She is not dead. I would know. I would feel it in my heart if she were dead."

"I'm sorry, Violet, but it's true. She is dead."

"When?" Her expression is lifeless.

"A week before Vegas." I swallow, waiting for the breakdown to come, for the tears to slip down her face, and her heart to shatter into a million pieces.

She shakes her head, causing blond strands to fly. "I saw her. I saw her in Vegas. She was there the night that you took me. I saw her, Ivan." Her voice is frantic.

"I already told you, Violet, it was the drugs. They messed with your head. You couldn't have seen her because she was already dead then. She's been dead for five weeks now, days before the auction."

"Five weeks? You are telling me, you knew she has been dead for five weeks and you... you didn't say anything this whole time?" She starts to pull away, but I can't let her go, not when she's angry, not like this. I try to grab her hand again put she just pulls away farther.

"Do not touch me," she growls, shrugging out of my hold. I'm angry at myself and at my need to love and care for her. If I didn't want her so much, if I didn't love her, then maybe we wouldn't be in this situation right now.

"I didn't tell you because I didn't want to hurt you."

She gives me a sour look. "No, Ivan, you didn't tell me because you didn't want to. You had numerous times to tell me. You chose not to, probably because you didn't want me to stop fucking you, or ruin our little game of house, or whatever this is we're doing."

"This..." I gesture between us, my voice rising "It isn't a fucking game to me, Violet."

She tilts her head sideways. "Well, I couldn't fucking tell. Not since you told me that you couldn't keep me, or what was it, you wouldn't?"

I clench my teeth and reach out for the nearest object that isn't her. I need to break something, hurt something. My hands land on a fucking statue, and I toss it, watching as it breaks, shattering as is lands against the wall. I slam my closed fists down on the table, loving the pain that radiates up my arms. Then I toss the fucking thing like it weighs nothing.

Violet startles, fear fills her eyes, and she takes a couple shaky steps backward and away from me. Everything she said, she fucking meant, and it hurts. It feels like someone's stabbed me right in the fucking chest. Like I'm losing my sister all over again.

"Just go to the fucking bedroom!" I order. I don't want her anywhere near me right now. I feel out of control; anger ripples through me. Hurting her is the last thing I want to do. I'd kill myself if I ever put my hands on her like that.

"What the fuck is going on out here?" Roman appears in the doorway, concern etched into his features. He looks between Violet and I, shaking his head. Violet, of course, takes that moment to slip out of the room, running away toward our bedroom.

"What the fuck, Ivan?" Roman repeats his question but I still don't have an answer to give him. I just want to grab something else and break it. This anger overcoming my body needs to be released.

How could she say those things? I risked it all for her. I'm in here now because of her.

I want to throttle her, shake her until she starts to think clearly again.

"I need to leave... I need out of this fucking house before I do something that I can't take back."

"Well, let's go. You can let out some steam at the gym. Maybe I'll kick your ass in the ring for breaking my shit." Roman grins at me, walking toward the front door.

I follow him, clenching my jaw, holding in the anger. Why did she have to do this to us? Why did she have to keep pushing and pushing? Roman unlocks the car, and I climb into the passenger seat, slamming the door behind me. I don't even tell Violet that we are leaving. I can't bear to see her like this, and I don't want to be around her right now. Not when I'm not myself. Plus, she's mad at me anyway. The best thing for us is space, even if it's the last thing I want to give her.

We pull out of the driveway and start driving down the road. I stare out the window, wishing I had it in me to just talk to Violet. I hate leaving things the way that we did.

"You want to tell me what's going on?" Roman questions as if he gives a fuck.

"Nope. There's things in your life you don't tell me about, and there are things in my life that I won't tell you about. Violet is one of those things," I growl, clenching and unclenching my fists numerous times.

When we finally get to the gym, I head straight for the biggest bag I see and start punching the shit out of it.

Why didn't I just tell her? Punch. *Why did I hurt her?* Punch.

Questions swirl inside my head as I keep punching the bag until a sheen of sweat covers my body, my fist aches and my muscles are stiff. Only when it becomes hard to breathe, my chest constricting with each breath I pull in and the pain in my hands becomes unbearable, do I stop.

Roman appears out of thin air, shoving a bottle of water into my face. "Feeling better?"

"A little…" I wipe at my sweaty forehead with my arm. I suck in a ragged breath. "Fuck… how long have we been here?"

Roman gazes down at his imaginary watch as if mocking me. "An hour and a half."

My face deadpans. "Seriously, how long?"

"About an hour and a half," he repeats.

"Shit." A wave of guilt washes over me. "We should get going. I shouldn't have left Violet alone that long." I feel like such a douchebag. We just left Violet to deal with her anger and grief all alone. I mean, she might have not wanted me there, but I could've asked Roman to stay home with her. I start toward the door and Roman follows.

We are about ten feet from the door when it opens and a guy in a suit walks in. He definitely sticks out like a sore thumb in a place like this, and my first though is that he might be one of Rossi's guys. Roman and I both freeze, fists clenched, and ready to fight if need be. The unknown man merely holds up his hands, showing us his sweaty palms. He looks familiar but I can't place him right in this moment.

"I really don't want to have to use my gun, so please, let's keep this peaceful, gentlemen." He lets the door fall closed behind him and then he steps right up to us, holding out his hand as if he expects us to shake it.

Who the fuck is this bastard?

"We haven't met personally, but I'm Damon... Damon Rossi." The glint in his eyes is irritating as fuck. Neither one of us takes his hand, now that we both know who he is.

Damon fucking Rossi, one of Rossi senior's sons. Fucking Christ.

You should've called him. The thought repeats inside my head. For a moment, I think of Violet and if she's in danger. There is no way anyone would be willing to show up at Roman's house, not knowing who he is. But Xander, his men might think otherwise.

Damon drops his hand, and instead, adjusts his tie as if he's insulted. "First. you don't return any of my brother's calls and now, you won't even greet me as a guest should be greeted?"

I'm anything but happy that he is here. Though I can't deny that he has some balls walking in here by himself with only a gun.

"I don't greet guests who show up uninvited." I cross my arms over my chest. Roman and I are evenly matched in size. We could take him, but something tells me if he disappeared, his brother would be kicking down our doors, and the last thing I need is another Rossi attempting to kill me.

"Ivan," he smirks, looking me straight in the eyes. "My brother simply wants to talk to you, that's all. Is it really that hard to pick up a phone? It's not like he was going to try and kill you... or the girl."

Anger overcomes me, and I take a step toward him, ready to rip his throat out.

"Ivan," Roman warns, and I swallow down the rage, knowing beating his face in won't do me any good. The last thing I need to do is piss more people off.

Damon smirks at my reaction, which only makes me want to hurt him more.

How the fuck does he know about Violet though?

"What do you and your brother want?" I growl, barely holding onto my patience.

"Look, I'm serious, he just wants to talk to you. We might be able to help each other out with the bastard known as my father. I mean it. I didn't come out here to fight with you. That's just one of the things Xander would like to discuss with you." Damon looks as if he's telling the truth, but you can never be sure. I've seen Rossi joking with a man one second and pressing a gun to his head the next, splattering his brains all over the fucking place. A man's word means nothing... only his actions.

"What's the other thing?" I ask, hoping that it's not Violet he wants.

"Xander would also like to know what happened to the girl you took from the auction." *Fuck.*

"That's none of his fucking business. The girl is off limits and anyone who tried to hurt her will die. Got it?"

"Xander doesn't want to hurt her; he just wants to talk to her." Damon stays calm and collected even with me threatening, which is kind of impressive.

"Then why the fuck didn't your brother come here himself?" I sneer.

He looks around as if he is deciding how much information he should give me. Then he sighs as if he's made up his mind. "He didn't want to leave his girlfriend, and honestly, I didn't want to have to leave my wife either, but we can't all have everything we want."

Wife? Girlfriend? These men were criminals at their finest. I can't believe they are openly having women in their lives. Their father would never allow such a thing within his ranks. You don't get to marry the woman of your dreams... you don't get to marry anyone at all. Rossi Senior sees relationships as weaknesses, nothing more.

"What do you know about the girl I took?" He hasn't mentioned Violet's name yet, so maybe he doesn't know a lot, maybe she's still safe.

"I know that Violet's sister has been looking for her."

My heart slams against my ribcage, and I clench my fist with a fiery rage.

I speak through gritted teeth. "Violet's sister is dead. Your father told me so. So, don't come in here lying to me, because I already want to rearrange your fucking face."

Damon shakes his head slowly. "You really think my brother and I would just leave a helpless girl tied up to the bed? Do you think we'd just light the place up with someone innocent inside of it? What kind of monsters do you think we are?"

My eyes narrow. "I wasn't aware there were types of monsters."

Damon smirks as if something I've said is funny. "You have very little to be judgy about. We know what you were doing for the last couple of years, so if you want to throw around who the bigger monster is in all of this, we can, but I'm not sure you're going to like the results."

"Don't guilt me, asshole. I know what I fucking did." Even saving Violet wouldn't make the memories go away. I knew they hurt women... sold them, raped them, but I always turned a blind eye to those things. Until Violet, that is.

"Good, then you know that we're all monsters in this, and no one is above the other. The only person who needs to pay and die is my fucking father. If you were smart, you'd help us. It would benefit you just as much. You must be aware of the bounty my father has put out on your head?"

"And what if I don't do as you say?" I tilt my head at him, daring him to do something, to threaten Violet.

He rolls his shoulders, as if he's feeling tense. "Then my brother will come here and change your mind and believe me, you don't want that. It will greatly displease him and definitely cause an issue, since this is a family affair now."

His statement throws me for a damn loop. What do Ella and Violet have to do with Xander's family? Damon must see the confusion written all over my face, because a Texas-size smile pulls at his smug lips.

"Ella is Xander's girlfriend, if you haven't gathered that by now. The one you claim is dead. She saw Violet in Vegas at the auction, where Xander took her to rescue Violet. She saw you carrying her out the back door. She knows her sister is alive, and for your fucking sake, I hope she's well. So, I guess if you don't want to deal with Xander, you could always deal with her."

Fuck. All this fighting with Violet, this entire fucking time was for nothing. All I had to do was believe her. Guilt grips onto me. I need to get back to the house, back to her and apologize, beg and plead for her forgiveness, for breaking her heart, for hurting her.

"Okay, I'll fucking call him. I'll set up a meeting with him and see what happens."

"You'll call him?" Damon lifts his dark brow in question as he pulls his cell out of his pocket.

"Yes, I'll fucking call him. Isn't that what I just told you?"

"Yeah, but I wanted to double check." He types out something on his phone and pockets the device, looking back up at me.

"It was nice to meet you Ivan, Roman, I look forward to getting to know you both. Hopefully, we will be working together soon." He walks out of the gym with a smirk on his lips.

Roman, of course, chooses that moment to turn to me, a smile on his lips. "See, it wasn't that fucking hard, was it? No blood was drawn, and nobody died."

"Unfortunately," I whisper under my breath.

"Shut up. Let's get back to the house so you can make sure *Kitten* is okay. Something tells me you have a lot of apologizing to do."

I slug him in the arm. Fuck. I know I do, but that doesn't mean he has to rub it in.

"Wait till you fall in love. I bet she'll have you by the balls within a week."

Roman shakes his head, locking up the gym. "Nope. I don't do love, big bro. I do fucking, and that's it. I'm not stupid like you."

"Being in love isn't stupid," I growl, getting in his car.

Roman rolls his eyes, and starts driving us back to the house, back to Violet.

Fuck. I'm going to be on my knees for a while, begging and pleading for her forgiveness.

21

Violet

Hating him would be easier, but whatever I try, I just can't make myself do it. I know I have every right to hate him after what he did. I should not want him near me. I should want him to never touch me again and yet all I want is for him to be here right now and hold me in his arms.

He didn't believe me when I told him I saw Ella, because he knew something I didn't. He could have told me right then or all the other times I've ask him about her.

If she is really dead then part of me would be, too. I still can't wrap my mind around the idea of her being gone. It must be a mistake, right? I'm so confused. My mind is in disarray. What if Ivan is right, and it was the drugs? What if I didn't see her, and she is really dead? No, no, no... It can't be true.

I wipe at the tears streaming down my cheeks, and another sob rips from my throat, filling the empty room. I'm angry, sad, and just disappointed in myself and in Ivan.

The things I said. The secret he kept for so long. I think I might've been able to handle him keeping it from me if it weren't for how angry and dismissive he would get every time I brought her up. He knew how important she was to me, how important it was to me to let her know I was okay and the whole time... the whole time, he knew she was dead?

My head starts to hurt, my eyes feel swollen, and my throat burns like hell. I need to get up and get a drink. I get up from the bed and slowly drag myself to the kitchen. The house is unusually quiet, and I wonder if I am actually alone. Would Ivan have truly left me here all alone? The thought hurts me more than I want to admit.

"Hello?" I call down the hall in the open space. "Ivan? Roman?" Complete silence follows. "Anybody?" I sniffle, feeling tears sting my eyes. I walk into the living room and realize that for the first time in many weeks, I am actually alone, completely alone, and not locked up. I would have thought that something like this would feel good, but this freedom is not something I'm used to and to be honest, I feel lost and alone without Ivan.

I wrap my arms around myself and walk into the kitchen, going to the cabinet to get a glass. I grab one and head over to the fridge to get ice and water. When I pass the pantry, I hear the growl of my stomach in my ears.

God, I'm always hungry... always hungry, always tired. It must be all the stress, the worry of the unknown future that has me feeling these things.

I grab a granola bar and walk back out into the kitchen, taking a drink of water as I do so. A part of me wonders what Ivan and Roman are doing right now? Would he leave and find someone else? He was so angry when he left, and I don't even understand why he was. I'm the one who should have been throwing stuff around, not him.

It's not like I lied to him. I open the granola bar, sinking my teeth into it, and that's when I hear it. The sound of glass breaking.

My pulse picks up as I walk back toward the bedroom. I can't tell exactly where the sound came from, but I'll be safest in our bedroom, right?

I'm halfway down the hall when I hear the sound of heavy footfalls behind me. I twist around just in time to see a figure moving toward me. A scream builds in my throat, but it never comes out. I have no time to react to the intruder who slams into me, pushing me to the ground face first. The glass in my hand is thrown, and glass flies in every direction.

"Hey, bitch." Luca's voice turns my blood turns to ice. He's supposed to be dead. I shot him. I struggle against his hold as best I can, but he's strong so strong, his body pushes mine into the floor, even as I buck against him.

"I've been waiting for you to be alone so I could make you pay for shooting me. Should have made sure I was dead before you left me bleeding on the kitchen floor."

"L-Luca?" I stutter, not understanding how he is here right now.

"Did you miss me?" His face is so close, I can feel his breath on my skin. I shudder when he starts to kiss my neck. Bile rises in my throat as his erection pressed against my leg.

"What do you think Ivan is going to think when he finds you, thoroughly fucked, my cum dripping from your cunt?"

His words spark so much anger inside of me that I start fighting him... really fighting him. I buck, kick, hit, bite, and scratch. My body moves without thought.

Fight him at all costs, I tell myself. I will not let him do this. I will not let him touch me.

"I like when you fight me, baby, makes your pussy really tight." He laughs and grabs me by my shoulders. His fingers dig into my skin as lifts me up a few inches just to slam me back to the floor with lethal force. My head bounces off the hardwood floor like a basketball. An explosive pain erupts at the back of my skull, making the room spin around me.

I think I black out for a moment, my body is numb, and it hurts to breathe. Once I'm finally able to form a coherent thought again, I notice that Lucan has ripped my shirt off and is touching my exposed breast, sucking, biting at the flesh.

I try to push him off again, but he just chuckles, wrapping a hand around my throat, squeezing till I see black dots across my vision. I feel his other hand reach down between my legs and tears start to roll down the side of my face and into my hair.

Ivan, where are you?

I close my eyes and try to let my mind drift away. I want to leave this body, forget the sick feeling filling my belly. I want to have no memories of this. Just when I think nothing can save me, that this evil man is going to take something so precious from me, I hear the sound of squealing tires off in the distance. I open my eyes and look up at the monster taking advantage of me. Luca is so busy trying to rape me he's not paying attention to the noises around him, because he doesn't realize that someone is coming until the front door swings open so hard I swear the whole room shakes.

I don't have to look to know who it is that's come to my rescue. Luca is pulled off of me in the next second. He lashes out with his hands, trying to get away, but Ivan and Roman move with superhuman speed. I cover my exposed chest with an arm and scurry backward.

Luca doesn't take more than one step before Ivan has him by the throat, slamming him against the closest wall. I get up off the floor and run down the hall, my stomach churning, my entire body aching. I can't sit there and watch them kill him, even though he deserves it.

I hear Luca's cries of pain as I reach the bedroom and slam the door closed behind me. I strip out of my clothes and go straight into the bathroom, turning the shower onto hot. I step into the hot spray and let the water wash every remnant of Luca away. His disgusting touch, his smell and his sweat, I want it all off of me. Erased from my body and erased from my memory.

I let the tears fall, leaning against the tile sobbing, releasing every single ounce of pain from within my body. I feel myself breaking in two, no way to hold myself together.

"Violet," Ivan calls out to me, his voice frantic, and it makes me cry harder. I sink down onto the floor, huddling in the corner. I don't even see or hear him enter the room, but then I feel his hands on me, pulling me into his chest. I clutch to the fabric, and cry into his chest, feeling the warmth of his body encompass mine. I suck in breath after breath of his scent, pushing the thoughts of Luca from my mind. *I'm safe. I'm secure. Ivan saved me.*

After a long time of holding me, he finally speaks.

"Are you okay? Did he..."

I open my eyes and look up at him. Guilt and shame fill his beautiful gray eyes and I shake my head no.

"I need to get you out of this shower and onto the bed. I want to make sure you're okay." He picks me up like I weigh nothing and carries me to the bed, setting me down on it gently. I lay my head down on the pillow. Other than the thoughts of what almost happened swirling inside my mind and a pounding headache, I'm okay.

Ivan's eyes roam over every inch of flesh before he's cupping me by the cheeks, his lips pressing against mine so softly, so gently.

"I'm so fucking sorry, Violet. I'm sorry for walking away, for leaving you here alone. If I hadn't let my temper get the best of me, I would've been here, and he never would've touched you."

I can live with the things going on inside me right now, the pain will fade, but I can't live with Ivan feeling guilt and shame over something he couldn't control. This wasn't his fault, and I refuse to allow him to think that it was.

"Listen..." I try to sit up while talking to him but then the room spins out of control. I have to close my eyes to get a grip on the dizziness.

"What's wrong?" Ivan's voice is laced with concern.

"I hit my head on the floor. I think I passed out for a little while. I don't really remember." I lift my hand, feeling for a tender spot on my scalp. My fingertips graze over the spot, and I feel a huge bump underneath my fingers.

"All right, we're going to get you to a doctor, right now. Here, let me get you dressed." Ivan hurries to the dresser and starts grabbing clothes.

"You're going to take me to see Mac?" I whimper, unable to not feel the tender spot on my head now that I've touched it.

"No, a real doctor." He starts helping me into my underwear, and I almost want to shoo him away, but I'm so woozy that I actually think I'm going to need his help.

"Is that really a good idea, Ivan?"

Ivan gives me a stern look. "I don't really give a fuck what is a good idea right now. You're my ending and beginning, and if something is wrong with you then I'm going to take care of you before I worry about anything else."

He finishes getting me dressed and then helps me into a standing position. Now that I'm standing and eye level with his chest, I notice that his clothes are soaked from getting me out of the shower, but he doesn't seem to care about them. Actually, he doesn't seem to care about anything but me right now.

"Ivan..." The words are cut off when a piercing pain shoots through my head. I squeeze my eyes shut in hopes to ease the pain but there's no point. It feels like someone is carving deep inside my skull with a dull knife.

"Kitten, stay with me." Ivan lifts me up yet again and carries me out the door.

"Roman! Car! Now!" he yells into the hallway and before I know it, we are outside, cool air hits my clammy skin, and Ivan opens the back door put us in the backseat of Roman's car, his grip on me never slacking, not even for a second.

Roman enters the car just a moment later, starting it without question.

"We are taking her to the hospital. I don't care what the fuck you have to say about it..."

"Calm down, Ivan. That's where I planned to go anyway." Roman's voice sounds oddly calm. The complete opposite of Ivan's worry-stricken tone. My eyes drift closed as I listen to the roar of the engine as Roman starts to drive.

"Open your eyes, Kitten. Don't go to sleep," Ivan orders.

"My head hurts... and I'm so tired," I whine. I don't know if it's the way Ivan is holding me against him or the soothing motion of the car but the desire to sleep overwhelms me. Maybe just a small nap would be okay?

"Violet, listen to me, you need to open your eyes. We are almost to the hospital." Ivan's voice is drifting farther and farther away, and I'm close to letting the darkness take over me when his next words drag me back to reality.

"Kitten, you were right. Ella is alive. You sister is alive, and she is looking for you."

I pry my eyes open to study Ivan's face. *Did he really just say that?* Is he lying? Is he just saying this to keep me awake?

"Ella?" My throat feels dry.

"Yes, Kitten, you were right all along, and I'm a fucking idiot for not believing you. Ella was at the auction just like you said. She was there to rescue you." I can see the remorse in Ivan's gaze. I want to ask him a million more questions. *How does he know these things?* How did Ella know where I was and where is she right now? Before I can get the first question out, the car comes to a sudden stop. I peel myself from Ivan's chest and look out the window and realize that we are at the entrance of the emergency room.

"I'll tell you everything as soon as we're done getting you checked over with the doctor, okay?"

"Okay," I whisper and let Ivan carry me inside.

The next two hours are filled with such a long list of tests that I start to feel like a guinea pig in a laboratory. The official diagnosis is as I expected, a concussion, but of course, the doctor wants to keep me here overnight just to make sure I don't have any issues, and Ivan reluctantly agrees.

Roman somehow got the nurse to admit me under a fake name. I'm not sure how he did it but I'm sure a large sum of cash was involved, either that, or he used other persuasive ways. I don't know and I won't get to ask him because he left shortly after he took care of the *paperwork,* no doubt to clean up the mess left behind in his house.

Right after they bring me in a tray of food for dinner, the door softly opens and a petite woman walks in. "Hi, Rose, I'm Lindsey, the night shift nurse. I'll be taking care of you tonight."

I give her a smile and watch her open the folder she brought in.

"Oh, lord, you slipped in the shower and hit your head? I swear, I don't understand how we can send people to the moon but they can't make it so you don't break your neck in a tub when showering." Her comment makes me giggle, but when I look over at Ivan's face, he is still emotionless.

"Well, one good thing about this is that you are still early in your pregnancy, so the fall you took shouldn't have any effect on your growing baby."

I blink slowly, very slowly, unsure of what I just heard her say. She keeps on talking, but I don't understand or hear another word she says.

All I hear is the word *pregnancy*. My first thought is that she's got the wrong folder, wrong information or that maybe she entered the wrong room or that she is reading the test results wrong, but the more I think about it, the more I realize that I have all the symptoms.

The sleepiness, the hunger, the sudden nausea. I press a hand to my head. *Stupid. I'm so stupid.* I feel so dumb for not having put one and one together myself.

"Pregnant? She's pregnant?" Ivan asks the nurse. I can't tell what he's thinking or feeling. His facial expressions are skewed.

"Yes..." She pauses, looking up at him from the folder in her hands. "Wait, you didn't know?" The nurse looks at us with confusion.

Ivan pushes up from his seat and walks over to me, taking my hand into his. I'm assaulted with a thousand different emotions. Is Ivan going to want to keep the baby? I can't imagine he would want me to get an abortion or give up the baby, but I don't know at this point, not without knowing his thoughts.

"My apologies, truly, I thought you knew or at least someone would have told you by now. According to your blood results, you are early in your pregnancy. Maybe five or six weeks. The only real concern is that you have low iron, so if you've been feeling tired often, that is why. Taking a prenatal vitamin will help with that."

Ivan's eyes pierce mine, and he doesn't even look over at the nurse when he speaks. "Can you please leave us for a little while?"

"Of course," she murmurs and walks out of the room, closing the door behind her. Once we're left alone, I start to shake, afraid of what Ivan is going to say, of what we're going to do.

"Why are you shaking, Kitten?"

"I-I don't know what you are going to say to me next. I'm scared you not going to want this... want me with a baby."

He tips my chin up to look at him. "Do you really think that I'm going to make you get rid of *our* baby?"

My heart bursts inside my chest when I hear him say *our*. "You mean you don't want me to get an abortion?" I hate the way my voice sounds, like I'm afraid or something.

Ivan gives me a sour look. "Fuck, no. When I sunk deep inside you without a condom, I knew the consequences."

"Then... then that means we're going to have a baby..." My voice shakes, and Ivan smirks at me, happiness twinkling in his gray eyes.

"It sure does, Kitten. We're going to have *babies*."

"Babies?" I ask, confused, as he leans down, bringing his lips to mine. I release his hand and grip onto his shirt, wanting him, no *needing* him closer.

He grins. "Yes, I want you to be swollen with my babies... not one, not even two... I want us to have a full fucking house, Kitten."

I swallow around the ball of excitement and fear forming in my throat. "You want to stay with me? After everything that happened?"

Ivan doesn't answer me, he merely pulls me into his chest, kissing me with a passion, with a need that is unyielding. Our lips fit together like two puzzle pieces, and I mold into him, wanting to crawl deep inside of him. He pulls away just a little, our faces still so close than our noses are touching.

"I could ask you the same. Do you still want me after everything?"

"Always!" I lean into him again, continuing to kiss him like I can't get enough of him.

He breaks the kiss a moment later, and I suck in a greedy breath, my insides shaky, my body reacting to him in the only way it knows how, with pure unbridled need. He brushes a few strands of hair from my face and cups me by the cheek, his thumb caressing my flesh, making me lean into his touch.

"We had a fight, Violet, and people say stuff they don't mean when they fight. We'll have many fights in this life, but that doesn't mean I'm ever letting you go. You're mine forever... for-fucking-ever. Nothing you ever say to me will make me walk away from you. Understand?"

I feel myself nodding without even thinking, because I know he's telling the truth. No matter what, Ivan will be mine and I will be his. We've fought through the darkness together and found light on the other side. "I love you," I whisper, nuzzling into his hand.

"I love you, too, Kitten. Now are you ready for me to tell you about your sister?"

"Yes!" Fear and excitement zing through me. I can't imagine what she's been through trying to find me. The fear she's felt well wondering if I'm still alive.

"She's alive. I don't know if she's doing okay or not. I didn't get those details but from the sounds of it, she's fine. She's been looking for you and showed up at the auction with the intent to find you." Shame fills Ivan's features. "I should have believed you, and I'm sorry for that. I will never second guess you again."

"Don't. Will you hold me?" I ask, and he nods, picking me up off the bed, taking me into his arms and taking the spot I was just sitting in on the bed. The bed squeaks underneath his weight, and I hold in a bubble of laughter.

"What else?" I ask, burrowing into his chest, the sound of his heartbeat beneath my ear.

"The man that your sister is with is one of Rossi's sons..." My body stiffens and Ivan runs a hand down my back, soothing the tension out of my muscles. "She's okay, Kitten, or at least from what I can tell. Rossi has two sons. Both of them have their own illegal businesses but neither one works with or even talks to their father. Matter of fact, his sons have been trying to kill him for quite some time, almost succeeded once. I'm going to be setting up a meeting to discuss things with him, and maybe I can get him to agree to letting you see your sister."

"I would love that. I miss her so much. I mean, even if I just got to hug her, it would make my entire year." With his arm wrapped tightly around me, and my body cradled into his chest, I feel safe, cared for, and loved.

"Nothing is ever going to happen to you, Kitten. You carry my heart inside you and as long as I'm living, I'll protect you from all the bad in this world." His words bring tears to my eyes.

"You've been doing that since the moment I met you."

Running a hand through my thick blond hair, he whispers, "Because I know you needed someone to watch over you, guard you... I just never expected to fall in love with you."

"But you did?" I peer up at him, his gray eyes full of adoration, his face now relaxed, and his body at peace.

"I did, and I wouldn't change it for the world," he whispers, pressing his lips to my forehead.

22

Ivan

IT'S NOT OFTEN that I'm worried or nervous about meeting someone and honestly, I'm not really
anxious because I'm meeting with Xander. I'm more worried because Violet is pregnant, and my priorities now center around her even more than before.

It's important that I keep the peace between Xander and I, even if it's just for Violet.

"Are you nervous?" Violet whispers, looking up at me. She's sitting on the edge of the bed with her hands in her lap while I adjust my stupid fucking suit.

I hate wearing this shit. Since going into hiding, I haven't had to wear one and it's been great, but now that I'm meeting with Xander, I need to look and act the part.

"No, Kitten, I'm not nervous." I walk over to her, wanting to take her into my arms, but I can't because of this stupid meeting. "I just want to make sure you and the baby are okay. This meeting is to secure our future, so while I'm not nervous to meet Xander, I am nervous to see what happens."

Violet smiles, and her smile alone has the power to bring me to my knees. Since finding out about the baby growing inside her belly, we've moved into our own place. It's nothing fancy, a simple two-bedroom cottage secluded in the woods but it's ours, and it's close to Roman so I can still help out at the gym. I don't know what the hell I plan to do now but I can't go back to the shit I was doing before.

"Everything will be fine. I'm sure Xander is a nice man. I can't see my sister being with someone who is heartless. Rossi might be horrible, but you said it yourself his sons are better than he is."

I don't have the heart to tell her the things Xander has been known to do. It's better if she assumes that her sister is in the care of an angel instead of a psycho, which is what he is.

"Xander's a criminal, Kitten, the same as me, and the same as his brother. Maybe he's kind to your sister but at the end of the day, he always has his own interest at heart. Don't forget that."

"I won't, but I like to think that we all can find our own happily ever afters. I'm sure my sister found hers in him."

I smile because maybe she is right. Maybe her sister did find love in Xander, the same way Violet found love in me. I guess I'll find out today. I press a kiss to her forehead and unbutton the top button on my dress shirt. This fucking thing is making me sweat.

"I've got to go down to the restaurant. You're going to go with Roman and sit a couple tables away. I don't want you out of my sight."

Violet nods. "Make sure to ask him a lot about my sister. All the questions I told you. Make sure that she's okay."

"Of course, Kitten." I take her hand into mine, feeling like a million bucks with her by my side. We meet Roman out in the hall, and he gives me a once over, a smirk on his arrogant face.

"You look like a lawyer, and you're sweating like a pig headed off to the butcher."

"Thanks, you look great, too, asshole," I respond, shaking my head.

"Why, thank you, I always look good." He crosses his arms over his chest. "I mean, I am the younger, better-looking version of you."

"Shut up. I need your head in the game. You're to make sure nothing happens to Violet while I'm at this meeting. Don't leave the room with her, and don't let her out of your sight."

"What if I have to go to the bathroom?" Violet asks, mischief in her blue eyes. Roman and her like to tease me, even more so now than ever, since I'm a little bit overprotective and a whole lot crazy when it comes to my girl.

"Then Roman will accompany you inside."

The smile drops from Roman's face, and Violet snickers under her breath.

"I'm not a babysitter, Ivan. If she has to go to the bathroom, I'll wait outside the fucking door. It's not like anyone is going to want to try and go inside with me standing in front of it."

I clench my jaw, telling myself that someday Roman will understand what it's like to love someone more than he loves himself. "I don't care what you do so long as she remains safe."

Roman rolls his eyes. "Let go, I'm starving."

The elevator pings, and we all step inside.

Once inside, I turn to Roman. "You're supposed to watch her, not stuff your face." Of course, he'd be more concerned about his belly.

"Why can't I do both? Plus, how weird would it look if we just sit in a restaurant and not eat or order anything?" He cocks a dark brow.

"I'm actually a little hungry, too," Violet interrupts, smiling nervously. The elevator door opens, and we make our way down to the hotel's restaurant. I keep Violet close by my side, while Roman walks right behind us. I scan our surroundings for anything that looks unusual. Of course, we came here thirty minutes early so no one would see us coming together. That's what you do; you arrive first and leave last.

The hostess greets us and brings us each to the specific tables we have reserved. Violet and Roman sit across the restaurant but within eyesight of each other. I watch her from a distance when the waitress suddenly appears in front of me, cutting off my view.

"Sir, what can I get you?"

"Whiskey, neat."

She smiles and nods as she starts to walk away.

"I'll have the same." A deep voice makes me look up.

"Of course, Sir." I watch the waitress scurry away, clearly uncomfortable with two guys looking like us at her table.

Xander Rossi takes the seat directly across from me, looking rather pleased with himself. "Ivan, it's a pleasure to finally meet you."

"Can't say the same." Especially now that I see his face. His features are so similar to his father's. He looks like what I imagine Rossi Senior to have looked like twenty years ago, and I have to remind myself that he is not his father.

"You might change your mind about me when you hear what I have to offer you," he smirks, full of himself, just like his father.

"And what's that? What could you offer me that I don't already have?"

"Money, power, and of course, the most important thing... freedom. You would never have to look over your shoulder again. Never have to worry about someone coming for you." His offer is very tempting, very tempting, even more so now that Violet and I are expecting a baby.

"The question is... what do you want in return?" I cross my arms over my chest, staring him down.

His dark gaze doesn't waver from mine. "All I want from you is a location. Tell me how to find my father so I can kill him. That's all I want from you. Then we'll all be free from him and able to live our lives." Xander is very good at hiding his feelings; you have to be to survive in this business. But even he can't hide the flash of desperation in his eyes. He wants his father dead more than anyone else and that's saying a lot considering how many people want Rossi dead.

"Furthermore, once my father is dead, I'll need someone to take over his business in this area. I don't want to expand mine, but I don't want one of my father's goons to take over either. I could make sure that you get the position."

"How do I know you're not going to just stab me in the back later? I don't know you but what I've heard about you raises concerns about your trustworthiness to me, and those I care about. Maybe you're just blowing smoke up my ass now so you can turn around and kill me later, taking your father's territory for yourself."

"I can assure you that I have no need nor desire to do either of those things." Xander leans forward, resting his elbows on the table. He looks as determined as I feel. "I guess the real question is, are you willing to trust me to secure a future for you and the people you love?" When I don't answer right away, he continues, "Maybe we should ask Violet to come over here and see what she thinks."

Anger and protectiveness surges through me like I've been hit by lightning. I slam my fist down on the table, loudly. "Stay the fuck away from her."

The last thing I need is Xander hurting Violet and our unborn baby.

Xander chuckles and puts his hands up, trying to calm me. "No reason to get angry. Look, I know what you're probably thinking. I keep Violet's sister like my father keeps his women and if I'm being honest, I thought the same thing about you, but now that I see you and her." He glances over to where Violet and Roman are sitting across the room. "It's obvious that you care for Violet just as much as I care for Ella, and for that simple reason alone, I won't betray you. I won't do anything that would hurt Ella or her sister."

I can't deny the sincerity in his voice. I consider my options. He's not asking me for anything dangerous, anything that I can't give him. And he's right, hurting Violet would only hurt Ella, and if he cares for her as much as it seems right now, then I doubt he would do anything.

"If you fuck me over, I will come for you, Xander," I growl, and then look over to Violet. When our eyes meet, I wave her over. She sits there wide eyed for a second but then excitement grabs her, and she hastily makes her way over here with Roman on her heels. She sits down next to me while Roman takes a seat at the head of the table.

"You must be Violet," Xander greets her. "I've heard a lot, and I mean a lot, about you. I'm Xander." He holds his hand out to Violet and it takes a lot out of me not to pull her fragile hand away when she takes it and shakes it softly. He might actually love Ella and play nice with us, but I know the things those hands have done. I know the life he's lived.

"Is my sister here? Is she okay? Can I talk to her or see her?" She starts bombarding him with questions, excitement in her voice.

"She is not here, I'm afraid. She stayed home in North Woods because, quite frankly, I didn't know if I could trust Ivan yet. I wanted to come and see for myself before I put her in any danger. As for the rest, yes, she is fine. Happy and healthy. We can definitely set up meetings for you to meet as soon as I've taken care of my father. Which hopefully will be very soon." Xander looks straight at me, urging me to give him what he wants.

"Until then, maybe we can set up a secure phone line or even video chat? You could talk whenever you want."

Violet's eyes sparkle as she nods vigorously. She looks like she's about to jump up and hug Xander. I hope she realizes that I would never allow that. I barely managed to hold myself back watching them shake hands.

"Okay, Xander, I'll take the deal. I'll tell you where he is and how to get past his security. But I want your word, a blood oath. I don't want you turning around taking it back."

A triumphant grin spreads out on Xander's face, and he pulls a knife out. When Violet sees the metal of the blade, she gasps. I extend my hand out, watching as he slices the skin on his palm, before handing me the blade. I do the same, feeling the sting of pain as the sharp blade cuts through my skin, and then we shake hands across the table.

My gaze pierces his, and I know now we've just become family rather than enemies.

"I'll be in touch," He releases my hand and gives Violet a soft smile. "It was very nice to meet you, and I'll be sure to let your sister know you're alive and well."

Violet opens her mouth to say something, but the words never come. I grab a napkin from the table and wrap it around my hand, watching as Xander drops money on the table and walks out.

Silence settles over the table, and I take a drink of my whiskey, letting it burn down my throat. Fuck, that was easier than I thought it'd be.

"Are we safe?" Violet looks up at me, those blue eyes of hers making me weak with need the same way they did the day I rescued her, taking her into my arms.

I smile, feeling like a hero. I might not have been able to save Mira, but I understand now that's not my fault. I can't control everything... but Violet, I could control her outcome, and saving her is the best thing I've ever done.

"Yes, Kitten, we're safe." I lean over and kiss her, a groan from Roman filling my ears.

"Are you guys going to fuck, too?" he mumbles, as I pull away.

I grin over at him. "Of course, we've been doing that a while. How the hell do you think you became an uncle?"

Roman looks at me, shocked, completely shocked. "You're having a fucking baby?"

Violet and I both nod at the same time. Roman, of course, throws his hands in the air, shoving away from the table. He leaves the restaurant without a backward glance, and I understand why he feels the way he does. We just reconnected and now I'm making a family of my own. He doesn't want me to forget about him, but he has no fucking clue the plans I have for him.

"Is he going to be okay?" Violet asks, her hand finding its way into mine.

"Of course, Kitten. He'll come around." I finish my whiskey and put some money down on the table. Violet gets up, pushing from the table, and I take the moment to wrap an arm around her middle and pull her into my chest.

A tiny gasp slips past her pink parted lips. "We've come such a long way, Kitten. Making you mine and putting a baby inside you is the best thing that could've ever happened to me. Thank you for saving me."

The smile she gives me is breathtaking, and my heart starts to pound deep inside my chest.

"Thank you for guarding me, watching over me, and keeping your promise."

"You were mine the moment I laid eyes on you."

"Yes, and you were mine." She pushes up onto her tiptoes and kisses me, and I know she's right. We belonged to each other that night, our hearts tethered to one another's.

EPILOGUE

Violet

NERVOUS ANXIETY COATS MY INSIDES, and I wipe my hands down the front of my jeans to rid them of the sweat forming against them. I've talked to Ella almost every day now, and I've even seen her when we video chatted, but none of those things compare to seeing someone in the flesh. In a few moments, she will walk through that door, and I will be able to see her right in front of me. I'll be able to throw my arms around her and hug her until my muscles give out.

"You okay, Kitten?" Ivan takes my hand under the table and squeezes it lightly. We are in some fancy restaurant. Xander rented out a whole room, and we have been patiently waiting for ten minutes for them to get here. Although it feels more like ten hours to me.

When I see the hostess come around the corner, my heart skips a beat. Right behind her is Xander, who appears with my sister on his arm. As soon as she sees me, she breaks from Xander's hold and basically pushes the hostess out of the way to get to me. I jump up and meet Ella halfway.

We crash into each other, and I wrap my arms around her, feeling the warmth of her body against mine. To many it might not be much, but to me, after assuming she was dead, it means the world to see her in the flesh, to feel her arms wrap around me.

We hold each other for a long time, not caring how crazy the hostess thinks we are. Neither Ivan nor Xander interrupts our little bubble of joy, most likely because they're afraid of what would happen to them if they tried.

When we finally break free from our everlasting hug, I pull away to look at her face. She is crying, of course, just as I am, but they are all happy tears. Besides her puffy and red eyes, she looks good, great even. She looks happy and I wonder if she sees the same in my face. Can she tell how happy I am?

"You know, you guys can sit down, too," Ivan calls from the table. I look over and see Xander has already taken a seat beside Ivan, and I take Ella's hand into mine, walking us to the table. Months ago, I never would've thought this moment could exist. A moment where we would all be sitting together as one big happy family.

"It's so nice to finally meet you, Ella," Ivan greets her but doesn't extend his hand to her. Xander's just as protective of Ella as Ivan is of me, and even though we're all on good terms, neither of them approves of the other touching their woman.

"Thank you for arranging this." Ella nibbles on her bottom lip, looking between Xander and Ivan, who both smile at her.

"I told you I'd give you whatever you wanted, Mouse." Xander's nickname for her makes me smile. Mouse? Does she know that Ivan calls me Kitten?

"I know but I just never thought this would happen."

"For what it's worth, neither did I." Ella gives me a half smile, as she takes her seat. I sit in the seat beside her and take a sip of water. I hadn't told her about being pregnant yet as I wanted to tell her in person. She looks nervous as well and I wonder if she, too, has something she wants to tell me.

We order lunch and the entire time, I'm jittery, wanting to spill the beans. Ivan keeps smiling at me, making me even more nervous.

"What's going on?" Ella finally leans over and whispers in my ear. Nothing has changed, not really. She can still tell when I'm nervous or if something is wrong.

"I'm...." The words sit on the tip of my tongue, and I look to Ivan across the table for permission. When he gives me the nod, I burst at the seams. "I'm pregnant."

Ella blinks, her eyes going wide, then as the shock wears off, she smiles, looking to Xander. He doesn't nod, all he does is smile.

"Me, too," she says with a joyous smile on her lips.

"Wait, you guys are having a baby, too?" I question.

"We sure are, and I cannot wait for the moment when her belly gets nice and big." Xander's eyes twinkle with love, with pure joy.

"Oh, my god, I can't believe it. We are pregnant together," I laugh. "Don't you remember we used to talk about that when we were kids? How we said we'd have babies at the same time."

Ella smiles. "I know. We said we would do everything together, including having babies."

Who would have thought that our dreams would one day come true? We might have planned getting pregnant together, but we definitely didn't plan on finding the men we love the way we did.

Our original plan included living next door to each other. Both houses with large connecting backyards and white picket fences. I don't know if I see that in our futures now. Maybe two mansions with high-voltage security fences is more likely. That's if Ivan and Xander can manage to live that closely to each other.

Either way, I'll take it. I'll take all of this. We might have not planned to end up with two mob bosses, but I am sure as hell not complaining now. I've never been loved or cared for more in my life. Ivan might kill with his hands, he might destroy, but when he touches me, it's with nothing but kindness, with a gentleness. Seeing him as that man when no one else gets to is something I'd never give up.

"Ivan and I are open to letting you both plan each other's baby showers if that's something you would like to do, Violet? Of course, it cannot be the typical baby shower, being we will need security, and such but it will be just as good, I assure you."

I look away from my sister and to Xander. "I would love that. I'm hoping soon that we can make a visit to your house? Maybe stay for a short while?" I look over at Ivan; he knows I'm not asking. I will make this happen. That's the one thing about me that will never change. Determination for the things I want and the people I love will be something that I never let go of.

Ella's eyes light up. "Yes, that would be so fun. Xander and I are considering putting a pool in so maybe after we get that done?"

"Now, now, don't be getting ahead of yourselves, we need to plan accordingly," Ivan warns, and I merely roll my eyes at him. Such an overprotective bear. I can't help but love him. I lift my gaze to Xander. I don't know all that him and Ella endured to get their happily ever after, but I'm sure it was just as much as Ivan and I had endured.

"Thank you for keeping her safe, for finding her..." I trail off, feeling tears sting my eyes. Xander's face is devoid of emotion so I have no idea what he's thinking but it doesn't matter to me. I don't care, not really. All that matters is that I said what I wanted to say.

"Things weren't easy at first, and I'll save you the story of how shitty of a man I was to your sister in the beginning, but I can promise you that I'll always care for her, love her, and make sure she's well protected. So long as I'm alive, no harm will come to her. I promise you that."

I nod, feeling my heart beat out of my chest.

Happily ever afters were something I lost hope in not long ago, but looking at the three people sitting at the table with me, at the man who safe guarded me and risked his life for me, I know that they exist.

I know because I'm now living my own happily ever after.

∼

Thank you for reading Guard Me. Can't get enough of Ivan and Roman? Next up in the Rossi Crime Family Series is **Tame Me**

ABOUT THE AUTHORS

J.L. Beck and C. Hallman are an USA Today and international bestselling author duo who write contemporary and dark romance.

For a list of all of our books, updates and freebies visit our website.

www.bleedingheartromance.com

About the Authors

Beck and Hallman
BLEEDING HEART ROMANCE

f CASSANDRAHALLMAN
AUTHORJLBECK

⊙ CASSANDRA_HALLMAN
AUTHORJLBECK

BB CASSANDRAHALLMAN
JLBECK

ALSO BY THE AUTHORS

CONTEMPORAY ROMANCE

North Woods University
The Bet
The Dare
The Secret
The Vow
The Promise
The Jock

Bayshore Rivals
When Rivals Fall
When Rivals Lose
When Rivals Love

Breaking the Rules
Kissing & Telling
Babies & Promises
Roommates & Thieves

Also by the Authors

***

DARK ROMANCE

The Blackthorn Elite
Hating You
Breaking You
Hurting You
Regretting You

The Obsession Duet
Cruel Obsession
Deadly Obsession

The Rossi Crime Family
Protect Me
Keep Me
Guard Me
Tame Me
Remember Me

The Moretti Crime Family
Savage Beginnings
Violent Beginnings
Broken Beginnings

The King Crime Family
Indebted
Inevitable

Printed in Great Britain
by Amazon